Acknowledgements

I write books because I enjoy the challenge of writing, and thinking, and of course everyone that writes novels enjoys the warm words of one's family, which I have received from all my friends and our clan. I smile when I call our family a clan. There were an even dozen kids, and with Mom and Dad, fourteen in all. Anyhow, I'm dedicating this book to my brother Jess Montoya because aside from his business acumen and sterling personality, he has humor. He has a memory for anecdotes and if you watched his facial expressions, he would already be smiling as if he knew you would laugh at what he was going to say. He can turn a smiling joke to a gut wrenching, gasping laugh. We all love Jess for his unique narrative, comical presentation, and his personal witticism. He is indeed the funny man of our family and we love him for bringing smiles to our faces. We love you Jess, and your positive disposition, and will keep you in our prayers.

Copyright © 2015 Joseph F. Montoya

All rights reserved.

ISBN-10: 1508696659

ISBN-13: 978-1508696650

This novel is a work of fiction. Names, character and places and incidents are products of the author's imagination or are interpreted as fiction. Any resemblance to actual event or locales or persons living or dead, is entirely coincidental.

About the title of this book, it is my wife's contention that during the early nineteen seventies when she worked as a court room clerk for Judge Edward C. Scoyen at the courthouse in Palo Alto, California, she heard the phrase "O' Dark Thirty," from the wily Judge Scoyen and believes he coined the expression. Though very serious about his profession, he had a humorous side that was compelling to Mary's own comical sense of wit, which of course, made for a most compatible working relationship with the now deceased Judge.

O' DARK THIRTY

Joseph F. Montoya

CHAPTER 1

The silent black Navigator rolled slowly up the dark Boolean's Poplar tree lined driveway and stopped a hundred yards from the large mansion. Six men in dark military uniforms, pullover cotton head masks stepped out into the quiet moonless night. One remained behind as the other four stealthily moved forward toward the stately home. When they reached the perimeter of the manor, the leader with arm and hand movements, directed each individual, raised his left arm and tapped his watch, then with his hand raised brought it down and each surreptitiously crept into the evening shadows. The lead man remained at the designated position. Less than twenty minutes had passed before one, then two, and finally all were back to the leader's side. In a hushed voice the four minions reported what they had seen. The lead man listened intently then, in a hushed voice delegated a specific task to each individual. There was a short pause and they synchronized their watches for the next meeting.

The five men entered the estate through the sliding door of the vast front room and advanced to the separate dining room, where voices could be heard laughing and making small talk in the adjacent dining room. A standing guard falls over from the zip of a silent bullet piercing his head, but he is caught by one the intruders and laid quietly down, dark blood oozing onto the lush carpeting. Only Mozart's Magic Flute could be heard faintly through the open door.

    The lead man entered the dining room and quickly fired a silent shot, which brought the nearest chandelier noisily to the floor, capturing everyone's attention. Two of the night stalkers bunched the maids and handpicked guests into the adjacent kitchen and locked them into a large walk-in food closet. Those remaining were the host, his wife, two children brought down from the upstairs, two lawyers and a medical doctor. The leader signaled to one of his accomplices, who expeditiously moved to the host's wife and shot her point blank in the back of the head, blood and bone splattering across the white table cloth, audible gasps from the two ladies, then moved away. The leader stepped behind the seated male host, seized a baby blue table napkin and draped it over the host's head, put his gun to the man's temple and fired. He pointed to another enforcer and directed him to the last woman. The man stood behind her in the ready, when she turned and looked up at him, he froze. The man stepped back and the leader shot him in the head, then he turned to the woman so that she faced him within two feet, their eyes locked momentarily then he shot her in the forehead. She dropped to the floor.

Three plus years later, as I opened the blinds of the large bay window, the darkness was still pervasive; my eyes were drawn to the metal streetlight and the falling snow from the light casting down on the street. I had a strange feeling I should know this scene, but as quickly as the moment came, it vanished. Maybe it was only because of my dear friend Michelle Gee Danese and all her gentle coaching about what I should know. Coping with what was real and what was illusionary wasn't any better now than it was after the terrible tragedy that had befallen me five years before. I was living here in this small, but beautiful, friendly receptive town, Wenatchee, because my life, according to Dr. Danese, was reliant on my anonymity. My long-term memory still, was all but gone, but my short-term memory was extraordinarily acute, if only from the last five years since my accident. Thank God. I think I still believe in God.

Even now it's hard for me to think the shock of what happened to me has completely blocked all the memories. I became aware of Barbara Streisand's beautiful soprano voice faintly singing in the den and I turned away and ambled to the kitchen. I reached for my favorite Starbuck's coffee cup and poured the only cup of coffee I would be drinking today. I sipped the steaming cup, eyed the kitchen clock and hurried to the bathroom and a quick shower, remembering that every day was special, because I really shouldn't be here, again I thank my friend Michelle for that phrase and there is no doubt they are true words.

As I disrobed in front of the standing mirror I studied my body. I was in need of losing some weight, not a lot, and even though I was working out with my friend Michelle every other day, I was going to have to do more. A trainer had been suggested just a few weeks ago and now I was going to look into obtaining that service.

I finished my lukewarm coffee, cleaned the coffee pot, and waited for my workout partner and friend, who would be arriving any minute. I looked at my daily planner and heard two quick knocks on the front door and Michelle came bounding in, "Carpe Diem, girl," she exclaimed.

"Seize the day?"

"Yup, let's get this road on the show, girl, and miles to go before we sleep," she smiled broadly, "I woke up full of it today Barbara Grevera and ready to tackle this cruel and insidious world girl."

This was my friend Michelle Danese and this was why we have always been good friends, at least that's what she has told me and I don't have any reason to dispute her every word. Miss Positive in the flesh.

"What are we doing this morning Doctor?"

"How about a long walk on, 'The Loop,' bridge to bridge."

"How about your knee? Will it take all the walking?"

"Put your hand on my left knee, girl and tell me what you feel?"

"A brace or knee pad?"

"That's right, it's a knee brace guarantee to walk a hundred miles, says my orthopedic friend at the local hospital."

"You are so crazy Michelle."

"I am she said with a sad face."

"No, you're sweet crazy and I love you so. What would I do without you?"

"And don't you forget that lady?" she smiled as we walked out the door, arm and arm to her Subaru.

"You want to walk South to North or North to South?"

"Does it matter?"

"Well, the eating places are better at the north end of town. That's about the only difference, and of course we can always cab it, back to the car, regardless of which end we start with."

"Well, that's a pretty good reason to end up in the North end Michelle."

"Alrighty, hope you brought your gloves girl, because it feels a little chilly on the paws."

"The cool air feels good."

"You're doing really well, hon, and don't worry about your memory it will come one day, I assure you. The only thing I don't know is when? When, when when? Egad, I'm starting to sound like some Psychiatrist, Barbara. Tell me to shut my mouth."

"Michelle, have you ever given any thought to marrying again?

"Oh my gosh hon. Where on earth did that come from? I'd have to think about the question. At this very moment, I would say no." She nodded, "yup, I haven't considered marrying again. I really loved Robert and even though it's been almost four years since his death, I'm still in love with him, but I try not to think too much about him or I get depressed. Besides, Barbara I have a friend that I love very much and right now she needs me as much as I need…you. You're part of this whole thing and you're here in the flesh. I'm going to remain with you as long as I live. Right now I don't need a man in my life and I can't think of anyone I would rather be around than you. Robert left me more money than I could ever spend in ten life times. Now Barb, if we don't change the subject you're going to cause me to tear up and bawl like some big baby."

"Sorry Michelle, I wasn't trying to get you all upset it's just that…"

"Pardon the interruption Barbara, you don't need to apologize. Believe me I understand."

They walked quietly for a short while.

"Do you still think there is a possibility that someone could come after me to do me harm?"

Michelle thought about her question. It was one of those things. Damned if you bring it up and damned if you don't. Barbara should *know* that it definitely is a possibility those bastards would come looking for her, simply because she had the good fortune of living after being shot in the head at close range.

"I'm sorry. I have burdened you with that possibility sweetie, but yes, I do think those people will come after you. At the time I told you this, I debated whether you should know or not know. I thought it was better to error on the knowledge of awareness than to be ignorant of the fact. I don't know if I have explained this well enough. I took it upon myself to let you know that someone might come after you someday, though now it seems unlikely. After all, it has been four years."

"I'm glad you told me. Yes it has played on my mind on occasions and I think I would like to be trained to my full potential in defending myself. Does that sound realistic?"

"Honey, you went to twelve years of school to become a fine doctor in your field, so I think you are able to become anything you want to be. If martial arts are your goal, we'll check out the local training facilities and find someone to teach you. How about tomorrow morning?

"Thank you Michelle, you're a real friend."

"We have an appointment with the Manager of Gold's gym on North Wenatchee Avenue this morning at 9 a.m. Are you sure you still want to find someone to train you?"

"You're so efficient Michelle."

"And don't you forget it hon," smiling from ear to ear.

Michelle and Barbara entered Gold's gym, walked by the entry desk and looked for an office. A tall handsome man stood to the side of what looked like a small office.

"Are you the manger?" Michelle asked.

He pointed to the open door.

"Come on in," a voice summoned from inside.

"Hi, I'm Tom Tamaru, and you must be Michelle Danese and Barbara Grevera."

"We are.

They were seated and Tom listened to their request to begin some kind of regiment of defense for the two of them. Tom explained that Gold's Gym was primarily for those who were looking to get in shape.

"I believe you're looking for someone that can teach you Martial Arts, an instructor of the Martial Arts, as it were. I'll introduce you to J. R. Bowman, a retired Navy Seal." He stood and peaked around the corner, "come on in JR."

Tom made the introductions, then, exited, allowing Bowman to interview the two women with a closed door.

JR and the two women sat looking at each other waiting for someone to speak.

"Normally I don't teach women. Most of my clients are men, young men, because my method is postured as a boot camp. The training is for sixteen weeks in the hills behind Saddle Rock. Are you sure you want to tackle something like that. It's pretty grueling. Essentially it's a Marine Corps boot camp with special instructions from me as a Navy Seal. Hand to hand combat with emphasis on killing your adversary with silent fervor. You will be able to kill your opponent with just your hands, no matter the size."

Michelle glanced at Barbara and saw no indication that she was thwarted by Bowman's words.

"Are you trying to discourage us from trying your boot camp Mr. Bowman," Michelle ventured.

"No ma'am I'm not, but you should know that many men that start with my boot camp don't make it to the sixteen weeks, but if you do, you will be adequately able to defend yourself with anyone that tries to accost you."

"Mr. Bowman, would you mind stepping outside while we discuss your offer."

He stood and stepped outside the door and closed it.

"What do you think?"

"I believe I'd like to try and do this sixteen week boot camp. What about you?"

"Barbara Hon, in a hundred and ten days, I never thought about doing some crazy Marine Boot Camp with some Navy Seal. I used to think those boys and girls were crazy to want to join up and get themselves all dirty and eat dirt, splash through water, get yelled at and called dirty names and all the other crazy things they have to do, but if you want to do this thing, I'm with you. Maybe we could see if he would train just the two of us. What do you think?"

"We can always ask."

Michelle opened the door and Mr. Bowman stepped in and sat down.

"How many men do you usually try to train at one time?" Barbara asked.

"As little as twenty and as much as thirty."

"How many do you have now? Today."

"Three, but they don't sound like they have the money. Money is tight nowadays and that might stop the three. They're all friends."

"How many would you expect to get, let's say, by the beginning of April which is only a week away?"

"Like I said, money is tight right now."

"How many would you like to have by the first of April?"

"The reason I need the bodies is because I can't afford to run the camp with less than twenty recruits."

"Could you step outside again, please?" Michelle requested.

The two ladies huddled and discussed the finances and called him back in.

"Do you run the camp all by yourself?" Barbara queried.

"Well, I have a Chef and my son is the gofer."

"When you have thirty recruits. What do you charge per head?"

"Two thousand for sixteen weeks with no returns after the first week of training."

"Would you consider training two women for the same price you would charge the thirty recruits?"

Tony thought for a few seconds. "Just the two of you?"

"Yes," they responded in unison.

Again he contemplated the offer. "No."

"Is it because we're women?" I thought there was no bias in the armed services. Barbara growled, surprising Michelle.

"No, I wouldn't charge that much because it wouldn't be fair to you two. I'd be glad to come up with an equitable offer that would be more favorable to you two. While I stood outside the door I had considered making you this very offer, because of the scarcity of money at this time. I don't think I could get ten recruits by June of July. This also would cut the time down because I could spend more personal time with each of you, making you more proficient quicker. Let me play with figures and come up with a more realistic price. Would that be all right with you two?"

The two ladies nodded and Michelle responded, "Sounds like a plan, Mr. Bowman."

"If I could get one of your cell numbers or any number, I will call you with the bottom line tomorrow."

The trio stood, shook hands and the ladies walked out happily.

In the car, they looked at each other and laughed freely, "He's good looking. Don't you think?" Michelle said shamelessly.

"Favors a young Robert Mitchum...manly," Barbara swooned.

Barbara and Michelle were engaged in conversation in Barb's house when there was a knock on the door. They looked at each other. "I wasn't expecting anyone," Barbara whispered and directed Michelle to open the door. Barbara walked to her bedroom and armed herself with a .45 caliber pistol and kept the door open enough to listen to the conversation and Michelle answered the door.

"Hi, I'm Arlene Voight, a neighbor and after talking to Dennis Seifert, I thought I should at least introduce myself."

Barbara came out of bedroom and joined her friend, without a weapon.

I'm Michelle Danese and this is my friend Barbara Grevera."

"We were having coffee. Would you like a cup? Michelle offered.

"Please, and coffee mate or milk will be all right."

They sat at the kitchen table.

"I hope I haven't interrupted anything."

"Not at all."

"Our neighbor Dennis, mentioned he had talked to you briefly at Memorial Park, Barbara, and was quite taken by you."

"Oh really. Taken?"

"Oh my gosh, here I'm gossiping and I'm so against the constant exchange of words that are nothing more than gossip.

O' DARK THIRTY

He just said that I should introduce myself and go from there. I'm ashamed I hadn't done this earlier. You've been here a long time; three, going on four years if memory serves me. Though I suppose it is never too late."

"Well, we haven't reached out to acquaint ourselves either Arlene, so if there is blame to pass around…"

"Dennis mentioned that you're a Psychiatrist."

"Yes, we both are. What do you do?"

"I teach at the local college…English, and I'm also the girls Basketball Coach."

"You look like you're in good shape," Michelle chimed in.

"Likewise, and neighbors do talk. Someone said you have been seen in the company of the local popular Marine Seal, Joe Doyle Bowman."

"Guilty," Barbara asserted, "three months of the most grueling physical punishment we've ever been through."

Arlene's cell phone vibrated and she excused herself and answered it.

"Sorry Barb and Michelle, I must be going. I'm really glad to have met you. I would love to have lunch with you sometime and get to know you better. My first impression is that there is lot mystery in your lives."

They all stood and shook hands and Arlene hurried out the door.

"If she only knew," Michelle smiled.

CHAPTER 2

In the small city of Samson, Colonial County, New York, lives the drug lord Dimitre Aristotle in a lavish mansion, known by its guests as, "The Ranch," where there were always elaborate drug parties, and this beautiful June day with the sun drenching it in warmth, was no exception. There were always beautiful women, with the tiniest of swimwear to appease the eye of any male, and some women, for this was the 21st century and almost anything went nowadays. The alcohol and drugs flowed easily around the large pool and the conversations were always about clothes, cars and homes; or the recent celebrities that visited the Aristotle expansive estate for favors or to be petitioned for whatever favor they might be able to offer, all for a price of course; sometimes even lives were bartered. His friends were many and varied and from all walks of life, Football players, race –card-rivers, basketball, baseball, hockey, soccer players, lawyers and judges. He knew people, some good and some very bad people. He managed to stay out of jail because he had money for the right lawyers and judges, plus he was recklessly intimidating, life meant very little to Dimitre Aristotle. His own subordinates were afraid of the menacing half Greek and half Cuban monster, as he was known to most of his friends - - without his knowledge.

Dimitre was observing the small crowd of casual friends from the second floor veranda but his eyes stopped and were fixed on one woman. From the distance between them, the woman was reminiscent of someone he had seen close up almost four years ago. Could this be the woman that vowed she would never forget my face and that someday---and his thoughts stopped? *Impossible,* he thought, *I was less than two feet from her head. Though the kill had never been confirmed. The strange memory had often rattled me and had even given me some sleepless nights, but I had finally been able to overcome the memory of the woman's face and even managed to forget her name. I stood and walked into one of Gina's guest rooms and beckoned her where she was playing Bridge with her friends.*

"Honey, could I borrow you for few minutes."

"Sweetie pie, you know I would do anything for you. All you have to do is ask."

He turned and walked to the Veranda, Gina in tow, and scanned the crowd for the woman.

"The lady in the red shorts and white tank top, next to one of the maids and the blonde in the pink swim suit."

"The one, now talking to the maid?"

He nodded.

"Her name is Summer Turco, works for the Dupree Law firm. I believe she's a Legal Secretary or novice lawyer at the firm. This is her first time here at the Ranch."

He turned at looked at his beautiful, adoring wife and smiled, "How do you do that?"

"Aside from having small tits, a big ass, long sexy legs, all that you love about me, I possess the most important attribute in my head, so you say. I have a photographic memory."

He reached for her, kissed and slid his hands down to her derriere and gently squeezed.

"Would you like me to cancel my card game?" She cooed.

"Too many people around. Would you have Hazel bring Summer up here. I'd like to talk to her please."

"Yes sir."

He walked to the bar in the room and fetched a Ginger Ale.

"Excuse me Mr. Aristotle."

"Yes, Hazel, thank you. Come in Miss Turco, would you like something to drink?"

"Is that a Ginger ale you're drinking?"

"It is. Would you like one?"

He opened the can and poured it into a glass.

"Do you drink alcohol Mr. Aristotle?

"Rarely, but yes I have a glass of white wine on some occasions. I've tasted the hard stuff and just don't like the taste. Beer, quite frankly looks and probably tastes like what I would imagine is urine."

"Interesting observation."

"Does it surprise you that I don't readily imbibe?"

"Yes, it does. Most of the Catholic priests, but not all, I know drink wine as well as the 'hard stuff,' as you put it and many clergy of the other faiths are not opposed to some wines. Has this been a lifelong thing, or did you have some kind epiphany?"

"I grew up in a house where my father was an alcoholic and my mother was a seven day Catholic. My mother's influence was greater than the falling down drunk of a father. That he drank could have passed with me, but he was also beat my mother, brother and me. That is, until I took it upon myself at a young age to rid our home of the bully and thug."

"I'm sorry," she empathized, *wondering what he meant by ridding the home of the bully and thug. Did he mean what I think he meant. Oh my God.*

"Don't be. I'm not sorry for what I did to the drunk that lived with us and nearly killed each of us over the years. I'd do it all over again. Men like my father should not be allowed to live and do what he did to his family. If it can be said, the only good thing that came of his brutal life is that I don't drink or smoke or use profanity around my family. The spinoff is with all the bad there appears to be, even in the worst of men, miraculously, some good comes from it."

"You're quite the philosopher Mr. Aristotle. Was Aristotle your father's name?"

"No, but the story of how we became the Aristotle's is quite interesting, even if I say so myself. After my father's unfortunate departure, our lives became harsh, grim, because though he drank excessively, he managed to put food on the table and that was sorely missed. My mother, who is still a beautiful woman and had managed to borrow enough money from her family and friends to secure a trip to Greece. To make a very long story short, we booked a ship to Greece and the owner of the ship was on a rare walk-through inspection and was leaving the ship with his entourage as we arrived on the large vessel. We had no sooner walked up the plank and stood aside, when Hector Aristotle was exiting. As he walked past us, he lost his step and fell against my mother and they both fell to the deck. Six months later he married Mom."

"Dim, Summer's escort is looking for her. Are you through boring her?"

"I am. My apologies, Ms. Summers, I hope I didn't over do it."

"Not at all Mr. Aristotle, you've lived a dauntless and intriguing life. At some future time, you must tell me the details of your mother's marriage to Hector Aristotle."

"I don't know what got into me, I believe, except for my wife, I have never told anyone, what I told you today. Thank you for lending me your ear. Now shoo before your escort leaves you stranded here."

Summer whispered something to Gina as she walked out.

"Wow, you obviously made quite an impression with Ms. Turco."

"I need to tap into that incredible memory you possess, Mrs. Aristotle."

"Don't you want to know what she whispered to me?"

"Not really, she's a classy lady. I'm sure it was positive."

She smiled, "I'm at your service sir."

"I'm sure you recall the terrible murders that occurred at my brother's mansion a few years ago."

She nodded.

"Were there any survivors?"

"Gina shook her head, "the paper didn't mention any. I don't believe anyone lived through that massacre. I'm sorry you have to remember any of that terrible day, Dim."

"I think I'm over that by now. Would you do me a favor and check it out, I mean about a survivor."

"Sure honey, I'll jump on it tonight after everyone leaves. Okay? By the way, were you able to satisfy your curiosity about Ms. Turco?"

"It was a business matter, but she wasn't who I thought she was. Turns out she's nice people."

"Good, our Bridge game is about to break up. You want to eat something?"

"I'm not hungry. I need to call the 'Fox,' and he touched his IPhone.

"Yes sir, Mr. Aristotle."

"I need to talk to you Jimmy? Meet me at the wharf in a half hour."

"Yes sir."

Jimmy the Fox Lamantia was a licensed lawyer with the state of New York, but he had gone rogue when he met Dimitre Aristotle a few years ago. He knew the law well, which is why Aristotle hired him, and he was ambitious with very little integrity, but he knew his place with his employer. Jimmy knew first hand and had witnessed the ruthless ways of his employer. If Aristotle could profit from killing his brother and his family, he would, with no hesitation eliminate *him* on a whim. Financially, he was well set and as long as he was a good soldier, he would remain above ground. He knew that his boss was up to something that couldn't be heard by anyone else or he wouldn't be meeting at the wharf, and he always had some historical question for him. The sun felt good on his face as he looked out at the expansive lake that seemed more like the Atlantic Ocean. He turned just as

Dimitre stepped out of his Acura and walked with purpose toward me.

"What presidents are on Mount Rushmore?" He asked and locked his eyes with mine. And what order are they as you look straight at them?"

"George Washington, Thomas Jefferson, Abraham Lincoln and Teddy Roosevelt?"

"What's the name of the tiny town that is closest to the granite carvings and what state is Mount Rushmore in?"

After a few seconds, "that would be Keystone, in South Dakota."

"What's the names of the last four President's, including the current President?"

"Barak Obama, George Walker Bush, William Jefferson Clinton and Ronald W. Reagan."

"Gina said that if you knew all that stuff, you probably had a photo memory, just like her."

"I don't think I do. I always liked History and the study of the United States except for what we did to the American Indian. We started out with good intentions but then we got greedy and…well you know the rest, I'm sure."

"No I don't, but then I don't really care, and I didn't know the answers to any of the questions I just asked you. Gina gave me the list because I told her you had a good memory. I think I have a pretty good memory, but only for what interests me. My overall opinion of this country is that its citizens are manipulated by our government, which is growing leaps and bounds. Anyway, I like that you have the memory you have, but the reason you're here now, is because I need to find out if the woman I shot at my brother's home is alive. Plus the lawyer that we killed that night had a wife that was not at Able's home. See if she's alive and where she lives. ASAP?"

Dimitre turned away and walked briskly to his car and was gone in a minute.

Jimmy 'the Fox,' Lamantia stood watching the Acura disappear in the distance. *Why can't he leave "well enough alone,"* he thought. *It was going to be three, four years, on March 17, St. Patrick's Day; I can imagine what he's up to.*

Jimmy went to his office after meeting Aristotle and opened his safe, retrieved the folder dated March 17, 2010. He placed the contents on his desk and began reading and taking notes, after a few hours he sat back on his chair. He didn't like where this was going, and there was no debating with Aristotle. He would need to make contact with his mole at the DA's office, which the contact would not like. Counting me and Aristotle, there were three others that had entered Able's mansion and slaughtered all that were there that night, including two neighbors wives, his own brother, which consisted of a family of four, and Able's two lawyers Berenski and Danese. The names of the two wives were never mentioned in any of the trial documents that Jimmy had in his possession, nor in the local paper. Jimmy's cell phone was ringing.

"Hello," and he listened for just a minute and then quickly stashed the folder into the safe and hurried out of his office and headed to Mercy Hospital.

Gina was in the hallway on the third floor waiting and when she saw me, hurried toward me.

"He's paralyzed from the neck down and is unable to speak at this time," she said crying.

"What happened?"

"Some kind of accident," she managed to cry out.

I thought, *it must have happened after he left me at the wharf.*

"How long has he been here?"

"I don't know, my mother's in the visiting room with my friend Lorna. He isn't talking, and he might die," she choked.

I reached out and brought her to me, "hey, he isn't going to die. He's to…tough to die."

CHAPTER 3

Barbara Grevera awoke with a jolt, sat straight up and stared across the room. She touched her face with frigid hands and thought she was awake, but was she, or was this still a dream? And was it a dream? Somehow down deep in her mind she was sure it was real. She placed her feet on the carpet, stood, walked to the bathroom and turned the light on, walked to the sink and splashed cold water on face. She peered into her questioning blue eyes. She even felt different, more alert, more in control of her body. She slid her nightgown off and stared at her body. It was thin and her arms and legs had definition. Had she been heavy at some time? She somehow knew that this was where she lived, but she couldn't quite figure out why. As she showered, she realized she had showered here before -- many times before.

Drying herself it occurred to her that she didn't see any indication of another person in her bed. Dressing quickly, she rushed out of the bathroom and opened the door across the hall, a made up bed, she went down the hall, opened another door, a closet, and still another door, no one. She lived alone she surmised. But I don't live alone I have a daughter and husband...I'm married.

She was sitting in the kitchen and was aware that she knew this room. Standing, she went to counter the and made a pot of coffee. *I do drink coffee,* she thought. As the coffee percolated she moved to the front room and opened the drapes over a large bay window to the lights of a waking up city in the distance. She knew which side the curtains opened. She sat on the large divan and pondered all that was happening to her. It was all foggy and yet some of it made sense. She knew where the light switches were in kitchen and the front room. She walked back to kitchen and sat down with a cup of fresh coffee.

There was a knock on the front door and a woman walked in, "Carpe diem, girl."

She was startled and spilled her coffee, then stared at the woman that had sauntered over to the coffee pot. She poured a cup and reached in the refrigerator for milk, poured, then ambled over to the table and sat. The woman looked over at her friend.

"You do know who I am, don't you Barbara? Are you playing with me? Why are you looking at me like you don't know who I am?"

"I…I feel like I should know who you are, but…I'm not sure."

"Do you know where you are? Where you live? Do you know your name? Oh my God, Barbara, I must be scaring you to death. I'm Michelle Danese, your friend…wait, my real name is Elizabeth Schneider, we grew up together, Schneider, Elizabeth, please remember me Deidre, Deidre, Deidre Berenski, that was your real name. Oh God, please let her remember me. We're best friends." She stood and hurried to the other side of the table, pulled her friend up to a standing position and hugged her closely. "Please remember me Deidre, oh please remember," she wailed, tears flowing down her face.

"And we had a friend...Veronica Aristotle, is that right?"

"Yes, yes we had a friend named Veronica and she had two kids, Blaine and Lucy. Yes Deidre and you've got your memory back, - - at least some of it?" She held her friend at arm's length and smiled through her tears.

They sat on the divan and hugged each other and cried till there were no more tears.

"I suppose we should use our latest names for each other if it will keep us alive longer...Michelle."

"Absolutely, hon."

"Briefly, before you came through the door I had been thinking about my foggy life and I was trying to decide if I wanted to keep living this way."

"I don't understand what you're saying, Barb. I thought you wanted to keep using our new names."

"I do, but life is getting shorter for both of us. Didn't we just finish the hardest Marine Corps Boot camp that Seal could put us through, and we should still live like coal miners? No offense against coal miners, assuming I still have a daughter and mother I would like to have them living with me. What's life all about except for the personal relationships with your family and close friends? Didn't the Seal say that he would proudly go on any firefight with us as a unit? Michelle we've been trained by the best and honestly I think I could handle myself against the worst. I truly believe what J.R. Bowman, hey I remembered his name, said about us two. Why would he say something that wasn't true?"

"I don't think he lied to us about our abilities. He said so little and when he did talk it was always precise…no wasted words. He said, except for a few instances, that we bitched less than most men and that we were two of the most positive recruits he had ever been around. Frankly, I believed him."

"I'm not afraid of any man now, Michelle. Boy, listen to me, I'm starting to sound like Mohammad Ali or Mike Tyson."

"Semper Fi, girl. You're just feeling your oats," and they gave each other a high five. "I couldn't have said it better, hon."

"How long have I been a veggie?"

"Almost four years."

"No way," she gasped and put her hands to her head.

"You haven't been a veggie, you just didn't have a long-term memory, except sporadically you do remember isolated instances of your past. Hey, you went through that boot camp with only a short-term memory, girl."

"Oh yeah, that's right. Some kind of Concussion Amnesia?"

Michelle nodded.

Everything is still off kilter in some ways. Let's go pump some iron, Michelle…we do pump iron…right?"

"Michelle, I will not live in fear again, so I want to go see my daughter and mother. How about you?"

"Hey, you really have awakened. It hasn't taken you long to get back to yourself. Don't forget you're

Barbara Grevera for a reason and I'm Michelle Danese for the same reason. You want to take a little time to think about putting what's left of your family in possible danger."

"I suppose I'm getting ahead of myself. It's just that…three or four years of my life have disappeared and I feel like I want to do something about it. Oh, Michelle, I'm so glad you're my friend, my check and balance."

"It's who you are, Barbara. Strange that Barbara is appropriate now. It fits you. When I gave you that name, it sounded awkward, but now…it's you. You were always our leader, the take-charge girl, feet squarely on the ground, no nonsense. Veronica and I always looked up to you and I still do."

Wow, you make me sound like Margaret Thatcher. Is Grevera Italian?"

"Not according to my brief genealogy research; it's Polish. Are you all right with being Barbara Grevera?"

"I am. Can we walk in a different direction?"

"May I get another cup of coffee?"

"What a host I am."

"We're practically sisters Barb," as she sat down at the kitchen table. Now what else was bunching up your panties?"

"Bunching up my panties?"

They looked at each other and burst out laughing. "Hey, it's a commonly used euphemism," Michelle responded.

Barbara nodded smiling. "Well, I want to work."

"As a shrink?"

"Maybe."

"Edward left you a lot of money, Hon."

Barbara's expression changed and she looked away.

Oh crap. Me and my big mouth, Michelle thought, *I would have to mention his name.* She stood and started around the table until Barbara put up hand to stop her.

"It's all right Michelle, I'm a big girl. There's no end to my gratitude to you. Shrink, lawyer, finance manager, caretaker, counselor, friend and who knows what else."

"What else are friends for, and furthermore I know you would do the same for me if the situation was reversed. Without a doubt I know that."

They stood, walked to each other and hugged for a few seconds, as the tears of joy flowed.

"Have there been any attempts on our lives in the last three years?"

"No."

"Let me try to explain to you what happened, without details about your specific situation and I'll try to keep down to five hundred words or less. The investigation of the massacre of the Able family, and those who happened to be at the dinner celebrating Veronica's birthday on that fateful day, was handled by the Assistant District Attorney. He went out of his way to keep the investigation down to a minimum of handpicked Detectives and police officers. Because of what happened to you, it was imperative to move you to different hospitals and clinics with the same medical staff to keep you safe. The assassins were not aware that *you* had lived through what should have been your death. The local paper was never given the names of all the fatalities, only those of the Able Aristotle family. After you were able to travel, we were uprooted from the city of Samson, Jeffersen County, New York in the dead of night and flown here, to Wenatchee Washington, the Apple Capital of the world and the land of the best Bing Cherries and fruit that has ever been grown, by one Father Reginald Collin Crosby, and in his own words, 'I would rather die than utter a word of what I've done.' Wow I should be in advertising."

Barbara rolled her eyes and shook her head. "I had forgotten what a ham you are Michelle."

"I hope you still love me with all my faults."

"Oh, I almost forgot, which has nothing to do with our present discussions. Gunnery Sergeant Bowman called me last evening and would like to take me out to dinner."

"Oh my God, Barbara."

Barbara and Michelle on their own, had been meeting at local Gold's Gym for several weeks after Gunnery Sergeant J.D Bowman had trained them in the proper weight lifting techniques and got them well past their weight in bench pressing. Bowman had said the two women were in superlative shape; as good as any Marine could have been after the sixteen weeks of the boot camp.

Two young men were watching the two ladies as they pursued their workout.

"They look like they know what they're doing."

"They do."

"What do you think?"

"Probably married. See any rings?"

"Does it matter?"

"Could be a couple or lesbians."

"Let's check them out."

"You ladies do well with the weights, like you've been doing them for a while."

Michelle and Barbara eyed the two young men with some suspicion, "and your point is?"

The taller man looked at his friend, "we were just trying to be friendly…is all."

"Well," Barbara spoke up, "we're both married and not to each other, and we're not looking for friends. Does that help you assess the situation?"

"Look, we're sorry for interfering with your workout," and they walked away in a huff.

"What was that all about Barb?"

"I'm fraught with all this crap, the intimidation, the fear, the worry of someone coming for us, to do us harm. All the training we've put up with, the running, Karate, the boot camp. Look at our hands, they feel like wood, all blistered. We're armed and ready for battle, Michelle. I have no fear anymore. I think we could put up a good fight with anyone. Do you?"

"I do, but you were rude to those guys."

"I think I'm changing, I even feel different now. I'm not sorry that I was rude to them."

Michelle studied her friend and felt sorry for her. Barbara was always a lady and in her previous life and would never have been so obnoxious. All this consuming transition had finally surfaced its ugly disposition to the sweetest friend I've ever known.

"We're both tired. Let's go get some breakfast," Michelle suggested and placed her arm over Barbara shoulders.

The two young men watched the two women walk out arm in arm.

"They're probably lesbians. Don't you think?"

His companion nodded with an insolent smile.

They walked over to their friend Ben Yamada, as he was working out.

"Hey Ben what do you think of the two ladies over there?" And they pointed to Barbara and Michelle.

He looked over at the two women. "They're very pretty, in great shape and very smart. Why?"

"Just curios," and they walked away.

CHAPTER 4

Summer Turco and Donald Dupree had been in Dimitre Aristotle's room and were only able to stare at the listless life of the most feared man in the city of Sumon.

As Summer observed the motionless body and all the connections to the vital machines operating quietly, she thought of the only time she had spoken to Dimitre Aristotle. He seemed polite, bright, friendly and gentlemanly, and yet she had recently heard things about him that painted a very different picture of this enigmatic man. It was very difficult to envision the handsome face she once seen, now covered with bandages and tubes in his mouth and nose.

Dupree touched her elbow and she looked up and he gently escorted her to the door and hallway.

"The gossip around the firm is that Dimitre is responsible for his brother's death three years ago, though it was never proven in a court of law."

"So I've heard, but the man I talked to a couple of weeks ago, in no way is that man, unless he has more than one personality. It's inconceivable to me, that Mr. Aristotle could be a person who would kill someone, especially his own brother and his family. I use to think I was a pretty good judge of character. But if it's true, that man lying near death is a murderer, I am a failure."

"I wouldn't say that. I have met and been to his 'Ranch' and found him to be all the things you said about him too. It's hard to judge someone bad, when they treat you as if you're special, accommodating, almost humble, because that's who he is at that time. I believe he does that naturally and without trying to fool you into thinking is anything but what he is…at that time. I would venture to say he treats his wife and his servants with the same courtesy without deception."

"Sounds like you've studied him."

"He's been in a few of our conversations when I get together with some of the shrinks and other jurists that I know. It's interesting mentally dissecting someone you know informally without ever coming up with a proper medical name. Some say he's a psychopathic, others think he's schizophrenic. Whatever he might be is very mysterious."

"Do you think he's going to die?"

"I was hoping to see his doctor or a nurse, but the only person was the guard at the door, and he didn't look too friendly."

A man was coming down the hall toward them and as he neared, he smiled and extended his hand, "nice to see you counselor."

"Likewise Mr. Lamantia. How's your man doing?"

"Doctor says we'll know in another three days, right now he's just here."

"Umm."

"Sorry, Summer this Jimmy Lamantia, Summer Turco."

"Nice to meet you Miss Turco, and now I hope you two will excuse me," and he hurried off.

"That is Dimitre Aristotle's right hand man, who also happens to be a very adroit, shrewd lawyer. Dimitre gives the orders and Jimmy 'the Fox,' Lamantia carries them out. Rumor has it that he has a photographic mind and remembers transcripts word for word.

"Why would a good lawyer want to work for someone like Aristotle if he's such a bad guy."

"Easiest answer, money. Long answer maybe he had a bad experience with the law, hates all the government controls, bad laws, taxes; who really knows except him and I'm not sure he knows."

The elevator door opened and Dupree and Summer stepped out to see four well-dressed men waiting to enter. The man in the lead, tipped his hat," counselor," and walked into the lift.

"Aristotle's minions," Dupree said quietly.

"Really, why do they look like the goons on those Mafia movies?"

"Yeah, you're right, they do look like those guys. Never thought about it before. Good observation, Summer."

Jimmy Lamantia was standing by the window of his summer home, looking out the window at the peaceful Wapato Lake, thirty miles from the city of Samson.

"Why did we have come out here to talk about business and Mr. Aristotle?"

Jimmy wasn't surprised by the question by the man, Tommy 'the Shoe,' Thompson, because he was always ready to speak his mind and Jimmy liked him for his candid perceptions.

"I want us to be able to converse here without wondering if someone has taped us. My grounds keeper has assured me no one has been in this cottage. I double-checked the premises myself earlier this morning. No tapes; no cameras."

"Before Mr. Aristotle had his accident he gave me some explicit orders to find out if one, the woman he shot is dead and two, one of the lawyers wives was not at Able's mansion that St. Patrick's Day, and if she is still alive."

Reggie Johnson spoke up, "hey I don't know about the woman that wasn't there, but everybody else in there was dead when we left the house."

"So what if they're alive, it's been four years since that went down. Forget about it," Rafael Esquivel expressed loudly, waving his hands in the air.

"Three years Esquivel, not four, Toby Erickson," 'the quiet man,' pointed out.

"Three years, four years those are not weeks or months man, those are years. Forget about them."

"You want me to tell Mr. Aristotle that you told me he should forget about it."

"Hey, so I've got a big mouth. No, I don't want you tell him even though he don't seem so good right now, Jimmy."

"Maybe they are dead by now," Rafael piped in.

"Nothing so far substantiates that, Rafael. I've done some investigations on my own and have discovered the names of both of the women, but their whereabouts is still unknown."

"No way that dame that the boss shot is alive, I saw it myself, Jimmy, point blank, in the head. She can't be alive."

"I hope you're right Jimmy, but we have to verify that for sure, and then one or two of you is going to have to go where ever that is, to make sure they never say anything."

Eliminating people was nothing new to these men. It was just business like Landscaping Engineers, whose job was to mow and keep lawns in good shape and the small mob's job was to keep people from talking or anything else their boss asked of them.

CHAPTER 5

"I'm glad we're working again, and that we still have time to keep fit. By the way how did your date go with Robert Mitchum?"

"He's really nice and old fashioned, opens doors, pulls chairs out. Respectful. All of the things that women dream about in a husbands."

"And - -."

"No ands. I'm not looking for a husband, and down deep I don't think he's looking for a wife. We've, meaning you and I, have bonded with this gorgeous man and his friendship is more important than love and - - or sex."

"Sex? I don't think I've heard you use that word in any connotation, ever."

"Oh for goodness sake Michelle, I'm not dead. Just because I don't engage in lascivious prose, doesn't mean sex isn't important to us all. There's a place for all of that stuff."

Michelle had stepped into a place she didn't want to be with Barbara. She thought too much of her to alienate her best friend.

"In my small group at 'The Shadows,' Barbara spoke, "we have a woman in her forties that I believe is in an abusive relationship."

"Go on."

"She's done everything the lead counselor has asked her to do and still he rails on her. She looks like he beats her because she wears all these clothes that cover her body, even when the weather is hot, - - and you know how warm it gets here June and July."

"Are there children involved?"

"She has two daughters, fourteen and sixteen, and both have run away because they hate their new stepfather. The mother denies he abuses them, for the same reasons that most women deny abuse of their children, fear and the inability to support the family without the income of the working abusive father.

"What do the counselors suggest doing about it?"

"There's the rub. She won't complain to the proper authorities, the police, and the police can only do so much without the legal restraints put on the stepfather. It's a vicious cycle, Barb. Personally, I'd like to give the bastard a little of his own treatment, however, Vigilantism is against the law."

"So is what the stepfather is doing, and he seems to be getting away with it."

"Michelle, do you trust J.D. Bowman enough to take him into our confidence?"

"I can't think of a better man to confide in girl. Give him a call."

"Should we ask him to come here for our little powwow?"

"That might not be a good idea. The neighbors see this huge Marine looking fellow in fatigues and they might get the wrong idea. What do you think, girl?"

"Yeah, he does dress in fatigues a lot. Maybe we could meet at his boot camp facility."

"Thanks Sergeant Bowman for meeting with us. I apologize for sounding so mysterious about it. What happened to your arm?"

"Broke the big bone, it's no big deal, stupid mistake. I don't know if I'll be any use to you at this time because I joined the police department, since I saw you last. I'm not getting any younger and my son wants to go to college?"

"That's great Sergeant," Barbara responded, they didn't know that much about him because he was one these men that didn't say much about himself. The more they learned about him the more interesting he became.

"Does that alter your plans for me?"

"Would you excuse us for just a minute?"

They walked outside and debated, then returned.

"You asked if your becoming a police officer would alter our plans? Right? No, we don't think it will."

"Well, then I'm at your service, ladies."

"However," Barbara espoused. "Would it be presumptuous of Michelle and I to have your complete confidence that you would never divulge anything we tell you from this moment on? As Psychiatrists, we take 'The Hippocratic Oath,' never to betray the confidence of any of our clients."

"J.D thought for a few seconds, and raised his right hand, "You have my word as a Navy Seal, that I would rather die than betray you, Barbara Grevera, and you Michelle Danese."

The two ladies eyed each other and nodded their approval, and for the next cathartic hour, Barbara and Michelle poured out their story.

"I'm completely on your side," Bowman nodded, "and I need to get you some night stalking attire and voice altering items for what you have in mind. I have a police friend that I believe will want to assist you in the surveillance aspect of it. He loves the mystery of it all, and he speaks our language.

CHAPTER 6

Sergeant Brandon Danielsen was a tall, dark haired, handsome ex-Marine who had gone into law enforcement when he left the Corps, and was now a detective for the local police department. He was a quiet man, unless he knew you, and then he could be quite communicative.

Barbara and Michelle had made an appointment to meet him at the Olive Garden Restaurant for lunch. As the two women entered the foyer, a tall man stood and spoke.

"My name is Brandon Danielson."

"Now, how did you know we were who you were expecting, Sergeant Danielsen?" Barbara queried.

"Bowman told me that you were both knockouts and I couldn't miss you. That was a perfect description."

"Spoken like a true gentleman, Mr. Danielsen."

They were seated and ordered the salads the restaurant was known for, followed by spaghetti and meatballs.

The conversation was light as they ate, but when the last dishes had been cleared and as they sipped their red wine the conversation took a serious turn.

After thirty-five minutes of coffee and tea, the three adults had come to the conclusion that they would work together to do some vigilante work for the good of those less able.

"You've been very honest with me and have divulged information that I have vowed never speak of - to anyone. I would like to state very clearly Ms. Grevera, Danese, that what we are embarking on is very serious, and has legal ramifications for all of us. I could be fired and/or end up in prison and the same could happen to you. It has to be said, though you may have already thought of it. Do you understand?"

"We do, but thank you for stating it out loud."

"Now, this man you are talking about is well known by the police department. Before our meeting today, I too, have thought about making him realize he cannot do these things to his wife and children, but because of my position, my hands are tied unless she makes a complaint, or someone else witnesses the abuse. You two are the answer, but after today we will only meet in secret. Do you agree?"

"Absolutely," Barbara responded.

Michelle nodded solemnly.

"You will only call me on the number I am going to give you now. It's a throw away phone that I will be using only with you two. I suggest that you purchase at least one, but if you can afford two phones that would be better. I'm available almost anytime by phone or you can text me if I don't respond immediately. I have a lot of meetings that I'm expected to attend. Now if we don't have anything else to discuss, I have something I must do."

"So what do you think of Brandon? Michelle asked.

"Well, we're tied together now and there is no turning back, though I think I like and trust him. He's putting his neck out too."

"Philosophically we walk the same path, which makes it easier for us to be confident in all that he said. Yes, he is putting his neck out too. We need to purchase those phones he recommended."

The following week, Barbara and Michelle were ready to begin surveillance on one Steven Grandstedt, bully. Steve was a plumber and worked all kind of diversified hours. As they followed him around and finally concluded he invariably ended up at the Elks Club for a round of beers with some of his cohorts. Consequently he was impervious to any consequences he might encounter while slightly inebriated: a bully with no fears. Perfect for Barbara and Michelle to sedate, overpower and have their way with the man.

On this particular rainy night, Grandstedt came out of the Elks Club walking erratically and was confronted by a person in a camouflage uniform.

"What the hell do you want? Outta of my way before I beat the hell out of ya."

He walked toward his car, which was parked beside a van. The uniformed person walked backward in front of him. The person spoke in a foreign language with a gargled voice. Suddenly another person dressed the same way appeared, rushed at him and grabbed his neck.

"What the hell? Where am I? Who are you?"

The cover over his head came off and a bright light was shining in his face. That suddenly was turned off and he could feel what had tethered him falling away.

A garbled voice still speaking in a foreign language spoke.

Grandstedt stood, still blind from the bright light that had temporarily left him without sight. He was now afraid."

"You cowards. Just let me get my hands on you and I'll show you---"

A blow to his midsection suddenly bent him over, and that was followed by kick to his face. He tumbled sideways onto a dirt floor. He felt two strong arms pick him and again he was hit in the ribs and he groaned. Then came a kick to the groin that sent him to the ground. He lay writhing in agony when a foot hit his kidney. The excruciating pain caused him to pass out.

He woke up in pain, facing a police officer.

"Were you in a fight? Have you been drinking sir?"

"Where am I?"

"You're in front of the Elks Club Mr. Grandstedt. We've radioed for an ambulance. It should be arriving very soon."

"Help me stand up. I don't need an ambulance. I'm fine."

Grimacing, he stood and wavered precariously. The police officer still holding his arm, kept him steady.

"We'll give you a ride home Mr. Grandstedt. We have your address and here is your wallet. Do you have any enemies that are Chinese sir?"

"No. Why?"

"This note was attached to your shirt."

"What? Let me see it."

"Do you read Chinese?"

"No, I didn't think so. We'll get it read by one of our Chinese interpreters and let you know what it says. OK."

It had been three days since Barbara and Michelle had taken Steven Grandstedt to Bowman's Boot Camp facility. They had vented some of the anger that had been building over the last few years and attached the Chinese note to his shirt collar. The Chinese dialect they had learned while teaching in China years before they became medical doctors. Now the language had finally become useful. She smiled, and yet was feeling some inner turmoil…maybe remorse. No! It was worth it all. What they did was right. Someone had to make it right. Justifying rationalization. Do I really have a propensity for hurting or killing? Don't we all? Perfectly innocent Army soldiers, Marines, and Air Force pilots go into battle with no personal reason for killing except for the *will* of their country to do so.

The knock on the door interrupted her thoughts and she was glad. She opened the door to an older man. He was smiling, which produced a smile from me. He just kept smiling and I finally asked why he had knocked on my door.

"I would very much like to talk to you Ms. Grevera. I like your name, Barbara Grevera. Is it Italian?"

He seemed harmless and did have a nice way about him that put me at ease. "Would you like to come in?"

"It would be a great pleasure to come into your home, Ms. Grevera. Thank you. My name is John David Salinger, no relation to Jerome David Salinger, the author of 'The Catcher in the Rye' novel, and I'm not Jewish, but I do write some."

"Would you like some coffee?" She said ushering him to the kitchen table, "and my name is Polish."

"Indeed I would, thank you. Polish? Interesting," he commented nodding.

"Are you a neighbor, Mr. Salinger?"

"John, please. Yes, and my den window allows a clear view of your home. May I call you Barbara?"

"Have you lived here long?"

"I grew up here and after my wife died I decided to come back and…well, my roots are here, though I did live in California for years."

Barbara noticed he faltered a little when he mentioned his wife. At least he's not from New York, she thought.

"Aren't you a little curious about why I would come over and introduce myself to you?"

"I am."

"I don't want this to sound like I'm stalking you, but you and your friend are quite compelling. Over the last few months I've seen that you engaged in the practice of military martial disciplines."

"Where are you going with this, John?"

"I suppose I have too much time on my hands. Could it be that I'm just curious? Hopefully not so curious that it kills me."

She smiled, "you appear to be in pretty good shape yourself, John."

"I am, for an old man. I take my Daisy on morning runs and sometimes for a walk in the afternoons. In the winter I work out at Gold's, where I have seen the best of you and your friend."

"Thank you. You have a dog?"

"I do, and I've been known to talk to her, and I think she actually understands me."

Barbara looked away, stood and walked to her bay window.

"I'm sorry I've evoked something from the past and---"

"You've done nothing wrong, John." she interrupted, "I too, had a dog, once, and up to this very moment, I had forgotten about it. You see, I have a very sordid past and maybe someday I'll tell you about it, but right now, - - I'd like to be alone."

"I understand completely Barbara. I'll let myself out. It was a pleasure to finally meet you."

She heard the door close, then, broke down and cried shamelessly.

CHAPTER 7

Brandon walked to Detective Goodlow's desk and sat in the chair beside him. "So what's the scoop on Grandstedt?"

"Isn't this the guy you said you'd like to spend ten minutes with alone," and Ron offered the report to him, with a picture of Steven Grandstedt stapled to it.

"Wow, who beat the hell out of him?"

"According to our interpreter it was a Chinese speaking person, who spoke a dialect used primarily in Bejing. Here's the note that was attached to Grandstedt when we found him in front of the Elks Club, still out cold."

"It's in some kind of Chinese."

"Right, and here is the English version."

"Who transcribed it into English?"

"The finance Manager at the bank. Her name is Pi Guo, her English name is Tracy."

"I bet it's accurate. She's a sharp cookie. I've met her and she really knows her way around money. She also manages equities for the bank."

"If you ever touch your wife again you'll end up floating down the Columbia River and it might be months before they find you down in Oregon. This also applies to your two daughters. If you're so sick, you can't stop, then you should consider leaving the state."

"Have any idea who's behind this?" Ron asked Brandon.

"I wish I did, I'd like to shake his hand."

"Do you think Grandstedt is smart enough to take this advice?"

"No, I don't.

"Hey Brand, let me ask Holbrook if you can work this case. After all you started with this one and you know more about this family than I."

While shopping in Macy's, Michelle picked up a blouse and studied the color and length and as she lay it back down, she wondered how it would look with her new black tights she had recently purchased and saw a man staring at her. Oh my God, do I know this man. He vaguely looked familiar; but from where? She dropped the blouse. The blood was running wild throughout her body. Could it be someone from Samson? Had she and Barbara been found out and now were in grave danger. She had to stop herself from rushing out of Macy's and what she should do. She stepped down on the escalator and looked around to see if she was being pursued. He was nowhere in sight. Maybe he wasn't staring and just happened to look innocently at me at the very moment I looked up and met his eyes. She reached the front door and stepped out feeling silly about the whole thing. She was starting to understand Barbara's unprovoked contempt for the boys at Gold's Gym. It was strange that after all this time, it would finally prevail…fear; sure that's what it is.

She dialed Barbara's number, "I'm so glad you're home. Could I come by?"

"Are you all right?"

"I think so."

"I'll make some coffee."

"Do you have anything stronger?"

There was a knock on the door and Michelle walked in and Barbara handed her a small glass of whiskey and she downed in a gulp, and immediately began coughing. Regaining her composure, "What was that stuff?"

"Jack Daniels."

"Wow, and I drank it straight?"

"You wanted something stronger, and I also made some coffee. Would you like some?"

"Please."

They sat at the kitchen table and both sipped coffee. "So what's got you all wound up?"

CHAPTER 8

"Thanks for meeting me here at the Loop, Barbara. Have any trouble getting the phones?" Danielson asked. "What's the story at your end with the Grandstedt family?"

"No problem with the phones. Michelle told me just today that Steve Grandstedt had been quiet for a few days after the beating he received, but is acting more civil to the family, according to Vada, his wife."

"Only time will tell if it sticks, though. Men and some women who do these things, never really change by themselves. He must get professional help and even then it's a long haul to stop."

Barbara concurred, nodding.

"By the way, I was very impressed with the quality of your handiwork on Grandstedt," Danielson said smiling.

"Quite frankly, Michelle and I weren't certain we could actually carry out this whole ordeal, but in the end, we felt relieved, almost…pleased."

"There's a lot I don't know about you or Michelle. It seems, you were born a little under four years ago, and I was really surprised that you wrote the note in authentic Chinese. What other properties do you possess that I would wish to know?"

"Well, I believe we informed you that we are certified Psychiatrists, we have teaching credentials. That's about it, and of course we speak and write one dialect of Chinese, Mandarin," and it happens to be Michelle's home language.

"And you have an M.D after your names."

"That's correct."

"Bowman wouldn't tell me much about you except that you were 100% all right in his book. I guess he must have sworn to secrecy."

"Do you really think that someone will eventually come here to Wenatchee for you and Michelle?"

"We went through Bowman's Boot Camp, because we can't afford to think otherwise. Not to anticipate someone's arrival could be terminal for us. We *must* be prepared. Our lives depend on as much anonymity as possible. And yes, I believe someone will ultimately show up to do us harm. The theory is that the man who put us this perilous situation, was not aware that I had lived through his onslaught of murder. Michelle told me that it was a miracle that I had been shot, point blank in the forehead and lived through it. The really strange thing is that now, trepidation has given way to confidence. I'm sure I speak for Michelle as well. We're ready and all the help we're receiving from you and Bowman has further prepared us to meet our adversaries on their level. It was essential that we that we change our mindset from helping good people to eliminating bad people."

"I'm glad for you and Michelle. Sometimes the law cannot be adequately applied to each and every situation and then it seems like the bad guys get away with murder. You two are the rectifiers."

"Thank you Brandon, I hope we never put you in a situation that will affect your job or life."

"I'm not worried. I think I'm working with some quality persons in you and Michelle. You're both strong willed, very smart and tough and that's a winning ticket. Let me know when I can be of service again Barbara. I've got to get back to the station.

Barbara sat in her car and thought about Brandon and all the work that Bowman had done to enable myself, and Michelle for whatever we would have to confront.

"You are not going to believe what I'm going to tell you Barb. Come over here to the divan and sit."

"Do I need a glass of wine first?"

"Yes! A glass of wine would be fitting. I would like one also."

Barbara stood and went to the kitchen cabinet.

"Oh crap," Michelle lamented," I've been so excited by the news I'm going to tell you that just this instant, it occurred to me, it might be bad news."

"Here, have a shot of wine and tell me anyway."

"Remember when I told you that I thought someone had recognized me? Well, someone did, a former college sweetheart. I'm going to meet him this Saturday and I'm excited about it, but right now it seems so out of place…Barb, I mean, I feel like…"

"Like you're deserting me? Barbara interrupted, "Don't. You should be excited. The situation we're in right now, is an imposition that was thrust on us and we're trying to make the best of it the only we know how. We deserve some cheerful excitement. Let it take us where it will. This is just life, in its complexity, surreptitiously raising its head of inexplicable confusion. We just have to deal with it and work it out."

"Oh Barb, you're so real. You just step up to the plate and take your swing." They hugged and then took a sip of their wine.

"So tell me how your meeting came about. I *am* excited for you."

"The day our eyes met, he wasn't sure it was me. It had been years since we had seen each other and we both have changed in physical appearance enough to create doubt. I had just walked out of Safeway and was walking to my car, when I heard someone yell, 'Kirsten,' and even though it has been almost four years now, I turned and looked toward the grocery store, but saw no one and guessed it was *not* for this previous Kirsten anyway. I no more than entered my car when he was at my door.

"Morrisey right?" He asked.

"And then I recognized Charles Gellately. He was on way to some meeting and we couldn't talk, but he wanted to get together this Saturday."

"Does he know?"

"No. Our conversation was brief. He knows nothing about me. What do you think? I mean he was an old boyfriend."

"You're a smart woman Michelle. You'll know what you should do and say. There is no way we can remain under the radar. We have to live our lives the way we want, not by someone's dictation. I'm not going down without a fight and they may win, but they'll know we were there. I would hope you feel the same."

"Oh I do.

"Are you all right Barb?"

"Yes, I met another one of my neighbors. He showed up at my door. I like him. He's older and I think he said he writes, along with keeping an eye on me."

"Are you saying he likes you?"

"I think so, reminds me of a middle aged Pierce Brosnan, quite handsome and humble. A quality I admire in men."

"Pierce Brosnan. Really, any interest on your part?"

"Not at this time, though I do like the man. He's not overly friendly and gives me space."

"All this from one meeting."

"He's a fast read, although I've been known to read wrong."

There was a pause.

"Have you heard anything about Grandstedt?"

"I'm glad you asked. Brandon saw a mug shot of him and was glad to see him with distinguishable bruises on his face. I guess Grandsted complained about his back and kidneys to the police, to no avail. He was also surprised by the note we left in Chinese."

"Really. Why? Surely he's aware that I'm Chinese and you taught English in Bejing, that you were subjected to learning Mandarin, Barb."

Barbara shrugged her shoulders. "Hey, what can I say?"

Barbara knew exactly what she needed to do. She had no more than entered her home when she rushed to the kitchen and started a two-cup pot of coffee. Her next stop was to a small roll top desk, where she picked up her ten year old Mac Computer and placed it on the breakfast counter and opened it. She sat looking at the blank page. Maybe she shouldn't put the information on the Mac. She closed it and set it on the stand beside the desk. She picked up a spiral notebook and set in front of her. Had Michelle already composed some kind of profile of my life? She couldn't remember, but if she was going to be alone from now on, it was most certainly essential. She needed an identity that she could recite at will, as if it were her *real* existence. Where had she previously lived? Did she have brothers and sisters? What schools had she attended? Where did she go to college? What about her parents? Were they alive? How did she end up here, in Wenatchee? What did she do for work before she arrived here? Was Grevera her married name? *Oh my God,* she thought. This is really opening up the proverbial can of worms. She sat back in her chair, put her hand to her neck and massaged it. How many times in her life had she been asked where she was born or what schools she had attended? Most people never ask those questions unless there is a specific reason.

One of my shortcomings has always been that I'm so damned honest. Somehow I would need to spin the truth, like our politicians do. Hadn't Michelle and Veronica always said that I was quick on my feet and with my mind? I don't need some stinking piece of paper to look at, and she closed the notebook. "I've got a quick mind," she said immodestly to herself.

I had no more than stepped out of the shower, when the landline phone began ringing. I wasn't going to answer it but its persistency drew me to respond.

"Hello."

"Is this Barbara Grevera, formerly Deidre Berenski?

My heart missed a beat and I had to think whether I should respond but before I could---.

The voice at the other cut in, "I understand your apprehension Ms. Grevera. Listen to me carefully, because I will not be calling you again; my name is not important. It is paramount that what I'm going to say in the next few minutes, be taken literally for what it is…a warning. I'm responsible for this leak that is now jeopardizing your life as well as your friend, Michelle G. Danese. You have my deepest apologies, but my life as well as my family's lives, have been imperiled and these people mean what they say. If it was only my life…but it isn't. This is a throwaway phone and so you don't need to worry about a trace. My conscience won't let me leave you without a caveat and so I pray you will leave where you are now living. Find another state or city. Arm yourself and know that we are living in a world where sometimes the only answer to our problems is that we become those who hunt us. Good luck and may God be with you Barbara J. Grevera.

I held the phone to my ear for the next few minutes. The towel had fallen to the floor and I was standing naked in the front room. A chill ran through me and I slowly walked back to the bathroom.

I sat on the divan and thought about what I should do about Michelle. I hadn't heard from her in the last ten days. Her meeting with her old boyfriend was the last time we had conversed. Stress, my gosh, when it arrives, it carries a big punch. Stop it Barb. You're not going to feel sorry for yourself. I want to talk to someone or at least be around a warm body. I peeked out my front window to see if I could see John at his computer in the den, to no avail. John was that his name? John, yes, Jerome David Salinger,' The Catcher in the Rye,' author, and he was John David Salinger.

Without thought, I reached into the closet and snatched a sweater and walked out the door. A walk had always been a good thing before and the fresh air couldn't do any harm now. I had walked about a mile when I saw a man with a dog approaching.

"Ah, Ms. Grevera, how nice to see you."

"So this is your dog…was it Daisy?"

"You have a very good memory. May I call you Barbara?

"I insist on it, John."

She leaned down on one knee and stroked Daisy's head, tenderly. "She's so gentle and trusting."

"She's a true lady, really. A little mischievous as a puppy, but when she grew up…all lady."

"How old is she?"

"A lady never tells her age. Two years past a decade."

"She's really holding up well. She's beautiful. You must love her very much."

John nodded and reached up and pinched his nose, and his eyes welled discernibly.

"I can't imagine life without her but then, life isn't forever."

"May I walk back with you two?"

He nodded and they ambled slowly toward the houses.

"I can't imagine you've never been married."

"I was married to a wonderful man John; a man that loved me as much as I, him; our happiness stolen by a madman, a psychopath. For the past three and a half years, emotionally my life has been a feather in the wind, lighting precariously and then with gusts swirling to the gales plea. I try not to indulge myself in the past for the obvious reasons, but sometimes the choice is not mine to grant, some sentiments so pervasive and inundating, one succumbs to their beckon. Forgive me John, I'm becoming sordid."

"No, no Barbara, you just want to talk. Please go on."

They walked on quietly until they reached his home.

"Would you join me for a cup of tea or coffee?"

She paused and then smiled, "Do you have any green tea?"

"Several."

"I can't think of the name of the tea that is often offered in Chinese restaurants. I think it's the name of a flower."

"Jasmine comes to mind?"

"Yes, Jasmine. Do you have Jasmine?"

"I do."

"I wouldn't be imposing on you, would I John?"

"I'd be delighted to have tea with you Barbara."

She sat at the kitchen table, but then stood.

"You're welcome to look around at the house," he offered.

She browsed leisurely at the paintings on the wall in the front room.

"I see you like Van Gogh."

"Not really, those were prints that my wife picked out several years ago. As paintings go, I prefer the southwestern flavor. I have one print by Georgia O'keeffe's, the apple family, the other prints by unknown artists, although some are quite prominent in New Mexico and Arizona. Our tea is ready. Would you like to sit in the front room or in the kitchen?"

"You're so accommodating John. The kitchen will be fine."

"Is that apple strudel? You're shameful John."

"Guilty."

"A thin slice please."

They ate slowly and sipped the tea.

"You mentioned earlier you were a writer. Is that what you did for a living?"

"No, writing is my hobby. I was an Industrial Engineer for IBM and Intel."

"And now you're retired?"

"Yes."

"Do they have an IBM or Intel plant or office here?"

"No, but I understand IBM is contemplating a plant in Quincy, Washington soon. I worked for both companies in California. The Bay Area is how it is referred to nowadays."

"I understand a lot of people commute great distances to their jobs, I guess even by planes."

"I didn't. Technically I still live there. You see I still have a home in Santa Clara, California."

"Do you rent this home?"

"No, I bought this home in '99 and thanks to the flexibility of my employers, I was able to commute here on weekends and time off from work. Essentially I was able to live in two different states at one time. Of course, it was easier when my wife was alive."

"You, as a person, are just the tip of the iceberg, John. There is so much to you."

"I think that's a compliment and I thank you."

"Ah, could I have another sliver of that strudel?"

"Less for me and that is good. Do you worry about your weight?"

"I've always been very careful about what I eat, although recently I lost a little over twenty pounds, which was brought on by...by," and she stopped the dialogue.

"Barb, if you ever want to get away for a while or even longer you can use my home in California."

"Oh John, you just can't stop from being nice and you hardly know me."

"If I can use your phraseology, 'you as a person are just the tip of that iceberg."

"Touche."

"Under all that protective armor, I believe is a gentle, wonderful, loving woman."

"That is definitely a compliment and I thank you."

"Would I be wrong to think you might be a professional person?"

"I'm not sure you want to go there, John. My life is very complicated and to involve a good human being like you would be a crime. But I am curious what you think I might be."

"Well, you're very direct, don't mince words, a positive attitude, protective of your friend. You sound a lot like my primary physician."

"A medical doctor," she responded, astonished.

"Hey Grevera, sorry I missed you. I need to talk to you my friend. Call me when you can. Michelle."

Barbara had a bad feeling about this call, she thought as she replaced the receiver down. Things are coming apart for me, but it might be for the best.

The knock on the door was usual entrance though somewhat solemn.

Barbara beat her to the punch, "It can't be all that bad Michelle," and they hugged in the kitchen.

"Ever the trooper girl. You're too much Barb."

She poured two cups of black coffee and they sat down, facing each other.

"It just happened, Barb, out of the clear blue, it just happened."

"It's not a bad thing, you deserve some happiness. Think about it? You've been babysitting me for almost four years. You have a life to lead too. If it happened to me, I would do the same thing."

"How long have you known, girl?"

"It's been almost two weeks since we've spoken and…well it's that inherent woman's intuition. Isn't that what they say about our psychic powers?

Michelle nodded, "Yup."

"So, what's up?"

"His company wants him to go to France for a couple of years and he wants me to go with him."

"I think that's wonderful, and that would get you out of harm's way here too."

"We think so, at least for a while."

"Is marriage on the brink?"

"We're going to play that by ear."

"Honestly Michelle, I think it's wonderful and I mean that from the bottom of my heart."

"I believe you and that you would be happy for me."

"Does he know?"

"Everything."

"Even me?"

She nodded, "I'm sorry."

"Don't be. Nothing is forever and besides, I'm ready for anything that comes my way. I have a couple of friends here that are very supportive of us, me."

"I can't elude the feeling of deserting you, Barb."

"I think I'd feel that way too, if it was reverse, but you're not abandoning me, for sure. I want you to go with all my love and blessings."

"You'll always be the best friend I ever had Barb and I think you know that. I'll keep you apprised of where I am, always. Thank God for throwaway phones. Pooh on the bad guys."

There was a short pause.

"When will you be off to France?'

"This Saturday."

"Wow, is there anything I can do for you before you leave?"

"Yes, remain my best friend," and she stood and opened her arms to Barbara. They hugged hard and then she kissed her friend on the cheeks, turned and rushed to the door, tears streaming down her face.

Barbara stood where Michelle had hugged her, eyes welled but no tears fell. She was happy for

Michelle and would not allow tears to diminish the bliss her friend had found. She was now alone and yet she felt secure.

There was a soft knock on the door. She touched her eyes with a tissue and walked to the door.

"Forgive me my arrogant intrusiveness Barbara, but I couldn't help but notice your friend leaving under some kind of duress."

"She's leaving Wenatchee."

"I'm sorry."

"It's a good thing John. She'll be happier where she's going and with someone she loves. I couldn't be more elated than I am now for her. She deserves all the things most us take for granted. Sit down John. I think I know you well enough to expose my soul to you." For the next half hour, she made a long story short and he sat dumbfounded.

"It all makes sense now Barbara. The military uniforms, the drill instructor, your training schedule for sixteen weeks, your living here for three plus years with very little interaction with neighbors, the rigid regiments with fitness centers, your apprehension to converse openly." He shook his head.

"There's more to the story, but this gives you enough to understand why it's good that Michelle is leaving Wenatchee. My only regret is that by enlightening you about my life, I have put *your life* in jeopardy."

"Not really. I don't think that even these people would want to kill everyone you talk to."

"I hope your right."

"Does this mean you will be leaving soon?"

They were unable to say anything for a few seconds.

"Would you like a shot of Jack Daniels John?"

"I certainly could use one, in a million years I wouldn't have--."

"I'm glad you're my friend John. I certainly need someone like you."

He nodded somberly.

"Hey, I need your strength Mr. Salinger."

"Yes, and I'm a hundred and ten per cent on your side, I thought you understood my unspoken loyalty."

Barbara nodded approvingly, then, noticed the curious look in his face, "do you have a question John?"

"Is your given name Barbara Grevera?"

"It is not and I'm not in a 'Witness Protection,' program, though I have changed my name, and I'm not going to change it again. This is whom I'm going to be from now on and that's a given."

CHAPTER 9

Barbara left her home, drove down to the old part of Wenatchee and parked. *I suppose it could be called, 'old town,' as the old parts of towns are called nowadays,* she thought. Managing to park in front of the old fifties ice cream shop that still had chrome and red Naugahyde seats, Barbara sauntered through the open door. She hadn't eaten a chocolate Sunday since…she couldn't remember when. The waiter was a young man in his teens, alert and eager to serve anyone that sat at the counter.

"Yes ma'am, what's your pleasure?"

"Can you make a single scoop Vanilla Sundae with a cherry and chocolate on top?"

"Absolutely ma'am, coming right up," he smiled and hurried off.

She had seated herself at the counter, but noticed the small tables by the window where she could sit and look out at the people passing by. As she settled at the nearest table she noticed an older man further down sitting by himself. A Starbuck's coffee rested on the table, with an empty ice cream dish. He was looking out the window when she sat, but as the waiter brought her Sundae, his eyes wandered over in my direction. I smiled inadvertently and he responded with the slightest dip of his head, hardly noticeable. I looked away, wondering why I had smiled. Looking down at my dish of vanilla and chocolate, I raised the spoon to my mouth and the creamy taste was delicately delicious, just the way I remembered it. Inconspicuously, my eyes ventured toward the old man and to my surprise he was gone. I quickly looked toward the counter and then out the window to see if I could see him, but he was gone. *Was I disappointed? The way my life had been going lately, I was probably more surprised than disappointed,* I speculated.

As I walked down Wenatchee Avenue browsing the store windows, I knew I wasn't looking for anything to buy. I just wanted to be among the living. I was…no, I wasn't going to admit it. I crossed the Avenue and walked up Orondo Street and found myself at the park below the courthouse. I walked over to the Cannon that I'm told, has been there forever, and started to read the inscription, but changed my mind and instead I sat on the bench beside it. I had only been there for a minute before I was looking for a tissue to wipe away my streaming tears. The dam that I had been filling all day had finally reached its apex and was flowing over in buckets.

"Here," a quiet voice offered and I looked through blurred vision and saw the outline of a man. He placed the tissue in my hand and I patted my face until I could see my shoes clearly, then looked up to see the old man from the ice cream shop.

"I don't understand."

"You need me, and so here I am, Barbara."

"I don't understand."

"Why are you crying? Why did you smile at me at the ice cream shop?"

"I don't know."

"You do know."

"I do?"
"Talk to me."
"I don't understand."
"You've said that three times."

I reached down to get another tissue and when I looked up, he was gone.

"Oh crap," I muttered as I began crying again.
"Here," he said again.
"Are you for real?"
"As real as you want me to be."
"You know I'm a Psychiatrist?"
He nodded.
"Am I delusional right now."
"You're circumventing the reason I'm here."

"My life is a mess right now and I don't know what to do about it. You see, I really should be dead, but I'm not and because I'm not dead, my life is the shits."

He nodded.

"I lost three years of my life, my husband was murdered, my best friend has deserted me and my daughter and mother live three thousand miles away. For three years I was totally unaware of what had happened to me, except for what my best friend was telling me, which I accepted as the truth. Michelle my dear friend and companion, all this time had to take it upon herself to sell my home and liquidate all that I owned, except what my daughter could carry away. There was never any closure. I don't even know where my husband is buried or where my daughter lives. I'm an empty shell of what I was, once. I didn't get to say, my goodbyes to my husband's mother and father that were killed a year and a half ago. I could be having a meltdown right now, and quite frankly I don't give a crap."

"Excuse me, ma'am."

I looked up to see a man in blue suit looking down at me with addled concern in his eyes and in his voice.

I felt foolish in front this man and couldn't think of what to say for a few seconds. "Well, I believe that proper Psychiatric term is a 'mental breakdown,' sir. Actually I was talking to someone, but he has obviously left me talking to myself, therefore your concern."

"I wouldn't dispute that. I mean I believe you were talking to someone. I stopped because I thought I recognized you, though I've never talked to you. Do you live on Red Apple Way, on the hill?"

I stood, "My name is Barbara Grevera, and yes, I do live on Red Apple Way, on the hill."

"I'm kind of your neighbor, same street though further up the hill a few houses. My name is Dennis Seifert. The neighbors across the street from you have mentioned you on occasion when we've gotten together."

"They probably think I'm some snob."

"Not at all, quite the contrary. Mary said you were pretty, had beautiful legs and appeared to be in great shape."

"You're being polite to me, of course."

"I suppose I am to some degree, but those words came out of Mrs. Hudson's mouth, and her husband Joe, agreed with her in her presence. Knowing Mary and Joe, they wouldn't deny it, in your company."

Barbara extended her hand, he looked down and accepted it. "Thank you Mr. Seifert, you may have stopped a meltdown. I'm grateful, but I must be going. I do have an appointment."

She walked away with purpose in her gait.

"Ms. Grevera," Dennis yelled.

She stopped and turned, "I totally agree with Mrs. Hudson and Joe."

She turned and continued walking and raised her right arm in the air. *Wonder if he's married,* she thought.

She lives with another beautiful woman, maybe she's gay, he thought, *a smile crossing his face.*

Barbara rose early Saturday morning, ate a light breakfast of fruit and drove to the Walla Walla point, to begin a run on the Apple Capital Recreation Loop trail that was ten miles long. She had mapped out to run from the Walla Walla point to the bridge and back again. She was there primarily to think about her life at this pinnacle and this was her mind cleansing therapy. She slipped a pair of cotton gloves on her hands this crispy morning and a light Adidas top. She stretched for five minutes and then started a slow jog that would increase slightly as her body adjusted to the routine.

She could see the variety of ducks and geese on the shallow pools along the Columbia River as well as on the trail. Runners no longer worried the birds on the asphalt runway as they ate of the lush grass along the trail.

Now that Michelle was on her way to France and hopefully a life of peace and happiness, her thoughts jumped to John Salinger's generous offer. If she had to move again she would certainly consider California. Maybe she could rent his home in Santa Clara. I wouldn't have to put my name on any transactions and I would be completely anonymous. How would they know where I lived unless I literally told them? From now on I would have to handle everything. Michelle was the genius that got us here and now it would all be up to me. I need to get a hold of Pi Guo and see what I would have to do.

Then there's my mother and daughter Katie, and oh my God, what am I doing. I'm getting way ahead of myself. Thank God I'm back. Stop this brain from going off the deep end.

It had been eight days since Michelle had left for France and loneliness pervasively began creeping in, creating doubt, apprehension, misery and then it was here. Barbara had just returned from a brief outing, approached the front door and noticed it was *not* completely closed. Its flaw was that it required a *slam* to close effectively. Just closing produced a false shut, and would open discernibly as one walked away. She turned and saw John walking briskly toward her.

"I saw him just as I entered the den, but just a profile and by the time I was outside all I could see was the back of a Volkswagen Jetta driving off. I didn't recognize him."

"I suppose it could have been anyone," she lamented, "or it could be one those who I've been expecting for almost four years. You know John, I actually feel some relief, I'm not afraid. I was a little startled by the realization that my door was not closed, but I didn't panic. I guess I've been waiting so long for this moment that it didn't have any punch. Would you like to come inside and have a drink?"

They sat quietly for a few seconds and each took a good shot of their JD drink.

"He was about five ten or eleven and thin, with I believe, was a dark mustache. He wore a dark sport coat and light chinos, maybe Latin. Do you think you should call the police?"

"Thin, you said he was thin."

"Maybe one hundred seventy."

"About the police, I was thinking about that, but I don't think I will. Bringing the police might work against what I want to do. Did you notice if there was anyone else in the Volkswagen?"

John put his hand to his forehead and thought. "I was more interested in securing the license plate numbers, but as I visualize the whole thing. I don't think there was anyone else in that car. Though I can't be for sure."

Barbara poured each another drink and gulped it down. He followed her lead.

"I think you should go now John. I think too much of you for you to be around me for the next few days. I want you to promise me, you will stay away. I absolutely feel like I can take care of this in my own way, and please do not call the police. You're my best friend and you'll just have to trust that I know what I'm doing. Promise?"

"I hope it's not Jack Daniels talking right now Barbara. But yes, however, with the greatest of reluctance, I promise not to call the police and to leave you on your own for the next five days."

"Now go. I have things to do, but first let me have the license number you obtained."

I had the license number checked out by Brandon Danielson and it turned out to be a rental with a bogus name and address, which I had anticipated. I had secured the medicine that was essential and rented a van with no seats in the back.

Everything was on a green light ready. The first night was eventless and she napped during the day. The second night was the same. The third night I heard the front door creak ever so quietly. From behind the door, I eyed the clock in the bedroom. It was a little after three in the morning. I was dressed in my camouflage uniform and could feel my pulse escalating.

The stalker pushed on the bedroom door slowly stepped in, stood for few seconds, allowing his eyes to focus on the bed for clarity. I stood motionless until he moved quickly to the side of the mattress and I followed him, syringe in hand, right hand reaching for his shoulder and neck and pierced his left carotid artery swiftly and he responded by throwing his arm around and lifting my body against the wall. I felt my head hit hard and then I felt myself losing consciousness.

CHAPTER 10

"Thank you for meeting with me, Mr. Lamantia. I was interested in whether you had sent anyone out for the two ladies that Dimitre wanted investigated."

"Yes ma'am, I sent Reggie Johnson."

"And have you heard anything?"

"No ma'am."

"What I'm going to tell you now Jimmy is to be held in the strictest of confidence by you, as well as me. Do you understand?

Jimmy he thought. Now she calls me Jimmy. What is she up too? He thought.

"The doctor who has been treating Dimitre has found a blood clot in the right side of an artery by the brain. He has tried using medicine to dissolve the mass to no avail and now he wants to remove it surgically. If it's successful, he would be up and around in a week or so, which would be good. If he isn't successful in removing the embolism, he could possibly have a stroke. Where I'm going with all this suspense Jimmy is, I'm thinking of suspending the investigation of the ladies in question by Dimitre's order. What's your take with all that I've told you?"

She wants me to agree with her so if things go bad, I would be a collaborator in her decision and very possibly end with a bullet between my eyes, he thought.

"Did the doctor give you any idea of what the possibility of a stroke would be?"

"Yes, he said Dimitre has a fifty-fifty chance of recovering."

"I don't know Mrs. Aristotle, your husband likes his orders carried out without arbitrations."

"I understand your apprehension, but what if he has a stroke and loses the ability to speak, which often happens with stroke people."

"Yes, ma'am. But do we dare take that chance?"

"You make him sound like some Gestapo General that would kill you if you didn't carry out his orders, Mr. Lamantia."

Now I'm back to being Mr. Lamantia, because she didn't like my answer. How do I get out of this?

"Maybe we could temporarily postpone our orders; wait to see the outcome of the operation, Mrs. Aristotle."

"That sounds like a viable proposal, Jimmy. I see why Dimitre considers you his right hand man."

CHAPTER 11

I had awakened on the floor, stood, looked around to see where the intruder might be and discovered he was standing against the bedroom door, moaning indefinable words. The anesthetics had kicked in but not enough to bring him down He was delirious. I turned the lights on in the bedroom and searched the floor for the syringe. I found it just under end of the comforter that covered the bed. The capsule was still half full, but missing the needle. It was still in his neck. I picked up the plastic capsule already with a needle and rushed to the perpetrator and inserted the needle in his neck and walked him out to my rental van, placed him in the back, tied his hands together and drove to the Bowman's Boot Camp.

Barbara woke up to persistent knocking on the door. She shuffled out of her bedroom in her slippers and finished wrapping her robe around herself at the door. She peeked out her side window, and opened the door to an anxious John Salinger.

"Thank God you're all right. I fell asleep early this morning after staying up half the night keeping an eye on you, for the last three nights, Barbara. Where's that van you rented? What happened last night?"

"John, John, come in and make us some coffee while I shower and get dressed, please. I'll explain everything and also, I want to have a serious discussion with you about California. The coffee is on the counter in the silver canister and well, you know how to make coffee in a Mr. Coffee, I'm sure. See you in twenty minutes."

CHAPTER 12

The transition from Washington State to the San Francisco Bay Area was luxuriously stress free. Pi Gau, my financial agent had picked out a home in a quiet cull de sac, in Sunnyvale, California. I was close to a main artery and only thirty-five miles from the legendary city, San Francisco. In that I felt alone, the peace of tranquility was here, though dubiously temporary. It made me feel lost in a prodigious and varied population of people that reside here. It would be a while before *they* found me again and by then I will have acclimated to these surroundings. The advantage would be on my side. But for now I was alone, free and loving life. I called my daughter and mother and offered an open invitation to come and live with me. Their response didn't sound inspiring, but they would give it some thought and call me later. Understandably, Katie would be leaving her friends and mother loved my daughter as much as I. I wasn't alarmed by any of this, no sir, I was free and I walked around with a big smile. Honestly, couldn't stop feeling giddied. I discovered that having a smile on your face sent the wrong message to some people, mostly men. I wasn't flirting or trying to entice anyone to me, I was just happy. One handsome man stopped and asked me if I knew him when I smiled at him.

"No, I'm just lighthearted and carefree," I responded and resumed my walk. I had been told I had a nice smile, but isn't everyone's smile nice. A smile on any face is alluring and will catch the attention of most who witness it, like crying has the same adverse effect. I think.

I peeked out my back room window and noticed the beautiful roses in my backyard. This was April and they were blooming. An old neighbor, in New York, had once told me that you could stick any flower or plant in the ground in most of California and it would grow, practically year around. I stepped out the back door and felt the sun hit my back. It felt warm and soothing. I had been here almost two months and never been in the backyard, or maybe I noticed the yard, but nothing caught my interest. Now it was inviting and it aroused my curiosity.

"She loves flowers and I think roses are her favorite. How do you like living here?" the neighbor called out from across the yard.

"I do, it's everything they say about the Bay Area."

"Darn it, I've got a call. It was nice talking to you."

And here I thought northern Californians weren't friendly. I went inside and rummaged around in the kitchen for a pair of scissors. In fifteen minutes I had three of the most beautiful velvety red roses in a small flower bowl lighting my kitchen table. The small teapot whistled its finished shrill and I dropped a packet of green tea in the steaming cup. Looking at the roses, my mind went up to Wenatchee and my conversation with John D, Salinger. He truly was a good friend. One of those people you meet and make you feel like you've known them all your life. They only see the good in you. That was John, and why not? I'm a good person, gone bad for a good reason. The law had their shot at Reggie Johnson and they let him go for whatever reason. I'm sure Mr. Johnson expected some feckless, inattentive, incompetent, sniveling woman. I didn't start this game of kill or be killed. He came to my house against my will and he ended up dead. The ambivalence of my deed did cause some consternation, but in the end. I was alive and he was not. Better him than me. I can still see the concern on John's face as he scrambled over to my house to see if I was all right. He was crying as he held me in his arms. It was so touching to have a man I hardly knew, have that much concern for me. He loved me as a genuine friend. How often does that happen?

I wanted to call Michelle Danese, but I knew she was probably trying to forget all that got us to Washington State in the first place. If she called me I would gladly talk to her, but I'm not going to call her. She deserves to put all this mess behind her for as long as she can, hopefully forever. My cell phone woke me from the trance I was in.

"Yes, this Barbara Grevera. Yes. Chillies? Well I don't know exactly where it is but I have GPS in my car and I'm sure I can find it with an address. I'm writing it down right now. Tomorrow will be fine. Can I have your name one more time? Rudolf, Del. Thank you. Five pm is fine. See you then.

"Barbara Grevera?"

I stood looking at an attractive Latin woman with a broad smile on her face. "Yes,"

"I'm Del Rudolph, Detective Delores Rudolph, John Salinger is a good friend of mine and informed me of your situation and I believe I can be of service to you. Did you have any trouble finding this place?"

"No, technology is amazing."

The two ladies entered the restaurant and ordered a meal making small talk all the while.

"So you've been here around two months. Do you like it here?

"Very much."

"Good. Would you give me the highlights of the last four years? I understand you didn't have any memory of your previous life until recently."

They had several refills of coffee and Barbara finished her most recent life story with very little said about the last two months here in Sunnyvale.

"The last conversation I had with John brought up a man that was found dead in Wenatchee about two months ago. Tell me about that situation."

"What did John tell you?"

"I want to hear it from you Barbara. If I heard correctly what our mutual friend said, I am completely on your side about what you did and want to do, I'm on your side all the way."

"The minute my memory was back, I immediately signed us up for a boot camp under the direction of a man by the name of Joseph Doyle Bowman, a former Marine Seal; after sixteen weeks of his training, my friend, Michelle and I were amply trained for what was waiting for us. I still feel that way. Michelle has gone abroad with my blessing, and I hope she stays away."

"Why are these men specifically after you?"

"The presumption was that I died by a bullet to the head by the man responsible for his brother's family death, and unfortunate friends that were gathered there to celebrate one of the families birthday. I was one of the unfortunate friends. My husband worked for Mr. Able Aristotle, the man murdered. Miraculously, I survived and have lived under the dark cloud of permanent fear, since I was aware enough to realize fear."

"Go on about the man in Washington that was killed," Rudolph prodded.

"I like to think that I was once a good citizen, obeying all the laws, working at my profession, trying to bring up my daughter, buying a house with my husband, paying taxes, all the things that Americans do, to have a good life. Out of the blue, I was in the wrong place, and someone decides someone should die and I lose a husband; end up in the hospital for months hanging by a thread. A bullet pierced my head and my life goes into limbo because of some nut abuses the law and justice does not prevail because of the lack of proof, adding to the misery, I find out that because I was blessed by a miracle to live, some…some bastard is sent to finish the job. How insane is that. Anyway, yes, I tortured the son of bitch until he told me what I wanted to know. I broke his nose, his left wrist, and all the fingers in his right hand, broke two of his ribs. I deposited his vile body in the dump. His name was Reggie Johnson. I believe he said he was Cuban. Do I regret it? Before I hung him I told him that he and his miserable friends had made a monster out of me, and that I was going to do the same to his friends if they kept coming after me. You know what he did, Detective?"

Rudolph just stared.

"He spit in my face and laughed, so 1 slowly began pulling the rope through the pulley until his feet were a foot above the ground. It took him forty-seven minutes to stop moving. The sad thing…I felt no remorse. It took almost a week before I broke down and cried."

Detective Rudolph reached across the table and held Barbara's hands in hers. She thought about the adjectives John Salinger had used to describe Barbara; beautiful, thoughtful, gentle, compassionate, hopeful and endearing of those she loved. Was this the same woman?

"I've brought some pictures," Detective Rudolph said, "and possible names of Dimitre Aristotle and his cohorts for you to look at. Right now that's about all I can do, but don't hesitate to call me for anything and if I can, I will. OK? We'll get together soon Barbara."

"Thank you Detective. You don't know how much I appreciate your assistance. I don't feel so alone. I have John as a friend, but you are a real bonus."

They hugged.

Barbara went home and hung the pictures of the men in her den. Now she had actual pictures of the loathsome bastards, and she stared at each man, fixing them indelibly in her memory.

"Hi mom, we tried calling last night but we missed you. Your friend John, thought it would be better if you came over to his house. Do you know how to get here?"

"Yes, I do and I'll be over in a few minutes. Are you still using the phones I sent you?"

"Yes mom, of course. I'm calling you on one now. Hurry up and come over. Gram's here too."

They hugged and kissed and cried until everyone was once again composed enough to converse, oscillating through Katie's school curriculum, machine gunning varied subjects and Sara keeping up with her granddaughter. Meanwhile John sat quietly in the nearby kitchen drinking coffee and listening to the grand reunion.

There was a lull in the discussion until Katie spoke up.

"You know the last time we saw you, was when you were still in a coma and…could I look at your forehead?" She stood and walked to where her mother was sitting and sat beside her. "Lean your head toward me Mom. Wow! It's almost gone. Grams come look."

"You were always a quick healer, honey. It's still hard for me to think someone can shoot another person inches from the head and still live. You're a miracle honey. God has something else planned for you Dee, and I'm sure they will eventually catch the man that did this horrible thing to you." She stopped and put her hand to her lips. "I'm sorry…Barbara, I'm not used to using your new name."

"I like your new name, mom. Do you like it?"

"Michelle christened me with it and yes, I do like it. Have you heard from her?"

"No, but John told us she was in Europe, France."

"Guilty," John responded, "Barbara, I hope I didn't jump the gun."

"It's perfectly all right. Yes, she's in France and I'm sure, enjoying her new life. I pray that she is never found out."

"Why do you have to keep moving from place to place, Mom? Nobody's looking for you and besides why would they? That thing happened almost four years ago. No one cares about doing anything to you. It doesn't make sense."

"I agree it doesn't make any sense, but the people that did this to me don't have any sense. I got it from an anonymous source that they are sending people, and I say people because some might be woman, I don't know that factually but one never knows."

"How do they know that you're still alive, mom? You changed your name, moved to a different state. How do they find out all this stuff?"

"The simple answer is intimidation. Someone on the side of law knows something that a person on the other side wants to know and money might be used to coerce that person for information that is needed. If money is not enough of an inducement on that person, his life or even his family or friends are used as a motivating factor. Good people are placed in an incongruous predicament where there is no good resolution, between a rock and hard place, Katie. Fair people don't want to compromise someone they might position to die because of the information they're forced to dispense to an in despicable coward. Almost everything these people do is by deception. You can't arrest them for what they think, but if they put bullet on someone's head and the courts find them innocent for whatever reason, then you are at the mercy of their treacherous endeavors."

"What about witness protection?" Sara queried.

"Mom, at the time I wasn't in a position to vote on that issue, but from what Michelle told me, it wasn't what we wanted. I concurred with her decision when it was brought to light later. I can't imagine living with someone looking over your shoulder for the rest of my life. That's not a life."

"So you're going to be a vagabond?"

"No honey, I'm not going to be gypsy. I've done all I'm going to do to prepare myself for whatever is going to confront me. Is anyone hungry?"

"Yes, grams and I haven't eaten all day and we're starving."

John nodded his head in agreement.

CHAPTER 13

Jimmy' The Fox' finally got word from Toby 'The Quiet Man' that he had sent to find out what had happened to Reggie Johnson in Washington State. Reggie had abruptly stopped communications with him. Then he thought he might have lost Toby. The Quiet man report was not a good one. Someone had beaten up Reggie, hung and left him in the Wenatchee dump. *Better call Gina Aristotle and let her know what's going on,"* he thought.

"Jimmy, I'll meet you at Starbucks on 33rd Street in Samson. The weather is good and we can sit outside. Is this about the women Dimitre wanted tracked down?"

"Yes ma'am. You see, I was able to locate the two ladies in question and at your request, the last time we met. Do you recall?"

"I do, and you sent someone. Right?"

"Yes, I sent a man by the name of Reggie Johnson to a small town in Washington State. At that time, which was well over a week ago, he had not come across the ladies. He was still trying to root out their exact location.

"I don't understand? Surely it wouldn't take that long to find two women in a small town. Does he have an Iphone? How about a phone book? What are the ladies names? I think you might have sent the wrong person, Jimmy."

I couldn't believe she said that, I thought, *Does she think these ladies are going to be carrying name tags on their lapels. I realize now why Gina was never allowed to go to the trial that Dimitre had labored through and finally been exonerated because of lack of evidence. She has always been kept in the dark about what Dimitre really does. She thinks he's an honest businessman because of the legitimate businesses that he has acquired from bad money. I was finally realizing that this woman had no idea what Dimitre did.*

"You're probably right Mrs. Aristotle."

"So were you able to locate the gentleman…Johnson was it?"

"Yes. He had been killed in an accident and Toby Erickson took care of the funeral arrangements in Washington State."

"Did he have a family?"

"No ma'am."

"Poor man, I can't imagine someone not having a family to weep over him. Sometimes I think the world is getting calloused and foreboding. Don't you think so, Jimmy?"

I nodded.

It was Wednesday, Brandon parked on Columbia Street and punched in Barbara Grevera's cell number. He had to warn her of a visitor she might be receiving. The phone kept ringing and he was about to hang up.

"Hi Brandon. Can I call you back in twenty minutes?"

He checked his watch, "That will be fine."

"Sorry about not being able to talk to you a few minutes ago. I had to shoo my mother and daughter out the house so I could talk openly with you. Are you able to talk now Brandon?"

"Yup, just got back in my car. I'm eating sweet peas from the pods. Ever eaten sweet peas from the shell? Just open the pod and roll the peas into your hand and into your mouth; nothing like fresh sweet peas. On a more serious note, that man you took care of here, before you went to California had a man from New York inquiring about him. I never met him, but my friend Wilbur at 'Paupers Graveside Services' called. Seems the man wanted to know how he died. Of course, he wasn't allowed to give that information to anyone but a relative, which this guy wasn't. Wilbur didn't seem to think that he had much familial interest, more like a Private Detective. It took them long enough to get the message that you're no roll over, Barbara. On the other hand, I don't want you to get intimidated by some guy that may or may not be associated with the person or persons that are after you. Just be aware that it could be. Here's Wilbur's description of the man who made the inquiry of his associate. He was tall, maybe six feet, blondish, going on grey, one hundred and eighty pounds, possibly Scandinavian, perhaps German or Swedish. He wore prescription spectacles."

"Thank you Brandon, for taking the time to inform me and I will continue to be aware that someone *will* eventually show up down here. I've met someone down here who is your counterpart. She's a beautiful Spanish lady that was originally from the other Las Vegas, the one in New Mexico. She's taken me under her wing here in San Jose and I'm comfortable with what is developing between us."

"I'm glad to hear that. I wouldn't want to think you would be alone in this thing. You're a good woman and if you ever need me in any way, I'm just a phone call away. You take care of yourself." Barbara. I've got to respond to a call I just received. Till I hear from you." Click.

Lingering in the room, Barbara thought about the new friends she had cultivated. Losing her best friend could have been devastating, but now she had more friends. She knew Brandon meant what he said when he offered his services for anything she might need. She didn't feel alone anymore. There have always been good people, you just have to reach out and they'll come to you. You have to make the effort for those you need. First I lost my fear as a consequence of robust training through the Marine Seal Boot Camp, by reaching out to someone, and I made it happen. Then isolation dissolved itself when others that felt the same way as me, shared those sentiments, and no, I've never eaten fresh sweet peas from the pod. The next time I'm at a Farmer's Market, if I can remember, I will try them.

I immediately went to my den and scrutinized the pictures on the wall. Blonde, one hundred eighty pounds, glasses, she thought, only one man had blondish grey hair, his name was Toby Erickson, and he could be German or a Swede.

O' DARK THIRTY

It had been almost three weeks since my conversation with Brandon Danielson concerning the next possible assassin's arrival and intermittently I had conversed with Detective Rudolph how I should ready myself for his coming. Her only caveat was, 'stay alert,' there is no handbook for *crazies* that kill people. There is only speculation of what might be. We can only react to their actions. When he will arrive, or if he will remain the person he is on a normal day; will he be alone or will he have someone with him? Will he try during the day or will he strike at 'O Dark Thirty?'

Jimmy Lamantia liked Chocolate, Strawberry, or Vanilla Sundae's with the cherry on top, so his meeting with, 'The Quiet Man,' Toby Erickson was at Tiffany's O'Rourke ice cream shop on fifth Street and Henry Drive in Samson.

"You know ice cream isn't good for you Mr. Lamantia."

"Everything that you eat too much of is bad for you Mr. Erickson. I'm treating. What would you like?"

"I don't eat ice cream."

Jimmy ate the last of his Sundae and cleaned his hands with a napkin and drank the water he had requested to get the sugar out of his mouth. "What kind of dessert do you like?"

"Mostly fruit, I like Mangos, some of the new apples, apricots, and of course cherries when they're in season.

Jimmy nodded, "All good stuff, Mr. Erickson. Shall we get down to business?"

"I'm ready when you are."

"I haven't discussed what happened to Johnson and at this time I don't think it's necessary to do so."

"No patience."

Jimmy eyes met Toby's and he thought about the quiet man. He didn't talk much, but when he did, he didn't mince words. "No patience"?

"That's right, Johnson did something wrong with those women in Washington and that's the reason he's never going to leave there. And you Mr. Lamantia, are too patient. You should have let me go to California directly from Washington. There's a possibility we wouldn't be having this conversation."

"We'll never know the answer to that Mr. Erickson, however I do concede, I should have let you go. Are you ready now and do you still want to pursue this thing?"

"Yes sir, I am ready and eager. Just say the word."

"I probably should have let you go in the first place. I want you to keep me apprised when you get there. I don't mean to tether you to a phone. Keep me in the loop. Okay?"

They stood and shook hands and Toby walked off. Jimmy followed his departure and then he spoke to him, "for what's its worth, Toby, I think you're the best at what you do. Good luck."

He turned and a discernible smile crossed his face, but said nothing and then strode off.

"Mom, can grams, John and I come over and have a barbeque. We bought some steaks and sausages and I made a tossed salad, and Marie Calendar has fresh Strawberry Pies, with whipped cream; John's going to bring a bottle of wine.

"Sounds good. What can I do?"

"You're supplying the house for the event. That's enough."

"I'll start the barbeque and clean the patio so it will be ready by the time you get here."

She had just finished cleaning when they came bouncing through the patio door.

"I brought three bottles of wine, which is about a glass for each of us, out of each bottle John offered," and went directly into the house to refrigerate them.

"Mom where's the platter for the steaks?"

"Kitchen counter, honey."

The steaks were on the grill and Katie was acting chef.

"How do you birds want your steak?" She pointed at her grandmother."

"Well."

"John?"

"Rare."

"Mom?"

"Medium rare."

"Wow, what a day. It's so beautiful." Katie shouted out loud. John brought out each a glass of red wine and they all clicked, "here, here in unison."

Mom brought a large bowl of fresh carrot sticks, cauliflower and potato chips with ranch dressing. A second bottle of wine was opened.

They sat enjoying their food making small talk about the weather, traffic and then, the subject changed to Barbara's safety concerns.

"Mom, Grams and I would like to come and live here with you. John agreed with his blessings, but thought we should at least debate it so we would all agree or agree to disagree and be happy about what we decide, one way or the other. What do you think?"

"I would like to live my life in the most mundane manner, but I'm thinking very subjectively, maybe even on the selfish side. Having said that, I don't want to jeopardize you or Mom's lives and I most certainly would be doing that. Don't you think?"

"Honey," Barbara's mother chimed in, "don't you think a lot of this is merely speculation on your part. You have set in your mind that some ominous individual will arrive and do away with you. Like Katie said earlier. It has been almost four years since that terrible thing happened to you and by your own admission, nothing has happened in those years."

Oh no, Barbara thought, am I going to have to expose our little dirty secret? Should they know? Yet I do want what's left of my family around me. Do I dare be this egocentric individual? I could ask John what he thinks? He knows my terrible, macabre secret.

"John, could I impose your candor on this subject. You know me and now you have reasonably assessed my mother and daughter. Take your time. What do you think?"

She has done me no favor for an honest evaluation, but I suppose I might very well be the most objective of us sitting here. Barbara wants a regular live, which I concur. She has stated so recently to me and I believe her, and there is always hope that the last person that confronted Barbara might be the last.

"With very little hesitation, I believe you should live the normal life you have requested Barbara. There will always be peril in living life, but why be alone. Your family is all that you have and I'm proud to be a part of it. I deplore violence but if shows its ugly head around here, we are ready for its consequence, and may poetic justice prevail." He stood and made a toast to the…"what shall I call this family name?"

"Mom's still a Berenski, so Berenski is fine John."

He nodded, "Of course."

They stood and clicked their wine glassed and in near unison, shouting. "Salud."

Toby Erickson arrived at Norman Y. Mineta feeling at ease. He had been stationed at Moffet Air Base in between Mountain View and Sunnyvale in California, years before.

As he drove up Coleman Avenue, he tried to remember the landscape; the Costco Warehouse was new. He entered El Camino Real in Santa Clara and observed Santa Clara University was still there. He drove through several streetlights and didn't recognize any buildings or particular structures. The whole avenue was different. He drove until he found the Stanford Stadium and then made a 'U' turn and headed back down to Santa Clara. *Leave for a few years and nothing is the same,* he thought.

After driving around and looking for a motel to rent he finally found one on El Camino in Santa Clara.

"I saw a huge structure on Tasman Drive. Looks like a stadium," as he lay down cash for two weeks rent.

"That would be Levi Stadium, the new 49er home, replacing Candle Stick Park up in, I think San Bruno. Don't know why they called it San Francisco 49er's it was still a few miles from San Francisco. Where you from?"

"Kansas."

"Oh yeah, the Chiefs are up there. Alex Smith was a forty-niner until Kaepernik showed up. Now Alex plays for your team. Here's your receipt for two weeks, Mr. Smith."

After placing all his clothes in the small dresser, he lay down on the bed, hands behind his head and thought what he would do next. He sat up on the side of the bed, and reached for his cell phone on the nightstand, pushed the numbers.

"Hello."

"I'm here."

"Keep in touch."

Toby thought about how easy it had been to get all the information on Barbara Grevera. He had an authentic FBI agent's card, and was able to get information by posing as the man. He knew exactly where this Grevera woman had moved from Washington State. If Lamantia had sent me in the first place…though I guess I don't really mind. I always liked the Bay area.

I walked down to Denny's Restaurant and as I was ushered to a table a man spoke abruptly, "hey Larry, Larry Stoval."

I sat and looked over to the man that had spoken He was talking to his wife about me. He stood, walked over and sat across from me.

"Ed Beckham, we were stationed here at Moffett. Remember?"

I did, but I wasn't happy about it, and I really didn't like this guy. Yeah, I remember the jerk. He was always giving me a bad time about my ears.

"So what are you doing around here, Ed?"

"I stayed here after I did my time at Moffett, and met my wife. That's her over there. I knew it was you when I saw those ears. Do you live here now, or just visiting?"

"I'm here on business."

"Really, what do you do?"

At first I wanted to tell him I killed people for a living, but I knew he wouldn't buy that.

"I work for the government."

"What, you going to tell me your FBI?"

"You were always a pretty bright guy Ed."

"Are you saying I guessed it? You're really FBI?"

"I didn't say I worked for the FBI."

"You work for the Post Office."

"We need to change the subject. What do you do Ed?"

He got this serious face and looked me in the eye.

"I work for Lockheed. I'm a Mechanical Engineer designing the air planes most of the United States flies and some of the planes other countries use."

I wasn't surprised. Blowhards always seem to rise to the top and boss people around. Ed Beckham was no exception. Although he was just one of many engineers that worked for Lockheed.

"That's good Ed."

"So how long you going to be in town?"

"Hopefully less than two weeks."

"Exactly what do you do?"

"Top Secret, Ed."

"Top Secret? Sounds mysterious." *Ed wondered if Larry really was FBI.*

Toby was sure Ed wanted to see his ID card and now he thought he might show him his authentic FBI card with a different name.

"You were always a hard guy to pin down for answers Larry."

"Yeah?"

"You were from New York. Right?"

"Excuse me gentlemen, here's your breakfast. Can I bring you anything else?"

I shook my head.

"Go ahead and eat your breakfast Larry. Before you do, look me in the eye and tell me if you're FBI."

I leaned forward, pulled the black wallet from my breast pocket with a badge and nametag inside and laid it on the table in front of Ed. He looked down at it, picked up and opened it to a picture of Larry with a different name.

"Well, no shit Larry." He stared at me in disbelief. "I'm sorry I doubted you. Hey, you know what I said about your---"

"It's all right Ed," I interrupted him, "Don't worry about it."

He stood, "It was good to see you Larry."

I finished my breakfast and walked back to my hotel. *You were right about me Ed Beckham,* I thought, with a smile on my face.

CHAPTER 14

"Ah, Detective Rudolph, good to see you. Will you be eating alone, today?"

"No, I'm expecting a pretty dish water blonde in a few minutes, but you can seat me now and I'll have coffee. I need the caffeine, Roberto."

Rudolph called the station and talked to her boss about Barbara Grevera and the possibility of hiring her to work for the Police Department. "She's trained, she's an MD in Psychiatry, all we'd have to do is bring her up to snuff on the police department's protocol, Tom."

"I don't know if it's all that simple, but I'll kick it around. Okay?"

" Thanks, I gotta go. Any trouble finding the place Barbara?"

"Just the parking. These one-way streets kept me wandering around. Directions have always given me fits, but now, with the new technology, it's a breeze."

"Original Joe's is one of my favorite restaurants when I'm hungry. I hope you like the food."

"On occasions I've been known to eat more than I should, but, one meal won't make me over weight, and today I'm famished."

They ordered their meals and Rudolph reached across the table and put Barbara's hands in hers. "I feel like I've known you all my life. I find your candid and openness very compelling in a person of your stature.

Do you think you have changed *inside* since your accident in New York?"

Barbara nodded slowly, "I do. I've changed and it has come about in the last few months. I've done something that would never have crossed my mind in my other life. My husband was a very successful attorney and I had a thriving business in Psychiatry; a profession I loved and if I may say so, I was very good at. Now, it seems distant; that life was someone else's. Yes, I've changed, whether it's for the good remains to be seen."

"You're still a good person, Barbara, don't forget that. That never changes. Our stories run along the same path and I identify with what happened to you. My father was a cop and so was his father, but I'm the first female in the family to become a police officer and the first to have my husband and son murdered by a gang I had busted. That all happened in Albuquerque and shortly after I got my revenge, I came out here to San Jose. My life changed. The bumps and bruises do alter us, no doubt, but I still believe under the layer of slime, liars, prostitutes, killers, muggers, wife beaters and every possible kind of reprobate - lies our true self, like a bright shining diamond. It just has to be dusted off every once in a while."

"I like that Delores," she nodded, " I really like what you just told me. Thank you."

"Would you ladies like dessert today?"

"We're going to pass, Roberto. Too much lunch, but thank you."

"I hope I don't insult you by what I'm going to ask."

"I don't think you would ask anything insulting, Delores."

"Well, you never know…would you ever consider becoming a police officer…wait, would you ever consider working for the police department in any capacity?"

"You realize you're asking that question with full knowledge of my current situation. Aren't you?"

"I am. We have a Psychologist that works with our department, to assist us when we need her. She also works with I.A, Internal Affairs. The thing is I was hoping you might be receptive to working as a Detective, right alongside me. I mean…. Wouldn't that be great? You've got the physical training already, you have the education and you're not ready to go back to your old job. I bet I could learn some things from you Barbara. Why not? Would you be able to exist on a police officer's salary?"

"Oh what a picture you paint, Delores. I need to think about your wild idea," she smiled, "and yes I would be able to continue my way of life on a police officer's salary."

"Really Barbara! I think it would be absolutely fantastic to work with someone like you. I talked to our friend John about it. I bet he would agree with my thinking. I really do. Let's get out of here."

"As long as you're with me, the city is responsible for you, so don't worry about anything Barbara. My boss thought it would be good for you to see what it is we do as detectives. Under normal circumstances I would be working with another detective, but we're under a hiring freeze because of the weak economy."

Rudolph drove down Julian Avenue until she reached 4th Street and turned right.

"There was an apparent homicide at one of the Victorian homes close to San Jose State and we're going to be first on the scene."

As they neared the site they could see people standing on the sidewalks close to the house where the possible homicide occurred.

A city police officer directed her car to the front of the house in question.

"Morning Detective. That's the house there," he pointed.

"How's the new baby Phil," Rudolph asked.

"See the bags under my eyes."

"Yeah, but I bet she's worth it."

"She really is and now Margie's thinking about another one. Can you believe it?"

They walked into the front room, where another officer was standing.

"You again, Sanchez?"

"Nice to see you again, Detective Rudolph."

"Has CSI been here?"

"Not yet ma'am, but they're on the way. I heard you were in charge, so I requested to stay and help out. That's the victim on the pull out bed."

"Any others?"

Sanchez shook her head.

Rudolph bent over and examined the man's head. "This the only bullet hole?"

"I didn't turn him over, but my guess, it is. New detective?" she asked, looking at Barbara.

"Almost. Gloria Sanchez this Barbara Grevera, yes, I hope she will be my next partner."

They exchanged smiles and shook hands.

"Tell me what you think happened here, Sanchez?"

"Well, we first noticed that the front door was not locked, so maybe the vic knew the person. He answered the door in his underwear and t-shirt, or yelled for someone to come in from here. There were two bottles of Corona on the end table; one had been drunk out of, the other, maybe a swallow. CSI gets pissed if we loiter around before they get their hands on the scene, so we didn't touch anything, but Phil did go into the kitchen just to peek around. From the little he observed he thought drugs might be found on the premises."

"How long has this guy been dead?"

"Well, the Coroner is on his way, Detective. We'll get an estimate soon."

"If memory serves, the last time I asked, you were pretty close to the time, Sanchez."

"It's strictly a guess, ma'am…I'd say around ten last evening."

Rudolph nodded, "Duly noted. Was there more than one perpetrator?"

"I don't think so, and it might have been a female."

"Why would you say that?"

"There was a towel over his penis."

Rudolph reached down and lifted the towel from his body and indeed, there was an exposed penis. She then scrutinized the hole in the victim's head.

"Would you guess the bullet that put that hole in this man's head was a .22?"

"Yes ma'am, though I didn't see the spent shell around the body anywhere."

Barbara squatted on her knees and looked at the hide-bed- divan cushion the man was lying on and noticed a small hardly discernible hole. "What do you think this is, Delores?"

Detective Rudolph leaned down, "it looks like another bullet hole, Barbara."

They stood.

"All right. Thank you Officer Sanchez, you've got a good eye and you're quite observant. Oh, who found the body first?"

"His friend. He's outside in Phil's car. I told him you would want to talk to him."

"Very good. Thanks again."

I followed Grevera over to the kitchen where she stood just outside the door of a very messy, foul smelling, where food was prepared. He stood by the counter and peered down at an empty cereal bowel with a dead earwig floating in souring low fat milk, a thumb nail of black coffee that appeared to have evaporated over a few hot days, with two cigarette butts protruding from the dark sludge at the bottom. Two empty Heiniken bottles, a wine bottle that was on its side where wine had spilled on the counter, an almost empty carton of Chinese food, and a half eaten burrito. The sink was full of dirty dishes that spilled over to a gas stove crowded with pans, a rancid tray of butter and a pearl white stove that was sprinkled with different spillage.

"And they *call us* pigs." Rudolph walked over to the window leading to the street outside and saw the throng of people milling around. What are they waiting for? Yet she knew. She flashed back to years before when her father had taken her fishing at a local lake and the forest ranger had brought a body alongside where she and her father had a boat. He had shooed us away. We had stood a few yards back feeling constrained to witness the bloated body.

Death was compelling, and for many it was a spectacle, or maybe it was just plain curiosity. She walked back to the front room.

"Did anyone call the landlady?"

"She's waiting inside the front door for you, Detective," Sanchez responded.

"Are you the lady that owns the place?"

"Nellie Marrone is my name, Officer. Are you in charge here?"

"Yes ma'am, my name is Rudolph," and I handed her my card.

"Is he dead?" She asked nervously.

"Pretty much so," she nodded. "I'd like you to ID him if you can."

"Do I have to? I'm not family. Can't someone else do that, Detective? I just rented the place to him, and are you sure it's Mark Stevens?"

"Is that his name?"

"I knew he was going to be trouble," she lamented.

"Let's go have a look see, Mrs. Morrone."

"Oh my God, the place is a mess. I hope that's not a blood stain on my new pull down."

Officer Sanchez had placed a sheet over the body and Rudolph inched the white cloth down so she could see his face.

She put her hand to her mouth, "is that a bullet hole in his head?"

"I'm afraid so. Is he your renter?"

She nodded, "yes, that's him."

Rudolph ushered her back to the door.

"Did you bring any information on your renter's lease?"

"Yes, here you can look it over."

"Can I keep it temporarily and collect the info I may need. I'll return it in a day or two. You've got my card if I forget, Mrs. Marrone. Thank you for coming in."

"Let's go see Officer Phil Bright, the cop with the new baby. He's got the friend that found Mark Steven this morning in his car. We need to ask him some questions."

"His name is John Dagget. He works at the Chicken Coup Restaurant just up the street and he should already be at work," Officer Bright offered.

"Sorry to be so long getting here, Mr. Dagget. I'm Detective Delores Rudolph and this is my associate, Barbara Grevera. I understand you should be working right now. We just want to ask you a few questions and then if need be, we'll have you come to the station later. All right?"

"That's cool, I called it in. My boss understands."

"Tell us what happened this morning."

"Mark and I grew up together and every once in a while I stop by on my way to work and get the latest word from my friend. Today I found him lying in his front room with a hole in his head."

"What kind of guy was Mark?"

"He was all right, friendly, more on the quiet side, had a good job."

"Did he do drugs?"

"We smoked weed once in a while. Nothing more than any other college smoker."

"Was he attending college here?"

"Ah no, he graduated a few years ago, but liked living here around college kids."

"Was he selling the stuff to these college kids?"

"I don't think so, but I don't know for sure."

"What about Meth, or Coke?"

"I never saw him with any heavy stuff. If he used it I didn't know about it."

"I guess he was a local?"

"Like I said, we grew up together here in San Jose." His mom still lives in South San Jose."

"Do you have her address?"

Dagget wrote it down on Rudolph's note pad.

"All right Mr. Dagget, sorry to detain you for so long. Give Officer Bright your phone number and address. We may want to talk to you later. Let me know if you plan on leaving the area for any reason, all right?"

"Delores," Barbara said tentatively, " I think I saw the man that's here to kill me. I'm not certain, but it left me unsettled. I'm by no means psychic, but maybe only remotely delusional. I had this feeling earlier, when I was in Valley Fair shopping center that I was being followed and then, twice, I caught the same man eyeballing me. Retrospectively, he does resemble one of the men you gave me a picture of. I purposely kept shopping, to see if I could catch him following me. But it was not to be. I think he might have become aware that I noticed him."

"Or he might be trying to intimidate you. Putting the fear in you so you start unraveling. Some of those bastards are weird Barbara. Were you coming in today?"

"Yes."

"Stay there and I'll pick you up in a few minutes."

There was a light knock on Barbara's front door. "It's just me Grevera. Where are the pictures I gave you?"

Barbara pointed at the man in the picture.

So you think that's the man?"

She nodded reflectively, "Yeah, I think so."

"He probably knows where you live. We might have Divone come in here to see if your place has been bugged."

"Think so?"

"I'll call him from the office and ask if he's got time to check it out for you. Do you still want to come with me?"

"I sure do, I'd go nuts sticking around here today. Too much to think about."

"What about your family."

"I sent them over to John's house."

"One of the things about you, Barbara, is that you're not, and I don't mean this as a negative, what I would call emotional; this whole situation doesn't freak you out. You're not afraid."

"Well, I wouldn't say I'm not afraid. For the better part of three years, I only knew what my best friend told me about myself. But when I woke up from my amnesia, she and I made a commitment to try and live our lives as normal as possible. Mundane was our goal."

"Speaking of mundane, that's what we're going to be doing today. We're going to pound the pavement around the Mark Stevens home questioning the neighbors for any information."

They started on the opposite side of the street.

"I didn't know the man. Most of the young people that live here are students at San Jose State. Sometimes they're a nuisance, too much partying and occasional fights, but most of the time, I don't even know they're around," a permanent resident stated from the doorway.

"All I know about the guy is that he did not actively attend State, and that he had a regular job. I didn't even know his name," a young female student offered.

"Hey, he was cool, man. Yeah I smoked a joint with him every once in a while. Sorry to hear that someone offed him. I knew his name was Mark, but nothing else. Good luck."

After two dozen knocks on doors, they still had nothing. He was practically invisible. Low key.

"Let's go back to his mother's place Barbara, maybe she's home now."

The drive to South San Jose was quiet.

"I suppose interrogating people reminds you of what you used to do."

"Pretty much so, Delores."

"I think you're going to be a great detective, Mrs. Grevera."

Rudolph displayed her badge and ID, Mrs. Stevens allowed them into her home and ushered them into the front room, where they were seated.

"I remarried a year ago and my last name is Vargas now, though I believe it will only be temporary as I'm alone again. So what kind of trouble is Mark in?"

"He's dead, Mrs. Vargas."

The expression on her face didn't change. She sat motionless, then blinked as her eyes, welled and tears flowed down her face into her lap. "Excuse me," she whispered, stood and hurried into the kitchen, and came back, tissue in hand, and sat.

"I'm not surprised, Detective. Life has a way of punishing me for all my errors. Poor Mark. He followed suit, everything he did seemed to turn to dust. The same dark cloud seemed to follow him everywhere. He was a good boy, really. Each generation follows what their peers, at the time do, and Mark was no different engaging in drugs and the 'live for today attitude.' He was once an altar boy at Christ the King Catholic church, but then he meets the good as well as the bad and life changed for him. He didn't kill anyone, or burn houses down, or rob old ladies, however he did live on the edge of the law. He was well aware of what he was doing but chose to play with the devil. Kids get tired of parents lectures and stop listening. It's too bad young people have to age to become nice. I'm sorry Detective, I'm blithering."

" I can't add anything to what you've said, Mrs. Vargas. Do you know if he was trafficking drugs?"

"I don't think so and if he was selling, it had to be in a very small way. He had a good job, but he never had money and I wouldn't give him any, not that I have any to speak of."

"We met one of his friends, a John Dagget, the man that found your son. Did Mark have a girl friend?"

"I don't know if she was a girl friend or just a friend, but he did bring a young girl here one time. She was attractive, but she seemed…fragile, maybe that's not the right word. She was reminiscent of a Cocker Spaniel I once bought at a pet shop. When the shopkeeper took her out of the cage, the puppy coward as I leaned over to pet it. It was scared, nervous and very tentative and kept shrinking away. This girl had the same visual image when Mark brought her into the house. I liked her."

"What was her name?"

"Adriana Molski, she said very little in the short time she and Mark were here. But she left me with a good impression of her. I'm sorry I don't know where she lives or anything else about her Detective, nor any of his current friends, except John."

"Thank you Mrs. Vargas."

As Rudolph and Grevera walked to the car, Rudolph's cell phone rang. "That was Divone. Your house was not bugged."

"Good. Thank you Delores. That's good to know."

The desk Sergeant waved Rudolph and Grevera over to his desk. "You've got this gorgeous little blonde waiting for you in interview 1." He twirled his finger around his sideburn, "says she's here to confess to some murder."

"Did she state her name?"

He looked down at a sheet on his desk, "Smolski, Adriana."

"Wow she came to us. Can you believe it Grevera. You said Room I. Right?"

"Good luck," the Sergeant waved with his hand.

Rudolph and Grevera stood looking into interview room I through the one-way mirror at Adriana Smolski.

Adriana looked around the desolate room, then placed her hands in front of her, eyes fixed straight ahead, as if she knew what was coming and accepted it.

She appeared smaller than she was, petite, frail, pummeled by life's abuses, and wrong choices. Wrong solely because they were the only choices available. Alone, because of the layers of guilt and shame which enveloped her and kept her invisible to everyone. Her life was a constant battle to survive and nurture her love child, a child sired by a heartless lover. Her daughter, the object of her infrequent smiles, her passion for survival, the endless outpouring of unrequited love so pervasive it would alter her existence, however inconsequential that might seem. Her soul exposed by the scars she carried from an early age because of her drunken father who entered her room and took her innocence, over and over again until she was but an empty shell, oblivious to everything but survival. She had finally answered back, her angry existence, the neglect, and oversight of her life. Her daughter the inspiration and she had become alive, fighting back and having a goal for all those who had trampled her innocuous, poignant reality.

Rudolph and Grevera entered Room 1, sat down and listened, rarely interrupting until Adriana had completed her story. Grevera occasionally stood and walked to the picture less walls but listened intently, while Rudolph dabbed her eyes occasionally. An officer was called in and ushered Adriana Molski out. They followed Tom Wilson to his office.

"Rudolph, would you check the part of her story about her father's death, talk to her mother, and get me a copy of her confession."

Grevera and Rudolph had spent the better part of the morning trying to locate the whereabouts of Olga Molski, Adriana's mother, and finally found her in an assisted living center in East San Jose.

Rudolph displayed her ID at the front desk. "She's got company right now, but I think she went across the street to get some coffee, our machine isn't working, officer. I'll have someone bring you two more chairs. It's the third room to the right, and Mrs. Molski will be in her chair, probably asleep."

They scrutinized the room, where three others were sitting in chairs, by their beds.

"Excuse me, who are you looking for?" a woman with a cup of Starbuck's coffee asked.

"Olga Molski," she responded displaying her badge.

"She's over there," she pointed. "I'm her sister, Sister Vivian."

An orderly brought the chairs and they sat facing a sleeping Olga Molski.

"I hope what you came to inquire about is not vital, because she is no longer coherent. Drug abuse and alcohol have depleted my sister of any comprehensive information," Sister Vivian offered. "I sometimes sit here for hours waiting for her to wake and when she does, she just blithers. However, Olga's all that's left of my dysfunctional family, except for her daughter Adriana."

"Are you a local nun, Sister Vivian?"

"I am a Dominican Sister of San Jose."

Rudolph nodded, "Tell us about Adriana,"

"She grew up with the devil in her home, and a mother, who was no more than the devil's advocate. She feared her parents. Poor girl had no chance for a normal existence. Adriana is always in our prayers for those in need and the deceased."

"Do you think that Adriana is capable of inflicting harm to anyone?" Rudolph asked.

The woman of God gazed at me quizzically, "What do you mean specifically?"

"Do you think she could shoot someone in the head?"

"Sister Vivian looked me straight in the eye, raised her hands in the air, "As God is my witness, I have prayed with Adriana on the ground and she has forgiven her bastard father and her worthless mother of all the sins they imposed on this wonderful woman.

This beautiful child may carry a heavy cross-laden with sin, guilt from all the abuse, these contemptible parents imposed on her…but inside the girl has the pure innocence of new born babe." Without hesitation she blurted out, "no way, absolutely not."

The two officers stood, thanked the good Sister, offered their cards and were given Sister Vivian's address for any future needs.

They sat in the car.

"Sister Vivian was quite convincing with her story of Adriana. Don't you think Barbara?"

"She was indeed, which goes along with my perception of Adriana Smolski. Why would an innocent person admit to killing someone?"

"Happens all the time, Barbara. Sometimes that person believes they actually did murder someone. Sometimes they're covering up for someone they really like, that they think *did* kill someone, sometimes just for the prestige. The reasons vary from person to person who admit to something they didn't do."

CHAPTER 15

Toby had been waiting for a cloudy evening and tonight was perfect. He checked his watch and stepped outside his motel. Scanning the sky he nodded and walked back into his room. His alarm went off at two-thirty AM and he dressed in a camouflaged uniform, walked quietly out to El Camino Real. He was at his destination in less than ten minutes. He parked a block away and walked deliberately to his objective. He would slip into the darkness of a home yard, if presented by headlights on the street. The penlight displayed three AM on his watch. *Most people were well asleep by this hour,* he thought. He stood in the darkness of huge Sequoia Pine across the street and observed the home he would be entering shortly. The city light in the middle of the block and a single porch light were the only visible illumination. Off in the distance he could hear a dog barking and the faint sound of fire siren to the north of him. Stepping out of the mask of darkness, he slinked his way up to the front door and carefully turned the doorknob. Locked. From the small pouch around his neck he pulled out a small pin and kneeled in front of the locked door and the door opened easily. He stood just inside and closed it gently, allowing his eyes to acclimate to the dark room. Stealthily he crept down the hallway, stopping at the first room. Putting his ear against the flat of the door, listened for any sound and after a minute, edged to the next possible bedroom. His eyes were adhering to the night and could see that there appeared to be at least four bedrooms. He thought he could hear someone breathing from outside the entrance he was standing in front of. Opening the door he listened and could hear the steady sound of someone's breath. Silently, he closed the door, but did not latch it. He moved quickly to the lump in the bed and as reached the bedside when the phone on the nightstand began ringing. He froze, confused, turned and hurried to the door.

"Hello," a sleepy voice answered, simultaneously, there was pounding on the front door. Toby stopped in the hallway quickly thought about which way to go. He opened the door next to the one he had just been in and saw a window and he rushed to it, unlatched it and was out in seconds. He ran to the fence and managed to climb over it and was running up the street until he reached his car two streets over, heart beating wildly and breathless.

As he drove to his motel, he thought someone had seen him go into that woman's home and alerted the police or someone in the neighborhood. He had been so careful, yet, no matter how careful, it seemed there are always eyes that can't sleep at night.

O' DARK THIRTY

CHAPTER 16

"I need to talk to you Delores," Barbara said confidentially, can we go somewhere we can talk privately?"

"Barbara you're scaring me. Is everything all right?" She asked as she led her to the ladies bathroom in the Police Station. She checked the toilet stalls and locked the door.

"He came into my house last night."

Rudolph nodded and listened for the next fifteen minutes.

"You're right, you were lucky and sometimes it's better to be lucky, than prepared. Do you want some time off today?"

"Absolutely not. I need to be here today Delores. I'm okay."

"Great. We've got Sister Vivian waiting for us, let's go talk to her."

"Thank you for coming in Sister Vivian." Do you remember my partner, Barbara Grevera?

"She nodded.

"We'll be talking to you in Room 2."

"I'm not a suspect, right? I can leave here anytime I want, right?"

"That's right Sister, we just need your help filling in some gaps about Adriana Molski. OK?"

Sister Vivian was astonished. "Have you already talked to Adriana?"

"We have."

"Why would you want to speak to her?"

"She came to us."

She pondered, "I don't understand."

"Do you think Adriana is capable of killing someone?" Rudolph queried.

She gasped and brought her hand to her mouth, "Like I told you on our first visit absolutely not. It's out of the question. What in heaven's name has she told you?"

"Do you have any idea why she would admit to killing someone?"

Sister Vivian's eyes froze on Grevera's and held. *She did have an idea but wondered if she should bring it to light. They would eventually find out, she thought.*

"The death of Adriana's daughter might be the reason," Sister Vivian lamented.

"Adriana had a daughter?" Rudolph probed. "What was her name?"

She nodded, "Virginia…Virginia Rosano."

Rudolph eyed Grevera, and changed her position in the chair and wrote something down on her pad.

"Was the father somehow involved in Miss Rosano's death?"

Sister Vivian thought, Adriana admitted killing her father?

"Adriana kept Virginia away from her parents, which wasn't hard because they had lost interest in Adriana and Virginia…except for the one time Adriana caught the father in her apartment with Virginia. Nothing had happened, but she threatened him with a pistol and told him she would kill him the next he came to her apartment."

Grevera made a notation on her pad.

"So Adriana owns a pistol?"

"Yes, I bought it for her and Virginia just in case."

"What kind of pistol?"

"A .22, Ruger if memory serves me. She didn't kill her father, Detective."

Detective Rudolph took note of that.

Grevera sighed, "do you know a man by the name of Mark Stevens?"

The question was met with hesitation. *Oh my God, she has admitted killing that snake Stevens.* "I still read the paper even though it's full of decay, hatred and universal madness, sometimes there is justice, you reap what you sow."

"Is that a yes?"

She nodded and pulled a tissue from her purse and dabbed her eyes, "Virginia was special, became a nurse just like her great aunt," she blew her nose, "she was beautiful, smart and loved life. She was living for her mother, who didn't have a life, not a good one anyway, and she loved her mother. She could have worked for any hospital, but she chose the County Hospital because it helped the indigent. She was a good Catholic and was going to take good care of her mother." She paused and peered down at her hands. "Her only mistake was meeting Mark Stevens. I firmly believe it was her first time, and it killed her. She was not a bad person. I will never understand what provoked her to try the awful drug. She was her own person, not easily induced to try anything, she didn't even drink alcohol or smoke." Sister Vivian slumped in her chair and sobbed.

Rudolph eyed Grevea and nodded.

"Would you mind if I went home? You can call me in again, if you choose. I'm talked out right now."

"Would you like me to drive you home, Sister?" Grevera asked quietly.

"Thank you, but I drove over here."

"Yes, we may need to talk to you again. Thanks for coming in."

"Oh, one last question," Grevera asked the Sister as she stood precariously, "and you're free to go."

Sister Vivian stood staring at the Detective.

"Did Adriana know Mark Stevens?"

"Oh my God, she blessed herself, "I don't know."

"That's all right, I'll save that question for our next meeting."

Interview room 2

Rudolph and Grevera interviewing Dalton Taylor Jr.

"Are you ready Dalton? I'm going to turn on the tape recorder," Delores Rudolph announced.

"State your full name."

"Dalton Taylor Junior."

I'm Delores Rudolph and sitting in with me is Barbara Grevera.

"How long have you known Mark Stevens?"

"Ah, ah, I'm sorry, I'm nervous, I've never done this before."

"Relax, think of us a family talking, Dalton," She said quietly with a friendly smile.

"Most of my life. We went through middle school together and then all through Overdent High School."

"Would you say you knew him as well as anyone could know a friend?"

"Yeah, I think so, but not any better than John Dagget."

"Do you know John Dagget well?

"I knew him but not well."

Grevera wrote something down on her pad.

"Do you know if Stevens did drugs?"

Dalton looked toward Grevera and back to Rudolph. "Yes, he smoked a little weed."

Rudolph stared at him, "What about other drugs."

"Ah…I don't know about other drugs."

"Did he ever offer you marijuana?"

"Yes."

"Did you kill your friend Dalton?"

There was a pause.

"He was my friend."

"Did you kill Mark Stevens, Dalton?" Rudolph yelled.

"No ma'am, and I don't think I have to take this abuse." As he stood,

Rudolph turned the recorder off.

"Sit down Dalton! Sit down or I'll come over there and sit you down," and she rushed around the table and pushed him down into the chair with the chair banging against the table loudly.

"Can she do this ma'am?" he asked Detective Grevera, "I mean can she bully me like this?"

"Like what?" Grevera answered innocently. "We can hold you for forty eight hours. Do you know of anyone that would want to kill your friend?"

Dalton stared at Grevera and then to Rudolph.

"Maybe?"

Grevera wrote that down.

"Were you aware that he was dealing?" Rudolph asked.

"It might have been what got him killed, the fool."

"So, who do you think might have killed Stevens?"

Grevera queried.

"Holliday knew Virginia and I believe he was upset when he heard how she died."

"And?"

"You asked me if I knew who might have killed Mark and I'm saying it might have been Scott Holliday."

Grevera wrote the name down.

"Your free to go now."

"Let us know if you leave the area, Dalton," Grevera requested.

"Did you hear her Dalton?"

He turned at the door, "I'm not going anywhere."

When he left the room Rudolph turned to Grevera.

"I have a meeting with Tom Wilson tomorrow in the morning that might take most of the morning. Would you mind checking out that story on Scott Holiday. Dalton might be stalling."

Grevera thought Delores's interrogation methods were a bit aggressive, however she managed to get results and that was the bottom line in police business; especially now, with the shortage of personnel.

San Jose's population had just reached the million mark, and still growing.

"I'm going to go see Sister Vivian's superiors at the Catholic Convent in the morning, then I'll try and get a hold of Scott Holiday's address and find out what I can."

"Good." Delores responded.

CHAPTER 17

Grevera hated to think Sister Vivian might have a motive for killing Stevens, but there it was --- Virginia Rosano. She parked on Market Street, walked up to the Basilica Cathedral Catholic Church and ran into young priest distributing pamphlets in the pews.

"Hello there, can I help you?"

"I'm Detective Barbara Grevera," as she displayed her badge and ID. I'm looking for the person in charge of the Sisters of San Jose."

"That would be Mother Superior, Sister Ruth, but she's out of town. Maybe I could help, Detective."

"You would have to know Sister Vivian pretty well to be able to help me Father…"

"Manuel Garcia. My friends call me Father Manny. As it turns out I do happen to know Sister Vivian very well. Would you like to sit down?

Grevera looked around.

"We could go somewhere else if you like."

"If it's all right with you, I don't mind."

"You're not Catholic, are you?"

I'm a nonparticipating Catholic of late and so I didn't respond.

The priest took her silence as a no, "You can call me Manny if you like."

She nodded, and observed the statue of St Francis of Assisi over Manny's shoulder. She had always liked St. Francis and his love for animals.

Father Manny raised his eyebrows as he caught the subtle smile, but let it pass.

"How long have you known Sister Vivian?"

He crossed his arms and paused, "I knew her when she was a nurse at the Veteran's Hospital in Palo Alto. I'm a veteran, and spent a little time in the good hospital, after a two year tour with a Marine division in Afghanistan. Nothing serious, just a little depression."

She raised an eyebrow.

He took notice, "Yes, even priests get depressed Detective Grevera."

She nodded, "That's right, even the clergy go to war. Something the average American probably doesn't realize. I've never given it much thought. How long has Sister Vivian been a nun?"

"I don't know the exact date, but around eight years. Yes, eight years," he nodded.

"What can you tell me about her niece, Virginia Rosano?"

"He shook his head, "a travesty, 'the good die young' is an appropriate adage for Virginia Rosano. She was everything a parent could want from an offspring. Most of the time when we make a mistake, we can learn from it and try never to do it again. Virginia didn't get that oport-unity. God had a different purpose for her and took her to heaven. It is not for us to question why…sometimes there are no answers for the whys. It is what it is."

"Father do you think Sister Vivian is capable of…of

"Killing someone?" he finished her question.

She nodded.

"I think under the right circumstances we all have the capacity to kill. The wars tell us that. Do I think the good Sister Vivian killed the unscrupulous low life Mark Stevens? No."

"Did you know the man?"

"I tried to talk to him, to no avail."

"Where did you talk to him?"

"At his house on 4th Street. I got the address from Sister Vivian and went to see him."

"Do you remember the day?"

"I think it was on a Wednesday or Thursday," I hear confessions on Friday, so it must have been on Thursday, yes on Wednesday I visit the sick at County Hospital. It was on a Thursday, in the morning."

"You're sure about the day, and that it *was* in the morning. What time in the morning?"

"Umm, eightish," he nodded.

Grevera wrote that down, "What did you talk to him about?"

"Essentially...I wanted him to stop seeing Virginia, to leave her out of his way of life."

"And."

"He was insolent, said that it was up to her, he had no control over what she wanted to do. She liked having sex with me."

"And."

Father Manny stood and looked toward the altar, He sneered, "I lost my composure," Father crossed himself, "and I lifted him from his chair, threw him across the pigsty room he lived in, and back handed and punched him without restrain until he yelled out, 'and you're supposed to be above all this, you phony bastard, bastard.' I looked down at him. I looked at that bloody face, and punched him one more time. I wanted to kill the grimy little, little…I turned and left."

"Did you kill Mark Stevens, Father."

"I wanted to kill him, he was arrogant and brash, but no, I didn't kill him, just thought about it."

Grevera thought, Father Manny could be a suspect, there was motive…hate and the capacity to kill…anger.

"Do you know if Sister Vivian ever talked to Stevens?"

"I'm not sure, you'd have to ask her."

"Why do you think Adriana's aunt had so much involvement in her sister and niece's lives?"

"You mean besides loving them because they're family and that she financially supported them."

"Financially? Does the Catholic Church pay their sister's and priests?"

"No. We take an oath of poverty and are subsidized by the Catholic congregation. Sister Vivian had a retirement coming from the thirty some years she spent as a nurse and she proudly bequeathed it to her niece."

Grevera nodded, "Very generous of her."

"Do you have any other questions, detective?"

She stood, "No, not at this time, but I may need to talk to you again, Father."

He extended his card.

"You've been very helpful. Thank you." She stood and took a few steps and stopped, turned, "did you know a man by the name of Scott Holiday?"

Father thought for a few seconds, "no, it doesn't ring a bell."

"Thank you father."

CHAPTER 18

Dimitre Aristotle's broken bones had healed but his memory was still in limbo and unable to take charge of his company. Gina Aristotle, with the help of Jimmy 'the Fox,' was running the daily functions of his businesses and doing a remarkable job with very few problems. The businesses had responsible people managing them and reporting any significant complications. Jimmy was happy for Mrs. Aristotle, she was very smart and was a lady. Never raised her voice and spoke to her subordinates as equals, unlike Dimitre, without the gun at her side. The Fox, had never seen her be abusive to any employee. Today she had summoned me in for, I worried, was an old direct request by Dimitre to locate two possible living persons that were overlooked in the Abel Aristotle murders.

"Mr. Lamantia, I've called you in today, because my intuitive juices have alerted me that Mr. Aristotle will soon remember most, if not all that has been blocked from his mind. If memory serves me, he had given you some viable instructions to ferret out two missing adults in the deplorable murder of his brother's family. Is that correct?"

"Yes ma'am."

"I think you should act on his orders, because as you know, Mr. Aristotle demands results. Wouldn't you agree?"

"Yes ma'am," *how could I forget*, he thought, *one of his own men is killed for pausing to do his job. Aristotle had not dithered to put a bullet in the man's forehead for merely hesitating.*

"I haven't pursued you for any results on this matter because it would have been inconsequential at this time, but now might be a good time to resume your task."

"Yes ma'am."

"I think that covers everything I wanted you to know, Mr. Lamantia, and you may go."

"Yes ma'am," and he turned and began leaving the house.

"Oh, Mr. Lamantia, would you please get back to me when you have *any* results."

"I will."

The thing about Gina Aristotle, Jimmy had often wondered, as he sauntered to his car *was, how much did she actually know about Dimitre's business ventures? Like today, 'the deplorable murder of his brother's family," was an implication that she had no knowledge of Dimitre's involution. How can that be? And why was he given the task of finding two people that were connected to the persons murdered in the Abel Aristotle home? Surely she would know why and yet, I don't think she really knows. This brilliant woman, doesn't smoke and I don't believe drinks, with a photographic memory and the morals of a nun…doesn't make sense*, he thought, *and she has no indication she lives with a psychopath.*

CHAPTER 19

Detective Rudolph and Grevera had just exited the Bayshore Freeway and were now on Guadalupe Parkway on their way to talk to Adriana Smolski.

"What' your take on Sister Vivian?"

Barbara looked out the window, " I don't think that Adriana killed Stevens. I think it was a man. You're friend, police officer Sanchez, thought it might have been a woman. When she said that Stevens had allowed the person into the front room, I think Adriana or Sister Vivian would not have entered, but a male probably would have. Just a guess."

"Is that a dog up ahead running up against the shoulder Barbara? I think it is, maybe a German Shepherd."

"Crap, I'm going to stop and see if we can catch it before it tries to run across the freeway. Too much traffic for it to survive. Poor thing is probably scared to death. I'm going to
catch hell from Wilson, but we're going to stop traffic on this
'suicide for animals' freeway and fetch us a dog, Barbara."

"Since you're driving, let me out, and you stop the traffic.
Okay?"

"You must have had a dog?"

"I love animals, Delores."

Rudolph checked the rearview mirror, saw a break in the
traffic, put her Ford across the middle two lanes of Guadalupe Parkway, stepped out of the car and directed the traffic to the lane opposite the dog, and allowed the cars to move slowly through the bottle neck. Meanwhile she observed Grevera walking slowly toward the Shepherd and talking softly to the frightened animal. He saw the dog suddenly run across all four lanes and end up forty yards up where Rudolph was directing traffic. She immediately stopped traffic and allowed Grevera to pursue the dog to the other side. The dog lay down when she approached her and while trembling allowed Grevera to put a scarf through her collar and slowly walk her to the detective's car and she ushered it into the back seat.

"There weren't that many cars and just maybe no one will have complained about the wait," Rudolph announced.

"He's got a collar and I saw an address, 1624 Meridian Avenue, San Jose. Do you know where Meridian Avenue is?"

"Yup, and we're going there right now. It's about two miles from here. Crap, I bet this is Wilson on the phone. Yes sir."

"What in the hell are you doing, Rudolph? You know you stopped a city council member and he bitched to the Chief and guess whose ass he reamed?"

"Sorry Tom, there was a German Shepherd on Guadalupe Parkway and we stopped to rescue it. It barely took twenty minutes." Click.

"He'll get over it. He loves dogs too," she smiled. Okay, now what was that address?"

They drove slowly up Meridian Avenue looking for the 1624 address.

"It will be on your side of the street, Barb."

"We're on the 1500 block, should be the next one."

They parked and looked at the home. It had a nice fence around the house, but the gate was wide open.

"I'll go check it out, and when I signal bring him over here."

Barbara could hear Delores talking to someone and then waved from the porch.

"Is this the Davolos residence? Is this your dog, Sir?" Delores asked.

"Looks like Esther's dog," as he nonchalantly peered around Delores at the dog. "Does the nametag say Tidus?"

"Don't you know your own dog?" Barbara asked incensed.

"Did you say you were police officers?" he asked indignantly, looking at Detective Rudolph.

"Yes sir, we are."

"Is this the way you speak to the general public? Surely you realize this isn't the late 30's and this isn't Germany? That you're not the Gestapo. You must have a superior officer in charge of you, that you have to answer to."

Barbara was standing almost face to face with the man.
She stared into his face. "Is Esther your wife? Is Tidus your dog? Do you even care that we brought this dog from a freeway where it probably would have been

killed. Dog owners like you make me sick. Where's your wife?"

"I don't have to put up with this nonsense and I'm going to report you to your superiors."

"Where is your wife, Mr. Davalos?" Delores asked.

"She's in Hawaii."

"I don't think we should leave this beautiful dog in your care, Mr. Davalos. You don't seem to care enough to keep your gate closed. I'm sure your wife would be upset with you if she knew you were not watching Tidus, and he was wandering around on a dangerous freeway. How long has this dog been out of the back yard?"

"It's none of your business."

Barbara grabbed him by his shirt collar and pushed him against the wall, she faced him directly, eye to eye. Angst
bubbling in her veins. She released him and he straightened his shirt.

There was a knock on the door. He walked briskly to answer it.

"I see these women have brought Tidus back. You ought to be ashamed of yourself Mr. Davalos. Esther would never have gone three days without calling someone. Tidus could---"

Mr. Davalos slammed the door in her face.

"Three days!" Barbara chided, "You bastard. Get us a leash and we'll take this dog where it will be safe." She reached into her top pocket and laid a card on the kitchen table as he rushed off to secure a leash. "I will personally care for this dog, Mr. Davalos until your wife is back."

Leashed, Tidus walked out with the two detectives.

"Do you have some place in the backyard for Tidus?"

"I do, and I'll see how he fairs in the house. I'll have my daughter and mother watch him during the day. Do you think Davalos will call Wilson?"

"No, he knows he did wrong by that dog and it would only make it worse for himself with his wife. He won't call. We'll drop this dog off at your house and we'll hoof it down to Smolski's. Okay?"

Grevera knocked on Adriana's apartment door. The curtain moved slowly to one side as a sad face looked suspiciously out to see who was at her entrance.

"Who are you?" she asked through the closed portal?"

"Detective Rudolph and Grevera, Adriana. May we come in? We'd like to talk to you."

The door opened and she stood aside allowing the two detectives to enter.

Grevera noticed the apartment was sparsely decorated.

"I'm sorry. I didn't recognize you. You can never be too careful."

"That's right," Rudolph responded, standing awkwardly in the middle of the front room.

"Did you come to arrest me?"

"Could we sit down Mrs. Smolski?"

"Oh, yes I'm sorry. Please sit down. All I have is coffee to offer you."

O' DARK THIRTY

"We don't need any coffee, thank you," Grevera responded.

"You said that you killed Mark Steven, when you came to the police station. Would you mind telling us again how you did it? Where you did it? What kind of gun you used and where you shot him?"

Adriana placed her hands on her lap and pondered the question. "Well, I believe I was at his home on 4th Street and I shot him with a .22 pistol." She stopped talking and peered straight ahead.

Catatonic, Grevera thought after almost two minutes.

Rudolph glanced over to Grevera.

Grevera eyes met Rudolph's and she put her fore finger to her lips and sat quietly. Then Grevera stood and walked in front of Adriana and stood directly in front of her.

"You bitch, you know you killed the horses ass and you're proud of it. So don't sit there like you didn't mean it. Of course you did you moron. What the hells the matter with you? Fess up and quit your quiet sniveling," Grevera shouted, "You're—"

"Shut up you cow, and Adriana stood up to Grevera, you don't know what the hell you're talking about. She didn't kill anyone, she doesn't have the balls to kill anyone," Adriana shouted vociferously at Grevera.

Rudolph had stood in the ready for any physical confrontation with Adriana.

Grevera waved her away and stared at Adriana.

"So who are you supposed to be? Grevera asked calmly.

"I'm not supposed to be anyone. *I am* Danny and not some pushover like Adriana. I didn't like the way you were talking to Adriana. That's the reason *I'm* here. I won't take the crap you stupid people unload on some little mousy woman."

"So you know Adriana?"

"Of course. What do take me for? An idiot?"

Rudolph spoke, "Did you kill Mark Stevens?"

"Who in the hell are you and where did you come from?"

"She's with me, Danny."

"See, that's what I mean, you guys gang up and beat up on poor Adriana. It's not fair. No she didn't kill Stevens, though he deserved killing. Adriana's is wimp, a wuz, but she didn't kill anyone. I tried to stop her from admitting the shooting but she wouldn't let me out. She needs me to do the talking at times and that was one of the times I should have been let out."

"Has she let you out before this time?"

"Oh yeah, that piece of shit father that raped her most of her life is responsible for me getting out, and it took a lot of prodding at that—." He stopped talking, walked to the wall next to the kitchen and leaned his head against it.

Rudolph stood and started to walk toward Danny, but Grevera stopped her. Another thirty seconds past and a woman's voice came out of Adriana.

"I'm sorry. I guess you met Danny."

CHAPTER 20

Toby sat down at an outside table at Tiffany O'Rourke's ice cream shop and waited for Jimmy 'The Fox.' It was a warm day and he ordered a Strawberry milk shake. He had voluntarily come back to New York because that was the proper thing to do.

LaMantia walked up and sat down across from Toby. He waited for Toby to start talking. The waiter came to the table.

"I'll have a scoop of chocolate, vanilla, strawberry sundae please, with a cherry on top," he requested politely.

"She made me Mr. Lamantia," he said, looking past him, "it was as simple as that. She works for the San Jose Police Department now and I blew my only attempt to snuff her. After that they were waiting for me to try again. Maybe I'm losing my touch."

"Maybe, but you're right for coming back and we can figure out how to try again. Any ideas?"

"On the trip back I was thinking about Carmen Llamas. The problem is I don't even know if she's alive or where she lives."

"By coincidence, I too, thought of Carmen while you were on your way back and I have made contact with her. She's alive and resides in San Francisco and has agreed to talk to me. So I'm going out there this weekend."

"Good. Outside of me, I think she might even a better person for the job. Because she's a woman, it might be easier for her to get next to this Grevera woman. Now that she lives in San Francisco, which is only a stone's throw to San Jose.

Jimmy smiled at Toby's humility but nodded in agreement.

Jimmy rang the doorbell of the Llamas residence and waited, looking around the neighborhood. A young lady answered the door.

"Are you Mr. Lamantia?"

"Yes ma'am."

"Could I see some kind of ID?"

I pulled out my wallet and showed her my New York driver's license. She scanned the license and me and returned it.

"Please come in, my mother will be back in a few minutes. My name is Rachel Llamas." She had made coffee. "Would you like a cup of coffee?" And they proceeded to the kitchen.

"Sounds good."

She poured a cup of black coffee, with coffee mate, and placed a sugar bowl on a mat in front of me. I took a sip and studied Rachel for a second. She was reminiscent of her mother in appearance and her disciplined ambience.

"Did you have a nice trip from New York?"

I nodded, "uneventful and yes it was a nice trip. They have good coffee on those flights." This was no ten or twelve year old. She could have easily been a twenty one year old adult.

"Carmen said you had a job for her in San Jose."

Carmen, not mother or mom, I thought, "yes I do have something she might be interested in doing."

"Some kind of contract work?" she asked innocently.

"Yes," somehow I was feeling like the child in our conversation, she was pumping for information and I was responding like a good little boy. I heard the front door open and Carmen came bounding into the kitchen.

"Good to see you Jimmy," and she rushed to me and I stood. She kissed me lightly on the cheek. "Has Rachel been interrogating you like a police woman?"

"You have a very interesting daughter Carmen."

"I thought you might be surprised by what I have produced with my young child prodigy," she said proudly.

I guess I was surprised, but not really. Carmen had always been special, she could have been some CEO of a large company and made millions. She had a talent that would make most people very rich. She was extremely creative and knew how to handlepeople. She was aggressive and beautiful and could easily acquire what she wanted from any man. Women were not exempt. I had not been the recipient of her charming and alluring genius that she spun, but I would have succumbed to her inducement had she only beckoned.

"Rachel honey, go upstairs and practice your piano recital."

I watched as she gave her mother the, 'spare me,' look.'

"Can you believe that I brought this brilliant girl into the world, not by myself of course, but with the help of a man I had to erase afterwards."

I raised an eyebrow, "do I dare ask you how you ever began this life of crime?"

"May I be candid and immodest?"

She refilled his coffee and they moved to the front room.

"Are you still a teetotaler?"

She beamed a beautiful even tooth smile and crossed her beautiful legs.

"I get high on life Jimmy, I thought you knew that."

I did know that, I just thought life might have made her more cynical and amenable to imbibing occasionally.

"I'm not easy, but if I really like someone, I give my whole self to them and I expect some reciprocation. I certainly don't want to be thrown out like some old blouse. I admit when a person is young it is easier to be deceived by someone who has more years than you, especially if it's someone that carries some weight in the community. I have always been older physically and mentally than my chronological age, which could have been a problem, but I was also smarter. Well, I happened to get caught up in a love affair with a liar, cheater that was also a bully. Just because he was the mayor of our town of eighty thousand people, he thought he could use me and then intimidate me. He told me he could make life very hard for me if I didn't go along with his proposals. The first time I endured all the punishment, took it like a good mistress, but the second time it happened he got a letter opener in his back. What I didn't know at the time was that he had a lot of enemies, including the Chief of Police in our city, and several women came out the woodwork and added their complaints and showed their physical and mental scars. The man was a pig, narcissistic, tyrant who got what he deserved. That was my initiation to what would be, to this day, my life of crime."

Somehow this image didn't fit Carmen Llamas. I lost focus of the real woman. She still seemed out of place, even as she spoke of her nefarious deeds. Why would someone so together, so intelligent wear the mask of a killer. Most of the killers I knew fit their vocation. Toby Erickson, Reggie Johnson, Esquivel and Thompson were picture perfect killers. They looked, talked and breathed what they did. Only Carmen's credentials confirmed her true identity, a real terminator.

"Does that answer your question about my life of crime?"

"You're enigmatic, Carmen. That's what you are, a complete mystery."

"How so?"

"Honestly, I don't know how to answer that question." I could hear Rachel playing one of Mozart's concertos faintly upstairs and I fell into a trance without realizing it. Motionless I listened and suddenly I was wiping tears from my face with my hand. I don't know why. I knew very little about classical music and it had been years since I had listened to Mozart, but it was the only music Mrs. Stacci ever played in my grade school. I'm not even sure I liked classical music then, but I knew it was Mozart, because she had played it over and over again on a gray mobile phonograph player that she hauled around throughout my K-6 years. Nostalgia precipitated my tears and I wept shamelessly until Carmen touched my shoulder lightly. Astonished I looked up into a pair of very blue eyes that said she understood.

"She loves Mozart too, Jimmy. Don't you dare feel shame or apologize for the tears. I too, have felt the same pining from her music and derived the same humiliation." I stood and wiped my face and hugged Carmen.

CHAPTER 21

"Katie would you fetch Tidus from the backyard, gather his food bowl, dog food, and his treats together? That call was Esther Davolos and she's on her way here to take him home."

"I was hoping she had forgot about him mom, he's been here for almost three weeks. I love walking him and he's so handsome. All your neighbors rave about how nice he is. He's really a sweet dog."

"Poor Tidus, all he's needed was some TLC, some one that cares about him," Barbara offered, "animals need love too."

"Is Mrs. Davolos an older lady and where has she been for so long?"

"That clown she calls a husband, said she was in Hawaii, and I don't think she's in her sixties yet, however I really don't know. I've never met the woman."

"We've never had a big dog like Tidus," Katie said petting Tidus in the front room.

"It's not our dog, honey."

"How old do German Shepherd's get?"

"I don't know. I've heard that big dogs don't live as long as little dogs. I don't know how old Tidus is but he looks like he's young."

The doorbell rang.

"Katie would you get the door, please?"

"I'm Esther Davolos. Is this the Grevera residence?"

"You're at the right home Mrs. Davolos. Come in we have Tidus already for you."

Barbara extended her hand to Mrs. Davolos and ushered her into the kitchen, where Tidus was sitting. Barbara observed him as Mrs. Davolos entered the room. Tidus didn't sit up and come to her, and she didn't rush over to the gentle animal.

"Would you mind if we sat down for a few minutes Mrs. Grevera?"

"Would you like a cup of coffee or tea?"

She paused, our eyes met, "that would be nice and tea would be fine, any brand."

"Lipton?"

She nodded.

Katie walked into the kitchen and filled the teapot with water.

"You're a police officer Mrs. Grevera?"

"I am and you've been in Hawaii."

"I'm sorry about Harold and his attitude about dogs and animals in general. He's not aging well. He doesn't like Hawaii, but I don't hold that against him. A lot of people don't like the islands. We all have our prejudices. I like the idea of getting away for a while. I have a friend that I grew up with and she feels the same as I, so we hit the warm weather together. When you live with a man for almost all your adult life, you learn to give and take, the good with the bad. I'm blithering. I suppose I should get to what I'm trying to say. Would you be interested in keeping Tidus as a pet? My guess is that you like animals. Tidus is a very good dog in a home where only one person loves him. I like to travel and Harold isn't a good dog sitter, and in a way, I'm not a very good dog owner. I suppose I was compensating for Harold's lack of interest in my *life*. Tidus is just a bit over one year old and would easily make the transition to a new owner that loves him. That's all he really needs and I'm sure you have been good to him."

"Have you thought this through, thoroughly Mrs. Davolos?"

"I have Mrs. Grevera," she finished her tea and waited for an answer.

"We have grown to love your dog and he is a sweet and gentle pet."

Tears appeared in Mrs. Davolos eyes and she turned and kneeled beside Tidus and hugged him, and after a minute she stood, wiped her face with her hand, compassionately thanked Mrs. Grevera with her teary eyes and hurried to the front door.

Katie followed her and closed the door behind her, then wiped her own wet eyes with a tissue.

Carmen Llamas watched from her car as she observed the morning watch of the San Jose Police Department depart to their respective duties. She finally saw what she came to see.

Detectives Grevera and Rudolph engaged in conversation walked to their car and drove off to their destiny. It was her understanding that it was the only two women detective tandem in the police department. She opened her daily planner and looked for Grevera's address. This was almost too easy she thought as turned the ignition on her Beamer and drove to Sunnyvale.

Carmen parked at the end of the block behind a parked Ford 150 and pulled out a clipboard from the satchel that lay in the passenger seat. She walked with purpose to the third house on the block and rang the doorbell, with no results, then down to the next home with the same results. The fifth house found a lady answering the door.

"My name is Maria Gagliardi and I'm with the Census Bureau. Normally we don't survey on odd years ma'am but because of the diminishing population in our state we're trying to determine why this particular area is experiencing a spike in population and the buying and selling of homes in the Silicon Valley, which Sunnyvale is a part of and the increase of persons to this area which includes Cupertino, Mountain View and Palo Alto. How many people reside in your home ma'am?"

"Well, there's just the two of us. We've been here for about forty years, if memory serves me. I noticed you were next door and that would be the Williams and they have a young daughter, he's an engineer with Apple and I think she teaches school somewhere."

"All right, so that would be the Williams and the count there would be three. How about the home to your right?"

"It's a rental and I believe it's single woman that lives there. I haven't had the chance to meet her. She's been there for a few months now. I think she's a police officer but that's only a guess. And then there's the Wongs and there are three of them and he's also an engineer and she's connected to Mission College in some respect, but I don't know for sure what she does there. On the other side of the Wongs, is an East Indian family and there are four of them. I don't know what he does, but whatever it is? He's doing well with it. I'm not familiar with the family that lives on the other side of the Indian family, but I think they're Vietnamese. You would have to talk to them."

"Thank you Mrs.---"

"Lamb, Virginia Lamb."

That's what I was looking for. I went to three more houses and left the neighborhood, but not before surreptitiously casing the Grevera home.

CHAPTER 22

The Holiday residence was well cared for. There were three beautiful Hydrangia bushes with large pink and blue flowers, separated by deep red, pink, and yellow roses along the front of the landscaped home. A Chinese Maple sat on corner.

I rang the doorbell and could hear voices inside, then a big man appeared in the doorway.

"Mr. Holiday?"

"Yes, I'm David Holiday."

I reached for my credentials and displayed them to him, "I'm Detective Grevera, with San Jose Police Department. May I come in sir?"

"What's this about Detective?"

"Do you have a son named Scott?"

"Is this some kind of joke?"

"No sir."

"We just buried Scott. He's dead, leave the dead alone," he shouted as he turned and hurried off, leaving her standing at the open door.

She stood thinking he might come back, but was about ready to ring the doorbell again when a middle-aged woman came to the entryway.

"I'm sorry that David shouted at you Detective, but he's taken Scott's death pretty hard. Please come in." She ushered Grevera to the front room, where they sat. Can I get you some coffee? It's almost fresh from about a half hour ago."

"That would be fine, black please."

There was a picture of Scott in his uniform on a black stand up piano. She stood and walked to get a better view of the young man. *He was handsome, hardly looked the age to have been in a war. Most of the men and women in uniform nowadays were no more than babies,* she thought. However, even WWII personnel were also very young.

"He was too young to die, yet he kept shipping, over almost like he had a death wish. Why do they keep going back to almost certain death? He could have been stationed here in the states and never had to fire another bullet, but they choose to go back. Young people are hard to understand. Do you have a young one in military service, Detective?"

"I don't."

"Scott could have gone to any college he wanted, but he wasn't sure what he wanted to do in life. He thought the military might give him some direction, and he liked the idea of some kind of discipline. You know he didn't smoke. Sure he drank beer with his friends, but was completely against drugs. Even when his close buddies engaged in smoking pot or taking something stronger, Scott didn't, and he liked to wear his abstention like a badge. His pals were all right with that. That's why his father has taken all this beyond grief. Scott was special. He had convictions and eventually would have been a good citizen. I'm sorry Detective, you came here on police business."

"Scott's name was brought up by one of his friends in connection with a recent homicide in San Jose and---"

"Surely," she interrupted, "you don't think Scott is in anyway involved with a murder."

"From what you've said about him, I don't, however I still have to ask you some questions concerning his involvement, if there is any. Do you know if your son had a friend or acquaintance by the name of Taylor Dalton?"

"Yes, we know Tay, and he's a good boy. He and Scott grew up together, went to the same schools, and he's now attending Santa Clara University in Santa Clara. We know his parents. They're tops as parents and as friends. Is he the one that mentioned Scott's name?"

"Yes ma'am. Do you know if he knew a young lady by the name of Virginia Rosano?"

Mrs. Holiday thought for a few seconds, "yes, she was a pretty little thing. Scott brought her here one time and we got to meet her. You don't think for a second that he had something to do with her death. Scott was as mad as anyone could be about it. You should have heard what he said about that worthless Stevens. Her death was a travesty and Scott's life changed after that."

"How did his life change?"

She stood, walked to the bay window and stared into space. He wasn't thinking right. I believe Virginia's death caused his death in that God forsaken war."

Mrs. Holiday blotted her eyes and returned to her seat.

"Did he own a gun?"

"Yes, both, he and his father are hunters. He loved those guns. David had been in Korea and at a very young age taught Scott to respect any firearms. We have them down in the basement under lock and key. Would you like to see them?"

"Yes, please."

They firearms were lined up in a locked box with a glass door and all appeared clean and ready for use. She didn't see what she was looking for.

"I see a forty-five and western .38 pistol, but no other hand gun."

"I think he owned a .22 but I don't see it in there. I'll ask David if he took it with him to Afghanistan." She turned and started for the stairs, as David stepped down into the basement.

"I think you're right Susan, he must have taken it with him," David asserted.

"Is it important that Scott owned a .22 hand gun?" Susan queried as they walked up the stairs and David ushered her to the front door.

"Scott is dead. We've lost a wonderful young man. We don't like that the police are coming around asking questions about a man who fought for this country like he's some kind of suspect in a murder, Detective."

"David!" Susan shrieked. "Stop it. She's just doing her job."

He turned and walked briskly from the room and disappeared.

"I apologize for David's behavior Detective Grevera. We've had a difficult time addressing all that has happened."

"I understand completely, Mrs. Holiday. I may need to talk with you again, and I'm leaving you my card."

She nodded.

CHAPTER 23

Chief Detective Tom Wilson stood in front of his detectives and lectured them about trying a little harder for results in the pursuit of the criminals.

"I know we don't have the staff we used to have a few years ago, but we have the best criminal detectives I have ever seen right in this room, and I'm not patronizing anyone in here. It's the bald-faced truth. I'm not going to throw names out because I'll forget someone and I would never hear the end of it. You all know that you are the best. The Mercury News has been good to our department and I applaud them for it, and I'm not saying this because I've been thinking about retiring. I've been at this for the last thirty-three years, two months, 1 week, two days, three hours, and checking his watch, twelve minutes and nine seconds. I know some of you already knew that bit of news. As you can tell, I'm counting the time." No one said a word. "The truth is the San Jose Police Department homicide division was ranked number one in the U.S for cities with over a million population. I just wanted you all to know that this memo just came to the mayor of this great city early this morning and it will probably make national news. Congratulations. Now get your butts out there and confirm you are the best. Rudolph and Grevera, I want see you two before you go out this morning," he called over his shoulder as he walked into his office.

"Close the door, Grevera. Please sit down. So what do you think? Do you still like working as a detective?"

"I do. It's very challenging. Thank you for the opportunity of working in this capacity?"

"How's your personal situation?"

"There has never been an episode except the one you already know about. Nothing, nada."

"Good, just don't close your eyes to it."

"Rudolph, bring me up to date on the Stevens murder."

"So far we've got multiple suspects. There's the mother's sister that is currently a local nun, the daughter that has admitted killing Stevens, but no gun, two young men that knew him and had been seen with him, close to the time he was killed, and a soldier that was on leave, but had a strong motive for offing Stevens."

"I was there when the daughter admitted the murder, but I don't think she did it. Let's try and get this one buttoned up."

"By the way, did you hear that Grevera provoked another personality from Adriana Smolski?" Rudolph briefed.

"Yes, I did. I believe that came from your previous practice Grevera. It was the talk of the squad room, and duly noted. Thanks Detective, now get out of here, and close the door behind you."

"Well, if she's not home we'll go talk to Sister Vivian and the good priest, Father Manny Garcia. Did you have someone else to see?"

"Hey I'm with you Delores. You're my mentor. I go where ever you go."

All right, here we come Adriana Smolski," Delores shrieked.

"I still don't understand why Adriana isn't in some mental institution because of her multiple personality disorder."

"You heard what the chief said. She wasn't a danger to herself or anyone else, plus we all agreed that even though she said she killed Steven, we didn't buy her statement. Personally, I don't think she could kill anything, not even a fly."

I nodded, but somehow it didn't seem right, I thought.

"Tell us about how your father died, Adrianna? Wasn't your Aunt Vivian involved with his death?"

"No, no way, that's all settled. Someone killed him because he didn't pay back some debt."

"Didn't she buy you a .22 pistol for protection against your father?"

"Yes she did buy me a pistol. I was afraid of my father because he had abused me and my aunt threatened to…she felt it would be safer for me to have some kind of weapon in my apartment for protecting my personal rights."

Grevera considered her words, "Do you think your aunt is capable of killing someone?"

"How can you say something like that? She was nurse in the Veteran's Hospital for years doing just the opposite and then she became a soldier of God, doing things to help all those who need help. She gave me her retirement pension and loved my daughter," and she began crying. "What kind of bad person does all that?" Through anguished tears she lamented, "yes, she gets upset with some of the things that have happened to me, but she's an angel. Go talk to Father Manny. He knows just how good my aunt is."

"One last question," Rudolph asked, "Do you still have the .22 pistol that you killed Mark Stevens with?"

Adriana stared back at me with desperate blinking teary
eyes.

Carmen Llamas was beautiful and smart, and never carried her benevolent attributes on her shoulder. She didn't need to, she knew who she was and kept it under a humble shield. She was watching her quarry from a distance and observing how she moved while unaware of anyone watching her. Carmen could see she was confident, well dressed, and completely in control of herself. She felt like she was looking at herself. Would it be wrong to actually approach this pretty woman and get to know her before she…Carmen speculated. The thought amused her, and she turned, walked away, a smile lingering on her beautiful red lips.

Unbeknownst to Llamas there was another person doing the same observation of her. He had placed himself in the vicinity of the ladies nightgowns and scrutinized the beautiful terminator from a distance she wouldn't notice. Now he left the area and followed her to the escalator in the sparsely occupied women's department, her delicate perfume wafting ever so indiscernible in the air. Here he stopped and browsed for nothing and proceeded to the moving walkway. As he neared the main floor, he could see Carmen Llamas making the exit from large department store, but no worry he knew where she was staying.

CHAPTER 23

"You know Mom, I'm really glad that we're all together again, and that you kept Tidus. I love the big dog once I started walking him. I don't think he was abused, unless not paying attention to him is abusing."

"Well, no one beat on him or didn't feed him, but bringing a dog into ones home and then not paying attention to it, *is* abusing the animal. I believe Esther Davolos wanted a dog for the wrong reason. Her husband didn't pay attention to her anymore and she felt like she needed something to compensate for that lack of attention, so she got herself a dog. That was good. However Esther likes to travel and Harold, her husband doesn't, so poor Tidus is left with a man who didn't want or care for a dog and you get abuse. Leaving the gate open where Tidus was housed was not a good thing and Tidus knew he was living in home where the one that liked him was gone, and the one that was supposed to watch him, didn't. He was certainly going to die where Delores and I found him. Freeways and animals do not fare well, with the animals usually end up being killed. Can we change the subject Katie?"

"Did I say something wrong."

"No honey, you didn't say anything wrong. It's on me. I haven't been the best mother lately and I'd like to think I am still your mother. Have you given any thought about where you would like to go to college? I'd like to be a part of your ongoing life, please."

"You know what? I miss you too" and she walked over to her mother and they hugged.

"Does it seem like it's been a long time ago since we talked like mother and daughter?"

"Mom, it was a long time ago. A lot has happened since I was a eight grader."

"Oh my God…has it been that long?" She wiped a tear from her eye with her hand. "Eighth grade. Oh Katie I'm so sorry, honey. I can't believe I've been so…thoughtless."

"Mom, mom, have you forgotten that a bullet from those bastards guns pierced your head? You laid in several Intensive Care Facilities, completely oblivious that you were alive. Even when you woke up, you didn't know me, your mother or anyone else that you had known previously. You're a miracle Mom. You're not thoughtless—"

"You're a wonderful mother Deidre, and you'll always be my sweet daughter," Sarah Sloan interrupted walking into the room, "it's a wonder you're not crazy with all that has happened to you. You're still beautiful and very bright. The woman you've always been with a little bit a muscle added to the already tough minded girl." Sarah gathered the two in her arms and they rocked quietly for a few seconds. "Fill us in on your knew job, honey."

They sat at the kitchen table, "It's different in a lot of ways and yet some things I do aren't much different than being a shrink. I still have to probe for information about the person, though in a little different way. Following police protocol is important, but there is some give and take. I love my partner, Delores Rudolph and our chief detective, Tom Wilson. The scuttlebutt going around is that Tom might be retiring because of a nagging disability, and that Delores might be the new Chief of Detectives."

"Is that a good thing for you, I mean, that you would be losing your partner," Sarah asked.

"Probably a bad thing, however if Delores becomes the Chief, I firmly believe she would try to find me a partner that would be compatible for me, having said that, I don't know if she has any leeway for that to happen. At any rate, I'm a big girl and I think I could handle the situation without too much concern."

"Mom, I know you like what you're doing right now but why aren't you going back to your profession. I realized you can't go back to New York, at least not to Samson, but you could start a practice here Silicon Valley. Nobody's seems to be looking to harm you."

Katie's question was a good one, and I thought I had answered it already. I hope I'm not losing it again. "I thought I explained that someone was looking for me to do me harm, Katie."

"Yes you did, but no one has appeared in so long."

"It doesn't mean it's not out there."

Katie thought she should drop the subject and not add to her mother's problems by being a pain in the rear.

"Well, the truth is I *have had* some negative episodes that were thwarted by me and my guardians, that I have managed to garner in keeping myself safe. In taking care of myself I think I can also keep you two safe. All right. And I want you both to know that I haven't forgotten how many years I spent becoming a psychiatrist and I'm not going to forget that I'm very good at my chosen vocation. Now can we please stop talking about me and get back to you Katie. Mother what do think about Katie going San Jose State or Santa Clara University?

"I think that should be left up to Katie."

"I guess what I'm trying to say is, are you happy living here in the Bay Area?"

"We've discussed it while you've been working and as long as we can live with you, we don't care where we live. I like Sunnyvale and so does Katie."

"You two birds are all I have in this world and I don't think I could go on without the two people I love most in this crazy world," and they came together and hugged.

CHAPTER 24

Tom Wilson had been walking around with a cane that he hated to use. Everyone that knew the Chief knew he hated his situation with his health and never talked about it. His wife had told Delores that his pain was so bad that he was taking huge doses of Morphine so no one would know he was having pain, which had side effects on his very life. His doctor had argued for years for Tom to retire. Thirty-two years was enough time to give to his vocation, but Tom's life *was* the police department. His wife's opinion was that no one should have to give up the job that one loved, and she knew that Tom loved his job and the San Jose Police Department. Was his illness a prelude to a reluctant retirement? The unspoken words of a *small* percentage of retired veteran police officers, was that there wasn't a life after retiring from law enforcement. Some ate their guns. Every day was a new day for most police officers. Each day presented a new difference, its own excitement, danger, helping hand, discipline, knowledge, resourcefulness, each its own resolve. Tom the quintessential policeman, following police protocol and insisting the same commitment from all his subordinates and woe is he that doesn't. He is the big stick. Retiring was the ultimate step, it was so final, the preamble to…waking up to come to work was life, and interfacing with friends, a new day, new problems, mingled with old ones. That was living. Everything else was a precursor to that quest, and Tom Wilson was going to grip that goal until he couldn't walk.

Delores came out of Wilson's office and plunked down in the office she shared with Grevera.

"How would you feel about working by yourself for a while Barbara?"

"Is there a problem?"

"Tom's talking retirement, and believe me it's the last words he wants to utter to anyone. I can't give you the clinical terms for what he has, because I can't pronounce the words, but it's something about circulation in his legs. It's some bad stuff. The problem has gotten to the point where walking is a real problem for him and he's at the limit of his medication and still maintains a clear head. Anyhow, where this is going *is* that Tom is endorsing me to replace him. That's his recommendation to his boss, because I've got the time and experience. I like being a detective and everything that goes with it. Just between you and me, sitting behind a desk doesn't really appeal to me. I think I could manage the office but I'm not sure I would enjoy doing it. Tom was a great detective and every bit the fine administrator. I have my doubts about me though."

Barbara could hear the reticence in her voice. "Have you worked the position in your tenure here at any time?"

"Yeah, but I knew it was temporary and didn't mind the work. I just don't know if I could do it on a permanent basis."

"Have you considered that you might grow into accepting the job and working at it with the same zest that you apply to being a good detective?"

Delores nodded, "Yeah. Who knows? Maybe once I wear the collar for a while I will adjust to it, and love it. However, today I'm going to be here in the office and maybe for the next week, so you're going to be on your own."

"I don't mind that you're not going to be with me today. Psychiatrists don't normally work with anyone, anyway. You've taught me well, Delores, and I think I am able to work without a partner, though I will miss you, and I wish you good luck today."

I was still having some difficulties adjusting to the traffic, especially in here in San Jose in the late afternoon, but managed to arrive at the Holy Rosary College at the Mission San Jose. As I approached the door to the old seminary, now a school for young orphans and derelict children, and a dormitory for the sisters who worked here, a sister was coming out.

"Are you looking for someone?" the good sister asked.

"Thank you. I am. Her name is Sister Vivian."

"I'll see if she's here, come in. We have a waiting room just off the foyer."

I looked around the small room and noticed that as the priests give up everything comfortable, the same was applicable to the nuns. The living quarters were much the same. A lone picture of Jesus hung on one of the walls. I reminisced as a young girl I had wanted to be a nun. My friend Freida Lansbury and I would help solve some of the world's hunger problems. It got us accolades from the sister that taught us Catechism. We were so proud. My mother gushed when I told her of my intentions. My father only smiled, giving me his patronizing grin.

"I'm sorry for keeping you waiting, detective. I wasn't dressed."

"Are you well?"

"There's a flu going around and though I had received my annual shot, I think I might have been too late for it to do me any good."

"I can come back when you're feeling better and I certainly don't want to get whatever you have."

"I believe I'm past the contagious period and I do feel better than I did yesterday. Would you feel more comfortable if we walked while we talk?"

"Thank you, Vivian. A walk sounds good."

Market Street was the main artery of downtown San Jose and there were restaurants and small shops all along the street.

"Would you mind if we stopped at the park? I think we can talk there," Sister Vivian requested.

"Adriana doesn't remember what she did with the .22 pistol you bought her. Would you know the where-abouts of the hand gun?"

Sister Vivian stared out into space and worried her hands. "I probably should have told you earlier when we talked. It wasn't that I lied. You never asked me that question before. Adriana didn't kill that miserable excuse for a man. There're bad people everywhere and that's a fact. You must think I'm a poor excuse for a Catholic Sister, but we have feelings just like everyone else. What Mark Stevens did by giving Virginia Rosano that cocaine that caused her subsequent death, was that he killed Adriana too. Virginia was her whole life.

"Are you aware Adriana has another personality?"

"I'm sorry. Another personality? I don't understand," she responded, confusion, blanching her face. You mean like, "The Three Faces of Eve," with Joanne Woodward. That kind of personality."

"Yes, though I've not seen three personalities in Adriana, like Eve, but it wouldn't surprise me if she did have more than one. Her life has been full of stress, worry and hiding her true self, just to keep living in her miserable world."

"I wasn't aware of that. She's always been quiet and to herself, even around me."

"With you she was stress free, she had no need to come out as someone else to protect herself."

"Is that how it works? I never witnessed any multiple personalities at the Palo Alto V.A. while I was there, though I'm sure it was possible. It's a big hospital, full of veterans with all kind of problems and the various wards that treat different mental illnesses. Does having another personality have negative ramifications?"

"Generally speaking it doesn't, and since you were not aware she had another person inside of her, and you see her more than anyone else, that speaks for itself. I don't believe she is a danger to herself. I have met Danny, her other character, and though he displayed angst, no hostility was displayed toward me. Now, getting back to the .22 pistols. Adriana did admit that you had given her the gun when she had to worry about her father's sexual advances, but she is unable to remember if she misplaced it or gave it back to you."

Sister Vivian reached in her purse and pulled out a tissue. "I took the gun from her apartment about a week after her father died, without telling her. I didn't think she'd be in need of it anymore. I know I should have told her, but she had so much on her mind at the time."

That's why she was so confident that Adriana hadn't killed Stevens, Barbara thought. *She's still in my sights.*

"Do you still have the pistol in your possession?"

"Yes. I'll give it to you when we return to the dormitory."

"Did you purchase this weapon from an authorized gun dealer?

"Yes, I had considered buying one from an individual but Father Manny Garcia thought it would be better to buy from a reputable gun shop and have papers to prove it, if something onerous should ever happen."

I nodded, "It makes sense."

"May I call you Barbara or would that be improper? I mean you really don't seem like what I thought Detectives are like. You know, like the series "Law and Order," on TV. They're all business. No warmth in their personalities, just facts. That's all they have time for, I guess. Cold is the feeling I get from them. You're not that way…Barbara."

"Thank you Sister Vivian, but I think each situation presents a certain kind of reaction from law enforcement officers. You're easy to talk to and you respond to kindness, which is good. But not everyone does. Like I said, every action presents a reaction. Would you mind going back to the dormitory for the .22?"

"Oh no, of course not."

They headed back to the campus.

"Did you ever take it to a gun range and fire it?"

"No, primarily because I wanted Adriana to do that and she did go a couple of times, however later I found out she didn't use her own pistol. She rented one just like it at the target center. She didn't want me to eventually get back a used pistol. She's always been frugal."

They walked up the few steps to the front door.

"I brought an evidence bag, so I would like to go with you to where you have the weapon."

"I suppose it would be alright because you're a detective and here on official business. I'll just inform the sister in charge that you'll be escorting me to my room."

I nodded and waited in the foyer.

"Is Sister Vivian in some kind of trouble?" I was startled by the nun's sudden presence.

"Excuse me," I muttered, wondering where she came from and then noticed a small cubical to the right of where I was standing.

"She didn't do anything wrong. I know these things Miss Police Woman. My name is Sister Antonette. They think I'm crazy, but I'm not," and she gave this wide smile and giggled. "You see if I was crazy, I wouldn't be here," and she turned and ambled off twitting with her hands close to her ear.

"What did Sister Antonette say to you?" Vivian asked shaking her head and observed Sister Antonette walking away.

"Nothing important, really. Is she all right?"

"Did she say something that made no sense?"

"She said that you had done nothing wrong and that she knew these things and then introduced herself to me."

"She's not well," Vivian responded, "and I've got a problem."

I could see the consternation on her face. "What kind of problem?"

"The pistol is missing and I have no idea who would take it. This situation is very distressing."

"Would you mind if I went to your room with you so I can see where it was kept?"

"I suppose not. Am I giving up any of my rights doing this?"

"Sister Vivian, did you kill Stevens with this missing weapon?"

"Of course not. Why would you ask something like that? I've already told you I didn't."

"Good. Then you have nothing to worry about. I'm assisting you in trying to locate the missing gun."

The small austere room had three beds with mobile dividers separating the cots, each with a four-drawer cabinet for the storage of clothing, and one lamp stationed on the top of each of the cabinets, conjuring a seemingly semi-private atmosphere. An open door across the room indicated a bathroom, and adjacent to it a closed door.

"Originally I kept it in my underwear drawer," as she opened the drawer to indicate where it had been kept, "but a month ago I stored in the closet over there," and she pointed to the closed door next to the bathroom.

"May I go look inside the closet?"

"Oh, of course."

"We don't wear these Habits daily any more, but they are worn at certain occasions."

I nodded. There were small boxes built into the wall for shoes and a single shelf on top extending the width of the closet.

She stepped into the small room and extended her arm to where the gun was stored.

"This is where it's been since I brought it back, in this corner."

"Was it covered by anything, like a bag or holster?"

"Oh yes of course. It was in the box it came in when I bought it at the gun shop, and then I had wrapped it in a brown paper bag and told Sister Ruth Superior where it was stored."

"So she knew you had a pistol up here in this closet."

"Yes. Yes, you see she grew up in Cheyenne, Wyoming and her family had rifles, shotguns and many pistols in the house."

"Do any of the other sisters that share this room with you know there was a gun stored here?"

"Sister Superior didn't think it was necessary for anyone else to know, so I didn't tell them."

"Will the sisters that sleep here in this room with you be arriving soon?"

"What time is it, Detective?"

"Five minutes till five."

"They should be arriving in minutes to wash up for dinner."

"Do you think that someone in here might have inadvertently taken the box thinking it was something they had stored here?"

"No, I don't. They all knew that box belonged to me. I never told them what was in it, only that it belonged to me."

"I would like to talk to Sister Superior."

"She should be in her office, or in the mess hall for dinner. I'll take you to her office first."

She knocked on the door and then opened it.

"Come in," she greeted. I followed her into the office.

"This is Detective Grevera from the San Jose Police Department."

She stood and came around her desk, "Nice to meet you Detective," as she shook my hand. "What can I do for you?"

"First of all, no one is in trouble here, Sister Superior. I'm looking for the pistol that Vivian had stored upstairs in her dorm room."

"I see," and she glanced over at Vivian, "and the presumption is that it is now missing."

"That's right. I thought you might know something about its disappearance."

She shook her head, returned to her seat behind the desk and clasped her hands in front of her on the desktop.

"In Wyoming, where I spent my formative years under the tutelage of my father, every family owned guns. My home was no exception, I learned to shoot a .22 when I was six years old, a Ten Gauge shot gun at twelve, and a 30 ought 6 at fifteen, when I hunted mule deer in Wyoming. My father always kept the small arsenal of weapons under lock and key. I thought since most of the ladies here weren't into guns of any kind, it would be all right for Sister Vivian to keep the pistol in a box with a brown paper bag around it. If I had to guess, I don't think it has left the premises."

Grevera thought for a few seconds, "Why would you say that Sister?"

"No one except Sister Vivian and I knew the hand gun was upstairs and no one, intentionally, would take it. Whoever took it was not aware there was a firearm inside. If you'll give me some time to get to the bottom of this, Detective Grevera, I should have something to tell you soon."

There was something about Sister Superior words that convinced me she would indeed find resolution to the missing .22. I extended my card to the determined head nun, thanked Sister Vivian and left the two to ponder the mystery.

CHAPTER 25

As I started to back out of the parking lot of the Safeway on El Camino Avenue, I felt a thump on my rear bumper, drove forward again, and stepped out of my car. A beautiful blonde woman approached, "I am so sorry, it was my fault. I didn't realize you were pulling out of the space, though it doesn't seem too serious," she said leaning over to inspect the damage to my bumper. "My mind was on my shopping list."

"She's right ma'am, it was her fault," a young man standing close by offered. "I saw the whole thing. Would you like my phone number?"

I looked down at an insignificant dent on my bumper, "I don't think that will be necessary, but thank you."

The lady extended her California driver's license to me. I peaked at the name and returned it. "I don't think there is enough damage to warrant us giving each other our driver's licenses. I thank you for your consideration."

"I'm really sorry," she said as she walked to her car and parked.

I sat in my car, and considered my attitude toward the woman as she walked by on her way into the store, and then I stepped out my car and called out to her, "Miss Llama." She stopped, turned and walked back to me, "I think I might have a a little rude to you.

You were very kind to admit fault. My name is Barbara Grevera. Do you live here in Sunnyvale?"

The woman has a heart I thought, and she is not without empathy, "no I don't live here, I'm here on business."

"May I buy you a cup of coffee?" Barbara asked, "Safeway has a Starbucks inside the store."

"Thank you, I would like that. I haven't had my second cup today."

They sat and sipped their coffee.

"I was trying to remember the last time I had an accident that was my fault, and for the sake of me, I can't remember, though I have been the victim of two fender benders."

Barbara was observing this beautiful woman as she talked and realized she was transfixed by her natural beauty and easy manner. She carried herself with confidence and even her feline grace was lithesome and unassuming. "Are you a Californian?"

"No, I'm from New York. And you?"

Grevera smiled, "I'm also from New York."

Carmen had to be careful though she knew her cover resume read well. This was no ordinary woman, this Doctor of Psychiatry was every bit her match. What was her motive for going to work for a Police Department? Was she in over her head with this wonder woman? Yet, there was a draw toward the beautiful and talented shrink, now a policewoman. I wondered if she played Chess.

"The City?"

"Up state."

"Buffalo?"

"I'm almost certain you've never heard of the town, Samson."

"With an o or a u?"

"An o."

She was right, I had not heard of Samson, New York of course, that's not saying much. I haven't heard of well over half of the towns in New York. Now, why was she so adamant that I wouldn't know of the town or city of Samson?

"Your right, I've never heard of the place." I was in need of changing the subject. She had bested me on locations. I noticed she was wearing a wedding ring, and my natural curiosity insisted on putting my foot in my mouth. Why would she be pretending that she was still married?"

Barbara sipped her coffee and mulled over the Carmen's innocent interrogation. Was this very attractive woman *prying* and why did I feel that she was, almost like a warning compelling my suspicious nature to stand at alert. Hadn't Carmen's innocuous meeting been impromptu, an accident, that brought them together to this point? Of course, lighten up Barbara.

"Do you have children Barbara?"

"I have a daughter that will be entering college this fall."

Ah, now that was something that Jimmy Lamantia didn't bring up in our conversation, a daughter that lives with her I think. What else had jimmy forgot to tell me?

"I have a daughter too, and she's a hand full. She's a child prodigy."

Barbara thought she said it as factual and not to flaunt her daughter's special attributes. My cell phone was buzzing in my purse.

"I think that's your cell, Barbara."

"I have to answer it." Excuse me and stood, walked away and responded.

Carmen wondered if it was a personal or business call. This was working to my advantage, she thought, even though I knew a great deal of info on Barbara Grevera, yet, I didn't feel I had an edge on her. She seemed to know me as well. How could that be? Two men had tried to eliminate her and here I was attempting to know her better because of my auspicious benefactor, Jimmy Lamantia.

"I'm sorry Carmen I have to go. It has been nice talking to you. I would love to hear more about your gifted daughter. I've never really met a prodigy."

"I'd like that to happen, Barbara. Maybe we can have coffee again, soon.

"Did you get my address?"

"I have it, thank you. You'll be hearing from me."

Aside from John Salinger, It was the first time I had met a stranger that I almost instantly bonded with, Barbara thought.

"First of all, tell me about your new friend you met at Safeway. It sounds like you two hit it off well, even though it precipitated from an accident, that wasn't your fault," Delores beamed with enthusiasm.

"You know, I hadn't met anyone in so long, and then it was a stranger who became my friend, all in a matter of minutes. She was really nice and has a daughter that is a prodigy, primarily in Music, and is attending the University of Californian, in Berkeley. She's only twelve years old."

"Ever the skeptical one. Are you sure it was a spontaneous meeting?"

Barbara recounted the brief meeting, "There was a moment or two that I pondered that very thought but, I thought it was just me with a hangover from all that has happened to me and my friend, Michelle Danese. I suppose I wanted to meet someone that was not a family member or close associate. Anyway, how's the new Chief of Detectives doing?"

"Like I said before, I can handle this job for a couple of weeks. The problem is, I need the drama, the new case, the mystery, the pondering, the accelerated blood pressure. Maybe when I'm older and I can't move around as well, it might be easier to grow into this job. The guys we work with Barbara, are tops. You couldn't find a better group of individuals in any department, even with reduction of personnel, because of the cut backs in all the departments. We just dig in a little longer for the same results. It's tough on the home life for sure but hey, we knew that when we signed up for it. Whew! Listen to me blather."

There was a chorus of applause from the squad room.

Rudolph smiled.

Barbara smiled too. "If I wasn't already here on the job, I think I would have been ready to sign up for duty under you, Detective Rudolph. You make a compelling argument for becoming a detective here in San Jose."

"I believe that's called preaching to the choir," Rudolph cackled and looked down at the notes on her desk. "That call I made to you yesterday was from a friend of the Holiday's, Scott's parents, David and Susan. Here's her address and phone number. She might be someone you want to talk to. I told her you would be calling."

As she drove up Meridian Avenue, she recalled where the Davolos lived and thought about Esther and her husband. Titus was wonderful pet and she would stop one day and let Esther know that she was taking good care of her beautiful German Shepherd.

"Come in Detective Grevera, my name is Jean Haselback. I'm a friend of the Holiday's and I know Susan and David well. Would you like to sit in the kitchen or the front room? I made coffee and I have tea at the ready with some Apple Strudel that is to die for."

"Sounds wonderful Ms. Haselback, it's been ages since I had Apple Strudel and I even remember where I had it. A neighbor had bought some from a lady from Germany and all she made was pastry and sold it door to door. Yes, it was a pastry I remember well."

"I'll have us served in less than five minutes," and she hurried herself into the beautiful kitchen with the sound of dishes and silverware clacking. Pouring a cup of black coffee, she offered me coffee mate or real cream.

"Um," I moaned as the aroma of rich black coffee wafted into my senses, "black is fine. Are you going to inform me that you're an active Chef at some fine restaurant in San Jose?"

"Thank you, no though I do love cooking and trying different things, especially pastries."

Barbara sat quietly and took a small bite of the strudel and smiled, tears rolled down her cheeks and dropped onto the tabletop. She stood, "may I use your bathroom Ms. Haselback?"

"Of course, the second room on the left, down that hall," and she pointed the direction.

Barbara was gone for a few minutes and as she reentered the kitchen Jean started to apologize---

"It was your act of kindness and friendship that instigated those happy tears, Ms. Haselback. You need not apologize. You know nothing about which roads I've traveled that have set me down here in your wonderful kitchen today. Your sincere generosity and goodwill have brushed aside the mundane and touched a delicate balance with the good that also surrounds us. You're a wonderful hostess, an excellent cook, and your strudel *is* to die for, but I suppose we should get to why I'm here. It's easy to forget that I'm working with the generous hospitality you bestow on your guests, taking nothing away from your sincere friendliness."

"Thank you Detective Grevera, that's very kind of you. Yes, as I mentioned earlier, the Holidays are dear friends and we've been friends for years. My daughter knew Scott and at one time we thought they might get married. I don't know what happened between them and then Scott went into the Marines and of course you know the rest. I'm getting ahead of myself. I wanted to tell you something about the Holiday's that might seem like I have no scruples.

David and Susan loved Scott and they were a very close family. I believe David took their son's death a little harder than Susan. I tried to console them by taking food to them and by hanging out with them, but David would always leave when I would show up. That was not the father I knew. He was always very cordial and polite. I suppose a death in one's family has a different effect on each member. Susan was still Susan but David was…different." Jean looked away and lost herself for a few seconds, then turned to Barbara, "he tried to kill himself," as she dabbed her eyes with a tissue.

"Did Susan tell you that?" Barbara asked.

She shook her head. "Susan is very protective of her family, and I don't think that's a bad thing."

Jean stopped talking.

"How did David try to kill himself?"

"With one of the pistols David and Scott used for target practice. They were both quite efficient with the weapons they owned. Susan doesn't think he would have gone through with it but now we'll never know. She found him in the basement crying and the .22 lying openly on a chair."

"So he wasn't holding the gun in his hand or to his head?"

"That's right, but he was crying and the gun lay next to the chair he was sitting in."

Barbara thought, his crying with the gun next to him was not definitive enough to deduce a possible suicide.

Barbara recalled that one of the pistols was missing when I went to the basement with Susan to see the lock and key display of firearms David had in his home.

"I believe one of the hand guns was missing when I was in the Holiday's home."

"Well, if it was the .22, it's because I have it stored in my attic, what little attic I have."

I wonder why Susan didn't mention that fact. "I'd like to see it Jean."

"No problem. Would you assist me in holding the stairs that lead to the attic? I've never placed much faith in the stability of those dubious stairs."

"Lead on."

Grevera held on to the wooden ladder as Jean stepped up. Her head now reached the opening of the attic. "Oh my God, it's gone," and she stepped down carefully.

"Maybe someone moved it further into the attic. What about your daughter?"

"No, on your first question and Colleen's more afraid of this ladder than me and, she doesn't know I put the gun up there. There was no reason for her to know that."

Standing at the top of the stairs, and Jean was still pondering the question in her head. Suddenly, "Of course, but why would she take it back without telling me," she said as if I wasn't I wasn't standing next to her.

"Are you referring to Susan Holiday?"

"She nodded.

" Do you think she could have come over here and taken the gun while you were out somewhere?"

"She had a perfect opportunity to do just that. You see, Colleen and I travelled to Bend, Oregon to see my sister and I left the keys to the house with Jean." She looked at her watch, "let's go downstairs, Colleen should be arriving any minute."

The two woman talked about the draught California was now experiencing and soon Barbara, after checking her watch, made a suggestion.

She stood, "I'm going to call the Holidays and see if I can't drive over there to talk to Susan or David. Rest assured, I won't let them know I've talked to you Jean. All right?"

"Thank you Detective, I appreciate that."

The front door opened and Colleen walked in. "Hi honey, this is Detective Grevera from the San Jose Police Department.

She was a lovely blonde, with a generous smile and friendly demeanor, "Mother said she was going to call you, I'm glad to meet you."

Scott had good taste in young ladies and she favored the deceased Virginia Serano.

"Would you mind if I asked you a few questions, since you knew Scott about as well as anyone."

She nodded and we all sat down in the kitchen.

"Would you mind if I left you and Colleen to talk, I have something I need to do upstairs."

"That would be fine," and they waited until Jean left the room.

"Did you know Virginia Rosano?"

"I knew of her, though, never got to meet her."

"It is my understanding that Scott had some special feelings for her."

She hesitated and then nodded. "Yes, and his parents were disappointed by his infatuation with the girl."

"Were you aware Scott took Virginia's death pretty hard and was upset with Mark Stevens because of the circumstances that led to her death?"

"I heard the story and was saddened by what happened. She shouldn't have died. Days later, the gossip was that she was quite innocent about drugs, smoking and alcohol."

"Do you think Scott's anger could have carried over to the killing of Mark Stevens?"

"I don't know if I can answer that question honestly. Before he went to Afghanistan, I would have said no. Scott should have been living in the fifties like my grandfather. He didn't like smoking or drugs. He was clean-cut and respectful. He was out of place, born in nineties, though he did manage. I know he drank a beer occasionally with his father and might have even tried drugs and smoking, but I never knew about it, and I knew him all my life. But when he came home the first time from where ever he had been, he was not the same person. He had always been quiet, but not reclusive. His behavior was reminiscent of the late Pat Tillman's in a lot of ways. Academically, he excelled and could have gone to any college he applied to, and he was a wonderful athlete. The few times he would allow me to see him, he was distant, moody, is the term that comes to mind. He definitely had changed. I hate saying these things now, but I believe he could have killed Stevens. He was a Marine, and isn't that what they're trained to do, kill? Doesn't war change a lot of men and women? Maybe he was unable to distinguish where he was again. Don't many of our veterans think they are back in those countries when they do things here? Isn't that what's called Post Traumatic Stress Syndrome?"

I could see she was becoming distressed. My phone buzzed in my purse and I checked to see who was calling, "Thank you for sharing this with me, Colleen. I don't think I have any more questions for you. I have to go. Tell your mother I appreciate all the information she was able to give me. I might want to talk to you again," and I hurried out the door.

CHAPTER 26

Barbara had been thinking she needed to go to Macy's or Nordstrom's to buy some work slacks. Dresses and suits were almost out of the question when the doorbell rang.

She opened the door. "My gosh, if it isn't my very good friend J.D.Salinger."

"In the flesh, my dear Barbara."

"Come in," and she hugged him closely, grasped his hands and let him into the front room. I've been so busy lately, I had almost forgot about you my dearest of friends."

"Were you aware that I hadn't even been here for the last two weeks?"

"I'm sorry John."

Titus walked into the room and ambled to John.

"Oh my God. Does this bear belong to you? Is he safe to be around?"

"John this is Titus, yes he belongs to us, he's not a bear, he's a German Shepherd and because he's more human than dog, he knows you're a friend, just because you're here. You noticed he didn't bark."

John reached over and padded Titus's head and Titus then promptly walked back to where he came from.

"What do think?"

"There's a transformation happening right before my eyes Barbara. How's the sleuth business?"

"All right. It definitely pulls you in. Like I told Delores, there are similarities between the two professions. Questions, motives, run the gamut in police work as they do in the therapist profession. The perpetual quest for answers to the who, why and when."

"Then the 'all right,' means you like what you're doing."

Barbara nodded, "yes, I like what I'm doing for now. Ask me a year from now and I might give you a different answer."

"Do you still have someone looking for you?"

She paused, "would you believe he or she, now that I think back on it, came into my bedroom and almost made me past tense. Someone in the neighborhood had seen this person enter my house in the middle of the night and called the police and they called my home to warn me, simultaneously, a police officer on night patrol began banging loudly on my door. Whoever it was that was in my house got spooked and left via the adjacent bedroom window, and it is the consensus of Mother, Katie and myself that he isn't coming back."

"Another close call, wouldn't you say?"

"Only by the grace of God, John."

There was a pause.

"I was headed for Macy's. Would you like to come along? Maybe we can catch some lunch at Westgate's Valley Fair or across the street at Santana Row."

"Excellent Barbara. I've never been to that shopping center but I hear it's 'pricey,' is it true?"

"I've never bought anything there, I've only eaten at one of the restaurants, and I didn't think it was all that pricey."

"Good, I'm ready when you are my dear."

Barbara was driving east on El Camino, and as they crossed San Thomas express John gasped, " oh my goodness they've torn down the shopping center where I used to buy tee shirts," he exclaimed.

"I'm surprised you even recognize this stretch. Delores, my partner, was clamoring that El Camino Real has a brand new face all the way to the Alameda."

"I guess I shouldn't be so surprised, but since I'm usually driving and don't really get the chance to observe the not so subtle changes."

They entered the Macy's ladies department, located at the far end of the shopping center from where they had entered, which was the men's department. I always thought it was odd that Macy's had two separate stores in the same shopping center one for each gender, however it's genius, when you give it some thought. I stopped to ask directions to the suit department. Turning to the left they had only walked past one casual section when she caught sight of someone she knew.

"John, I think I know the blonde lady up ahead. I'll try not to be too long with her. Do you mind?"

A smile appeared on his face, "take as much time as you need my dear."

"She's also very bright."

"She appears to be smart, Barbara," John still smiling.

"Also sexy."

"Really?" Hadn't noticed.

"You're practically drooling."

He reached up with his hand to wipe his mouth.

"I can't believe it, you bump into me and now I practically bump into you. How are you Carmen?"

"It's always a nice to see you Barbara, and what are the chances of meeting you here in one of the biggest shopping centers, if not the busiest, in San Jose. " Her eyes turned to Barbara's friend.

"This is my very good friend, John Salinger. John, meet
Carmen Llamas."

"Would you by any chance be an author?"

"It certainly is by chance that I am an author, Carmen Llamas, however not the 'Catcher in the Rye' author."

Carmen and Barbara laughed.

"I read your book about the professional woman exterminator and was quite impressed with the reality of your story."

"Of course, it was pure fiction," he smiled.

"Yes, but then sometimes fiction mimics reality. Wouldn't you say?"

"True, you read, and do you also write?"

"No, although I have considered a memoir of some sort, someday. I'm sorry, I'm holding you two up from your shopping, Barbara."

"Yes, I'm looking for some slacks to work in."

"Do you keep a diary of some sort, Carmen?" John interjected.

"I do. Maybe you could give me some pointers on initiating my story."

She gave him a card. "When you have the time, give me a call and I'll meet you wherever you want, at your convenience Mr. Salinger." She hugged Barbara quickly, "see you again hon."

"She's delightful, Barbara. How did you meet that gorgeous thing?"

"The car she was driving bumped into me in the Safeway parking lot, initiating a brief car insurance meeting, and as a result we became fast friends for the oddest of reasons."

"Oddest of reasons?"

"It's hard to put into words, John. Initially it was all business, but because there was so little damage to either of our pumpers. I felt she was sincere and friendly, so I offered to buy her some coffee and it blossomed into each of us calling the other by our first names. Did you know she has a child prodigy?"

He smiled mostly to himself. "She's charismatic, wouldn't you say?"

"Fits her like a well-fitting pair of pumps, John."

"Pumps?"

"Ladies shoes," she laughed.

"Where are you right now, Barbara?" Rudolph asked over the police radio.

"Just off Lincoln and Meridian Avenues."

"I hate to do this to you, but we're short everywhere and you happen to be nearest to the next scene. There's a possible suicide in the Hirata home at the address I'm going to give you. Check it out and let me know ASAP. I'll try to get someone else in the interim.

"I'm on my way."

This was a peaceful and elegant neighborhood where people lived quietly, and the home I stopped in front of was no exception.

The door opened, "Is this the Hirata home, ma'am? I'm Detective Grevera." The woman was distraught and weepy. She held a tissue to her face and allowed me into the home without speaking. An older man was sitting in the front room. He only looked at me, then turned to stare at the wall. The woman led me down the hall and stood beside the closed bedroom door. I looked at her and she stared back, her hand still to her face. I reached for the handle and opened the door. The room was tidy, well-kept and the blinds were closed giving the room a gloomy presentation. A lone nightlight shown enough illumination to see someone was on the bed. The young woman could have been sleeping. I touched her forehead and it was cold, but there was still a little color in her face. There was no sound in the house, so it was easy to hear the doorbell ring. There was no indication that she had used a pistol, only a bottle of prescription drugs sat on the bedside stand. Avinza, which was a brand name for Morphine could be the drug she took. I heard a woman's voice as she neared the bedroom. I turned and waited.

"Hi. I'm the assistant Coroner, Marge Meany, and you are?"

"Detective Barbara Grevera."

"There's no statute against suicide. How did you end up here?"

"I happened to be close to the Hirata home, so my boss sent me here. I guess I was the first one here."

Dr. Meany walked over to the bed. "Looks like she's just sleeping. No blood?"

"I think the Morphine might have been the method, Dr. Meany."

"That's a pretty good guess. You familiar with brand names for drugs?"

"In my former profession I was a psychiatrist."

"An MD. I heard someone was working with Rudolph that was smart, a pleasure to meet you. So you think it was Avinza as she picked the bottle up. It appears to be half empty. It wouldn't have taken that much to do its job on the young lady. I don't think I'll be needing you for any of what is required of me here, Detective Grevera, so you're welcome to go about your other business."

"I'd like to talk to the mother and father about the young lady, so I'll hang out here for a little longer. Nice to have met you Dr. Meany."

"And back to you. Maybe we can get together for some coffee. I'd like to know why a shrink becomes a Detective."

"Yeah, okay."

I left Dr. Meany doing her testing and walked to the living room, where Mrs. Hirata, handed me a note.

I guessed that the Hirata's don't speak a lot of English in their home, so she directed me to their dentist on Meridian Avenue.

"Delores, I just left the dental office of Dr. Tiffany Kitamura and Mark Nishimura at 1198 Meridian Avenue where Phyllis Hirata, the young lady that appears to have committed suicide, was employed as a Dental Assistant. Phyllis's parents don't speak much English, so Jane Hirata, the mother, gave me a note to talk to a young woman by the name of Crystal Kitamura, the office manager, sister of Dr. Kitamura.

Phyllis had been employed part time by the dentist. She and Crystal were good friends."

"That's my dentist!" Delores exclaimed. "Did you get to talk to Tiffany? She's a doll and really knows her stuff and very professional, yet family like."

"Really."

"If you don't have a dentist yet, Barbara, you should try her. She's terrific. The whole office staff is just great. Anyway, go on with your interview."

"Chrystal was shocked to hear she had died. That's all I could tell her. She indicated that Phyllis did work for them as a dental assistant, she loved her job, and the staff all loved her. The patients really liked her too, and Dr. Kitamura felt she was an integral asset to her thriving business. Phyllis's friend, Chrystal, pointed out that she never mentioned her parents, and kept her conversations mostly about work here at the dentistry. Innocuous conversations mostly."

"Thanks Barbara. Did anyone show up there before you left the home?"

"Yes, the assistant Coroner, Dr. Marge Meany arrived just before I left."

"She's good. All right, Grevera thank you and continue where you were going before I diverted you, and thank you. Later."

CHAPTER 27

Susan Holiday opened her front door and was surprised to see Detective Grevera.

"Sorry to bother you Mrs. Holiday. Do you mind if I come in for a few minutes. I need to ask you some questions about the missing .22 pistol."

Susan thought about the question and realized that the Detective had probably talked to Jean Haselback, but she wasn't sure.

"Could we talk in the kitchen? I need to take some notes."

"Sure Detective. Would you like some coffee?"

"No thank you." She looked directly at Susan. "Did you ever find the .22 hand gun that was missing from your home Mrs. Holiday?"

"Well, ah, it was never really lost. A friend was keeping it for me because I thought my husband might want to do harm to himself."

"I see. So that's the reason you didn't mention it to me when I was here last."

"I'm sorry I mislead you, Detective and now I'm afraid it's left me in a bad light." She stood, walked to the kitchen counter and grabbed a tissue. "Our lives have become chaotic and filled with doubts and resentments. We've drifted apart to some extent and David and I are both having trouble sleeping without crying and pointing fingers at each other." Tears rolled down her cheeks and she dabbed her face. "Scott was our whole life and now that he's gone we're drifting on an ocean without paddles. We're falling apart."

"Is David home now, Mrs. Holiday?"

"He's upstairs taking a nap."

"No, I'm not," David interposed as he stepped into the room."

"I'm glad you're here Detective Grevera. Unless you've recently lost a loved one, you can't imagine the things the mind does to protect itself, including deception. We find all kinds of reasons to blame ourselves for something we had no control over. We should have done this or we should have done that. My God we have driven ourselves for one or both of us to have a breakdown, or heart attack. I think the reason Susan allowed Jean Haselback to keep the .22 was because she thought I was going kill myself. I wasn't going to do anything of the sort. The reason I was crying down in the basement was because I had read a note from Susan's doctor in regard to her last visit with him. Honey, I'm sorry I opened it before you and discovered you had a short lease on life. I assumed you didn't want me to know."

Susan stood and walked to David, crying as she embraced him.

"Honey, why would you want to keep something like that to yourself. Haven't we always shared our good, and bad news with each other?"

She sat back down. "Yes, but lately all the things that have been happening just kept stacking up and we've been unable to handle them. It's like we're out of sync and unable to think rationally."

Barbara sat taking the whole scene as if she were invisible.

The scenario before her eyes was very touching and tugged at the very essence of compassion, humbling, commiserating. Despite her compassion she had to interject herself into the setting that had formulated before her eyes.

"Do you have the pistol on the premises?" Barbara asked quietly when the conversation had stopped.

Susan eyes turned to David and their eyes met momentarily and without any words, he stood and walked out of the kitchen.

"I suppose you think we've gone crazy," Susan lamented.

"Not at all Susan. You two have been through a great deal of trauma recently and that has caused a strain on your everyday life. Your son is home on leave and someone he knows gets murdered, there's a lot of finger pointing as to the perpetrator, your son included, he returns to his overseas duty, then he is killed setting off an additional emotional minefield and your lives begin spinning with no apparent clear resolution. Considering all that has happened to you two, I think you're doing all right."

David walked into the kitchen with the .22 and laid it on the kitchen table, in front of Barbara. "It's not loaded," he said. She reached into her purse and secured a large plastic bag, where she placed the firearm, then back into her purse.

"You don't think Scott killed this Stevens character, do you Detective?" David asked.

"Hopefully this pistol will prove that he didn't kill him, Mr. Holiday. I want to thank you for your cooperation and now maybe we can get some clarity, some answers to our questions. Thank you David and Susan. I have another stop to make so I'll be going."

Susan stood and walked Barbara to the door. "I'm sorry I wasn't up front with you from the start."

"I understand Susan, try to have a nice evening."

Detective Grevera called Delores Rudolph to chat, but she wasn't available, so she drove to the police station and up to the squad room. After placing the pictures on the board she stepped back and examined each face introspectively as if one might jump out at her and admit the killing of Mark Stevens. It was glaringly true, all of the faces on her bulletin board could have shot the man. They all knew and most disliked him, some more than others.

Adriana Smolski could be the least likely, yet Danny is obnoxious enough and bold enough to carry out what he defended Adriana of. Sister Vivian and Father Manny Garcia, well, she almost had to give them the benefit of doubt…though. Scott…Scott Holiday, yeah, I suppose a war veteran that had received a medal for bravery and for disposing of several of the enemy in Afghanistan had to be taken as a serious suspect. Even his father and mother could be questionable. Sister Wilamina? That's right she hadn't heard from the good charge nun at the dormitory. Had the pistol been found and who took the firearm in the first place. Was it an accident? Wilamina was not an active nun anymore and was she psychotic enough to kill someone? Should she call Sister Ruth?

Grevera turned the light out in her office and closed the door. She could see one of the other detectives working in his office as she walked out of the squad room. *Could this be Sunday,* she thought?

Detective Grevera started to knock on Sister Ruth's door when a voice said, "she's not in her office, but she's coming back in a few minutes. Are you the detective that was here a couple of days ago?"

"I'm Detective Grevera, and yes I was here two days ago. May I ask who you are?"

"My name is Alyson Grayson. I volunteer for Catholic Charities, to assist where they need me. I don't know if I should be telling you this. I don't think there is any harm in your knowing and it might even be the reason you're here now…about the missing hand gun."

I nodded.

"It seems that Sister Wilamina had been in possession of the gun. I wasn't privy to why she had the weapon, only that she had confiscated it, because she didn't want Sister Vivian to get in any trouble."

The front door opened and voices could be heard.

"I believe Sister Ruth is here so…it's been nice talking to you Detective," and she sauntered down the hallway.

"Ah, Detective Grevera, I'm so glad you're here. I tried to call you yesterday morning. Did your boss tell you?"

"Unfortunately I haven't been able to see her. I've been too busy."

"I think it's nice that she's in charge of *all* the detectives. A woman, I mean. We have firewomen, policewomen, CEO of large corporations, mayors of towns, Senators and on and on. We have stature. I understand that you're a Medical Doctor with a license in Psychiatry. Your boss told me, I hope you don't mind."

"You're very kind Sister Ruth, and yes, women are slowly climbing up to the glass ceiling, however I'm on a mission to solve a very complex homicide. I understand you found the missing firearm."

"Come on inside," she gestured and, she circled her desk and sat. "Have a seat Detective."
She fetched a key from her purse and open a drawer, took out a small box and offered it to Grevera. "I don't know the history of this pistol, where it's been, if it has been fired, just that Sister Wilamina had taken it from its location upstairs because she thought she was helping Sister Vivian."

"Sit down, Barbara. Does the name Llamas mean anything to you?"

"She looked tentatively at the Chief, "yes, Carmen Llamas is the lady that bumped into my car in the Safeway parking lot, that I briefly told you about a week or so ago."

"I thought that name belonged to you somehow, though wasn't sure. She's in the Stanford Hospital ICU as we speak. Apparently the perpetrator confused her with a person that had killed someone this perp knew and he took retribution. She's alive, but that's about all. She took two shots to the body and one grazed her head near her ear. The doctor's induced a coma so they could work on her. I knew that name belonged to someone in the department so I went to Stanford for a look /see, Barbara. I got the name of the doctor so you can talk to her before you go to the hospital. It might save you a trip. Eric McDougal is handling the case, so if you need more information, you can see him. How are you doing with the Stevens case?"

"I've got a pistol for you to check out and see if it was the gun that killed Stevens," Barbara said and handed the plastic bag to Rudolph."

"Good, Has it been tagged?

"Yes, I hope so."

"I'll see if I can get a rush on it and get back to you."

Barbara walked to her desk and thought about Carmen Llamas. *Someone put two bullets in her body because they thought she had killed someone they knew, hmmm.* She stood and went back to Rudolph's office, but she could see she was on the phone. She waited, but then as she made the decision to forget about…Rudolph saw her and waved her into her office.

"I need to go over to Hedding Avenue, and talk to Ann Demming at the District Attorney Crime Lab," Rudolph said standing. "Did you have a question?"

"Do we have the person that shot Llamas in custody?"

"Unfortunately, he was killed when he resisted the two police officer that arrived. Llamas was clean, maybe too clean, not even a parking ticket. "She had no criminal record, Barbara."

Grevera stared into space.

"McDougal is good detective, Barbara and he'll find out just how innocent Llamas is or if there is more to her life than we have now."

"Thanks Delores, you're way in front of me."

CHAPTER 28

Barbara received a text message from Detective Rudolph. "The hand gun you gave me recently is not the murder weapon."

Barbara sighed in relief and walked back to her car. She was tired and happy with the news. She liked the Holiday family. She was going to go home, fix a light dinner, shower, crawl in bed and read a book. Instead she found herself driving up El Camino to Palo Alto and Stanford Hospital. Carmen Llamas had been on her mind all day and she was compelled to see her. Barbara refused to think cynically about the woman that had bumped her car by accident.

She displayed her badge at the nurse's station and walked down the corridor toward room 214. The medicinal smells instantly brought her back to her stay at hospitals. She stopped and leaned against the wall.

"Are you all right ma'am? A nurse asked.

She stared into the probing eyes and for a second, forgot where she was.

"May I sit for a minute?"

She was ushered into a vacant hospital room and sat. The nurse brought her a glass of water. "Are you sure you're all right?" the nursed asked again.

"Yes, I just need a minute to sit. Thank you."

"Is that a gun you're wearing?"

"It is, I'm a police officer," and I showed her my credentials.

"I was pretty sure you were, officer. Thank you. Are you here to see the Llamas woman in 214?"

"Yes."

"She's still under."

I stood, "thought she might be, but I wanted to see her, anyway."

"No problem."

I walked quietly into the room. I'm sure this must be what I looked like a few years ago. Tubes everywhere, and life machines making their distinctive sounds, I thought as I looked down at her face. Carmen was still beautiful I thought even with all the life paraphernalia engulfing her body.

"How well do you know this woman, Dee," a familiar voice asked.

I gasped in disbelief, as Ed appeared in front of me. "Ed, Edward, I'm not seeing you am I?"

"I believe you are in a way. I'm sure you would know the lingo. *Illusion* comes to mind."

"The last time I can remember becoming delusional was in Wenatchee at Memorial Park, but then, the person was a stranger. I've been working hard lately and not getting a lot of rest. Lots on my mind; might be the cause. You certainly appear to be real though."

"In your mind, I am real. I don't think you can touch me, but I don't really know. Do people that are supposedly crazy and think they see the things we don't see, really seeing those things?"

"If that's a question? Yes, I think they do see those things. It's real to them. Right now, you're real to me. I've been under stress for the last week and this is the effect. I guess you've been on my subconscious and this is the result. I'm glad you're here Ed." Tears rolled down her cheeks and she reached for the tissue box on top of the stand next to the bed.

"I've missed you Edward. We didn't get to say goodbyes. I guess you know I was in pretty much the same shape Carmen here is in when…when…oh my God." Barbara put her hands to her face and wept unabashedly.

"Detective, Detective," a clear voice spoke out.

"Barbara looked up to see the nurse she had seen earlier in the hallway.

"Are you all right? You were talking to someone and then you began crying."

I stood, "it's been a long day and doesn't look like I'll be talking to Ms. Llamas this evening."

"Mom, where have you been? I tried to call you all day," Katie probed as Barbara walked into the house.

Barbara reached into her purse for her iPhone and checked the charge. She had forgot to plug it in two days ago. "I'm sorry Katie, I'm having a bad day," and she sat down in the front room divan.

Katie plunked herself down beside her mother, hugged and held her, "You look tired and down."

"Both would be accurate."

"How about a glass of white wine with some White Clam Chowder from the Fish Market."

"Sounds good."

Katie sat the glass down in front of her mother. "Be back in five minutes with the chowder. I think I'd like to go to San Jose State next fall. I found a friend that is going there to become an engineer. She says they have a good engineering program and of course this is Silicone Valley. The chances of finding a job after graduating are great. What do you think of an engineering degree?" Katie walked into the front room with a steaming bowl of Clam Chowder. She smiled. Barbara had lay down and was sound asleep. Katie placed a light blanket on her mother, picked up the untouched glass of wine and walked to the kitchen table, placed the contents on the table and began eating.

Chief Detective Delores Rudolph dropped an envelope on Barbara Grevera's desk and walked into her office leaving the door open. She knew Grevera was punctual and would be arriving soon.

At ten minutes till seven Grevera arrived, sat and opened the envelope. She studies each picture thoroughly and sat back on her seat. She turned in her chair and looked toward the Chief's office and found Rudolph waving her in.

"Recognize any of the people in those pictures?"

"Yes, where did you get these and are they current. He's in a wheel chair."

"What's his name?"

Barbara lost herself as she remembered the evening that brought her to near death and in some ways did kill some of her spirit. At that time he was only a voice, because of the hoods they had worn. Barbara had never forgotten his voice, though she had managed to redirect her rage. Reminiscing created too much stress and anxiety. She had carefully built her own wall of defense and it held well.

"Dimitre Aristotle."

"Poetic justice." Rudolph carried on, "seems Aristotle was obeying the law when, he was hit by a person that had run a red light. His Ferrari was totaled and Mr. Aristotle wasn't much better off. Though the man was later found floating in his apartments swimming pool, evidently drowning by accident."

"Chief, I'm a little confused by all this. What are you trying to tell me?"

"I guess what I'm saying, and I don't know if I ever told you what happened to some of my family. You see, when I was a detective in Albuquerque, I was on a drug enforcement squad that had caught a well-known drug lord, was prosecuted and was doing time in the New Mexico Penitentiary, just south of Santa Fe. The bastard, while in jail, had my brother and father killed, to make a long story short, I took retribution on his gang, and I let him know that if he did anything else, his wife and family would suffer, as well as some of his good friend's families. That's all I can tell you about it, Barbara. That's why I'm here now, in California."

"Wow, you did mention that you were here for something that happened in New Mexico, but you left out a lot of important details to your story."

"Its just the way the law works. The bad guys are able to do anything they want, to anybody, and if they don't get caught, get away with it. But Placido, the drug boss, thought he could call on his friends on the outside to do his heinous killings, while he's inside and safe and thought the law was going to pussyfoot around with kid gloves, he was definitely wrong. Anyway, I'm trying to tell you, that you and I are going to Samsun,

New York and pay a visit to Dimitre Aristotle. We have three days to complete our mission. We leave on Friday and come back Monday."

"What about the Stevens case."

"We won't get any results on that pistol you gave me until the latter part of next week. My superior is allowing us to go. The only catch is we have to pay our own airfare. Will that be problem for you, Barbara?"

"Not at all."

"What about Katie and your mother?"

"Humm, they'll be all right, but I'm not sure I should tell them where I'm going. Maybe I should tell my friend John, so someone knows in case we run into a problem. Do you have some sort of plan on what we're going to be doing in New York?"

"I was hoping you would ask. You see I have a friend that used to be a San Jose Detective and he has indirectly ended up in your hometown of Samsun as a Detective. When I made contact with him a while back, he informed me that he had read the transcripts of the trial you were a part of, that ensued after Aristotle's blood bath in his brother's mansion, and all of the intimidations by him on prospective jurors and witnesses. Where I'm going with all this, is that he's a thug, murderer, intimidator and all around scumbag. By all your accounts, he's been trying to kill you with his hired minions that are no better than him. My friend, and I won't give you his name, because you don't really need to know it, for his good and well as yours, and has been studying his daily movements for a case that someone is trying to prosecute our pathetic scumbag. He thinks if we come out there, with his help, we could bag him and save the city a lot of money on another trial."

Barbara thought about the term, 'bag him,' and knew what Delores had in mind. Aristotle always seemed to circumvent the law in some way and stayed out of prison. But if I did this thing, I would be no better than Dimitre Aristotle.

"He's a cold blooded killer Barbara. By all rights, you shouldn't be here. Don't you agree? He's a psychopathic murderer. A person like him has no feelings for what they do. I'm sure you know that. People are no more than an annoying fly to that man, and he swats them with the same regard, and lays his head on his pillow at night and falls asleep. We would be doing *all* a service if we were to swat him."

Barbara thought, *Delores is looking right into my head and reading me like a book. She's a very smart woman. She knows people well. It wasn't like I hadn't done this very thing once before with Michelle Danese up in Wenatchee. It had emboldened Michelle and I. But is this what I was becoming? I couldn't even say it.*

"What if the next person he sends is successful, Barbara?

I nodded. I can't seem to let go of this vengeful train I'm on, not because of me. They won't let it go. They insist on my reacting, no matter my reluctance. Of course Delores was right, though she seemed anxious to do this terrible...almost as if she was enjoying talking me into it. Yes, she wanted this to happen. She had already planned the whole thing. We were just going to carry this thing out with her and her friend's schedule. Is this right? Does it matter? Obviously it matters, at least to me, it does. Delores, in her heart believes she doing something good for me. Yes me, and here I'm chastising her for it. 'No good deed goes unpunished' was applicable here and I was the *heavy* in it. Now I'm flagellating myself.

"I'm sorry Delores, of course you're right."

"You've got a whole day to think about it. No harm done if you decide against it."

Driving home I turned the radio dial to 98.5 and listened to, 'Journey,' by coincidence, one of my favorite bands, but then I turned the radio off. Quiet ruled the airwaves in my head. I had to think.

CHAPTER 29

The flight back to San Jose had been quiet. Neither Delores nor Barbara spoke about what they had accomplished in Samsun, New York. It was done.

Barbara flipped through the pages of the Sunnyvale phone book and found the number she was looking for. She punched in the digits.

"This if Father Kelly."

"Father Kelly, I need for you to hear my confession today at your convenience."

"Are you a member of our church?"

"I'm a modern Catholic. I think that's what I would be called nowadays, but I am Catholic."

"I hear confessions on the weekends."

"I would like for you to make an exception and hear my confession today. I'm sorry to sound so demanding but Father Kelly, I really need to confess something that is eating me alive."

"Do you know where the church is on Saratoga-Sunnyvale Avenue?"

"I do."

"How long would it take you to get here?"

"Fifteen minutes at the most."

"I'll be waiting at the front door of the church."

"Father Kelly."
"Yes."

"I'm the person that called you on the phone to hear my confession."

As they walked into the church, the priest spoke, "Do you want to confess face to face or have me in the confessional box?"

I thought about the priest's request. It was tough enough to just be here and then to speak openly. Face to face would be too difficult.

"It would be easier for me to do it in the confessional box, Father Kelly."

He led the way, and when both were ready Barbara spoke.

"It's been at least five years since my last confession, and in the interim I have committed two mortal sins. I believe I should preface my beginning sentence. Five years ago a very bad man stood in front of me with a pistol inches from my forehead, and shot. He thought he had killed me. It could have been God's will that I didn't die, which I prefer to think, or just plain luck. At any rate, I lived, at first precariously, then more out of desperation than harmoniously. I had to leave my family and escape where I couldn't be found, which was the state of Washington for the first years and then here in the bay area, since. Because I didn't die, the man that shot me sent a man out to finish the job in Washington, which I was fortunate enough to learn about and prepare for his arrival. When he arrived, with the help of several people, one being from law enforcement, I was able to capture and after grilling him for hours he admitted his mission was to kill me and a friend whose husband had the misfortune to be at the same assassination. She didn't even know the man that killed her husband and yet she was also targeted. Well, we killed the man and then fled here."

"I don't understand. Can't you go to the police and tell them you're story."

I stood and turned to open the door.

"Please don't go," he begged quietly, " I'm sorry I didn't mean to discourage you. It was the wrong thing to say to you. Please go on with your confession. I beg you."

I knelt, "the police know about the man. Father, he was acquitted after a lengthy trial. Men like him employ others to intimidate those who have information that could put them in prison. They twist our justice system and use it for their benefit. Some even work for the justice system, corrupting and manipulating this man's cause, money and fear rule. Children have been killed to sway a witness."

Barbara paused, she looked through the porous sliding wooden panel, at the priest sitting, taking this all in.

"I've been having trouble accepting what I did and thought that if I verbalized my sin, I could minimize some of the guilt and maybe get some sleep."

"What is it you did?" he asked sincerely.

I thought about his question. I was trying not to say what I did. The priest moved in his seat, anticipating the answer, I was afraid to give. I was aware of the perspiration in my armpits and my clammy hands. My mouth was dry.

"Are you all right ma'am?"

Suddenly I was back to Aristotle and the moments before I faced the murderer. Since the actual assassination of the sociopath, it had been subliminal, but now it had invaded my consciousness and it was in your face real. I had taken my cloth hood off and stood directly in front the crazy killer, inches from his face. "There's still a scar where you shot me. Our eyes met. Look I yelled, and pointed to the spot. He stared apathetically never observing where I pointed. I was filled with rage and contempt ready to end his ruthless, contemptible life. You had no compassion when you allowed us to witness each murder. We were, each of us a witness to all the shootings of our loved one and friends. It was so callous and abhorrent and you went about it as if you were swatting flies on a wall. What makes men like you, I shouted? Why couldn't you just leave it alone? It was a miracle that I lived and you had ruined my life. You killed my husband and my best friends husband and you still pursued your vicious venomous ways. What compels you to keep killing and destroying lives? I just wanted to be left alone and try to put some of my life, that you turned upside down, together again, but no, you had to keep sending someone for me, until I turned on you. Yes, you made me who I am now Mr. Aristotle. The wounded stag turns on the rifle less hunter and gores him to death. Tell me why?" She raged in his face. "It was over and done a long time ago." Seconds went by as she observed his apathetic, listless eyes.

"Then it happened Father. His eyes told me that he didn't care what I was about to do. I did what someone should have done a long time ago to this psycho. I put the muzzle of my .357 to his temple and pulled the trigger." Barbara began crying, hands to her face and rocking back and forth. No words were uttered.

CHAPTER 30

"How long have you been here this morning Barbara?" Delores asked.

"A while."

"It's still resonating in you, isn't it?"

Barbara turned in her swivel chair and peered at Delores for a few seconds. "It will probably never leave my mind. Things like that don't easily leave one's memory. I rid myself of one worry and put another in its place."

"What we did was right, Barbara. If nothing else we saved lives that otherwise would be lost. Yours comes to mind."

"True, but it was *me* that pulled the trigger."

"We were complicit in the whole ordeal Barbara, I might just as well have put a bullet in his temple, too."

"Yes, I suppose you're right…it's just that…"

"Every law enforcement officer dreads the day he or she has to choose whether to shoot someone in self-defense or be shot. Each of us dies a little with the guilt. Don't think for a second your situation wasn't the same. It was you or him. No difference. Mr. Aristotle wouldn't have hesitated to end your life if he had the opportunity. He sent two, maybe three people to kill you, but it didn't work out for him. You're still alive Barbara because you didn't wait for him to come to you. You took the fight to him. Something, I'll bet, he never thought would happen. I liked what you said to him, about the 'stag goring the rifle less hunter to death.' It was perfect Barbara. You may never forget what you did, but it was right and one day you'll accept it. I believe it's what Marines and Soldiers and all personnel go through when they have to kill someone. Let me change the subject now. There appears to be some discrepancy with the handgun you turned into me for AFIS, so I'm going over to Hedding Street to check it out. Why don't you go see your friend that was shot at Stanford Hospital?"

I nodded, "thanks Delores."

I showed my badge at the nurse's station and asked about Carmen Llamas.

"We moved her into a room with a younger patient with a broken leg, at Mrs. Llamas's request," The nurse responded.

"Has she had any visitors?"

"We still have a guard at her door. He could better give you that information.

"I displayed my ID to the guard and whispered about Carmen's health."

"She's doing all right health wise," he said, "but she's only had two people come to see her since I've been here. A Nanny and her daughter."

I thought about that as I entered the two-bedroom ward. I walked to her bed, stood over her, looked down at a very pretty woman. Her eyes were closed and she appeared to be sleeping.

"I don't think she'll know you ma'am," the roommate said quietly.

I moved to her bedside.

"Why would you say that?"

"Are you a friend?"

I nodded.

"Do you know that she was shot?"

I nodded. "How long has she been with you?"

"Two days, don't know how long she was in the IC ward."

So she's been here five days as I calculated mentally and she's only had her daughter and the woman who took care of her when Carmen was working.

"They have a guard outside the door, but no one has come to see her," the young lady said, with her broken leg extended in the air a few inches.

"Why do you think she won't recognize me?"

"Well, yesterday when her daughter and the woman who brought her, were here, and she didn't remember either one of them."

"Is that you, Barbara?" Carmen asked quietly from her bed.

I peered at the young woman and she stared back perplexed. I walked over to her bed and returned Carmen's smile.

"I'm surprised to see you Barbara. I mean I'm pleasantly surprised that you're here."

I sensed she recognized me, but in a hazy kind of way. There was just a hint of doubt in her eyes - or was it something else, I wondered. Trauma has its own face and it can seem normal but also deceptive and elusive.

"What do you remember about me, Carmen?" Egad, I was sounding like a policewoman.

"Is this a trick question?"

"I'm sorry, disregard that question."

"I am having lapses in my memory, but I recognized your voice and it prompted some recall. Our inadvertent meeting was in the Safeway parking lot in Sunnyvale. I bumped into the back of your car. If memory serves me, you're a police officer. Right?"

Police officer? Had I mentioned I was a police officer, I wondered. *The conversation had been born by her bumping into my car. Carmen had carried most of the dialogue, without saying much about her own person.*

"Did I say something wrong, Barbara?"

I was still too paranoid and almost certain I had never mentioned being a Detective, however there was some chance it had leaked into our conversation over coffee that day.

"No Carmen, you didn't say anything wrong."

"Have you been assigned to find out what happened to me?"

"No, the detective handling your case mentioned your name and I came to see if you might be the Carmen Llamas I knew."

"Thank you for coming. You're my first visitor and possibly, my only caller."

I thought about that. "Do you anyone that would want to…."

"Kill me," she interrupted. *I thought about Barbara's question. I didn't personally know anyone that would want to put some bullets in my body, but there were a few dead people that she was responsible for and they had friends that would want me dead. I might have pissed off someone out there for what a miss deed. Nowadays, it doesn't take much provocation* to get oneself offed. It happens every day with road rage.

"Did you see the person that shot you?"

"He looked young, but I didn't recognize him. Just another face in the crowd."

Barbara thought it could have been a wrong person shooting.

"Were you aware your daughter and her Nanny had been here?"

"No I wasn't aware, except that the young lady in the other bed said they had been here."

"I'd like to get the Nanny's name, address and phone number Ms. Llamas."

"May I ask why?"

"Just police protocol."

"I thought someone else was in charge of my case."

I nodded, "we're short staffed and since I knew you, I volunteered to assist Detective McDougal, every bit helps in solving difficult homicides."

"Homicide? Hand me your note pad and I'll give you the info you wanted."

"You could have been a homicide case."

Carmen returned the pad to Barbara and added, "the address for Joanne Ambrosia is the same as mine. She lives with us, that's what most Nanny's do."

"Thank you Ms. Llamas."

A lady wearing a white long doctors coat and a stethoscope around her neck walked briskly in.

"Hi I'm Dr. White. How's our beautiful Mrs. Llamas doing today?"

"She appears to be doing well. I'm Detective Grevera with the San Jose Police Department."

"How's my friend Detective Tom Wilson?"

"Well, I think. He recently retired and I'm sure is enjoying his free time."

"Good. Ms. Llamas is a very lucky woman. We hope to be able to send her home in another day or two. Just a couple tests for possible infections from a bullet that passed close to her heart and she's out of here. I just need to look her over and you two can continue your conversation.

"I've got to go Ms. Llamas, but I hope to see you before you leave."

"Thanks for coming in Detective Grevera."

CHAPTER 31

"Are you sure you picked up the right .22, Barbara?" Chief Detective Rudolph queried.

"Why?"

"Neither one of the pistols you gave me are the murder weapon."

Barbara stared into space and wondered. Could there have been another .22 pistol involved? Have I missed a possible suspect? Is it one of the people I've already interviewed? I need confirmation that the handgun Sister Vivian gave me is the same one she gave to Adriana Smolski, and the very one I gave to you.

Do you have the serial numbers of the gun from Sister Vivian, Delores?"

"Yes, I also have the box and gun it was purchased in."

Barbara was driving down Market Street and as she neared the corner of West San Carlos and Market she could see a small crowd gathering and people pointing to the roof of Sainte Clair Hotel at the corner. She pulled over and stepped out of her car.

"Can you see what they're looking at?" a stranger asked Barbara, also gawking.

Someone up ahead also looking, shouted, " looks like someone is on the edge of the Saint Claire Hotel roof."

She put her phone to her ear, "Delores I'm at the corner of Market and West San Carlos. Have you received any calls of a jumper on Saint Clair's roof?"

"No, why?"

"I'm across the street on the side walk and it looks like there is a jumper up on the roof."

"Get up there Barbara and see if you can talk to the person."

"Are you sure?"

"Who better than you Barbara. Go on you're wasting time talking to me about. Go for it girl…please!"

Before she knew it she was running across the street and into the hotel. She showed her badge to the first person that looked to be in authority.

"Follow me. We have the elevator waiting for you."

"Do you know the name of the person that's on the ledge?"

"I haven't seen her to be able to recognize who's up there. She may not even be a guest here."

"Are you the manager? Is there anyone on the roof with her now?"

They stepped into the waiting elevator.

"I am the manager and no there is no one on the roof now, except the lady that's—"

"How did you know someone was on the roof?"

"I saw a crowd gathering outside, so I stepped out to see what they were gaping at."

"How long would you say she's been up there on the ledge?"

"Well, it's just a guess…maybe five minutes."

It must have just happened as I was driving by, Barbara thought.

The elevator stopped and the manager pointed to the door to the roof.

Barbara ran to the door and opened it to the crowd chanting, 'go ahead and jump' and surveyed the roof. She could see a lady at the edge nearest Market Street, so she moved to the opposite end so she wouldn't spook the person and raised her arms in the air and lowered them, to try to mute the throng that had gathered. The chant slowly subsided until all just stared up the new person requesting quiet. In a relaxed voice Grevera spoke.

"My name is."…*Oh my God, I can't tell her my real name…who*, "Delores Rudolph, and this is *new* for me so if I say something you don't like just tell me…okay?"

"You weren't sent here to stop me."

"No, I was driving by and saw the crowd gathering over here, so I stopped to see what was attracting all the attention. I could be putting myself in some kind of personal jeopardy by doing this."

"You mean if I jump?"

"Yes."

"Do you know who I am?"

"No, though I wish I did know something about you."

"Why did they let you come up here?"

"Because I'm a Psychiatrist."

"Yeah, I suppose I should have known that. I've been to a few of your kind. Well Delores, I'm burned out. I've managed to screw up my life with men and drugs and going nowhere. I'm tired of life and this is pretty much why I'm up here. I've alienated, the few friends I have and pissed off my parents, been a lousy mother to a wonderful daughter, everybody's better off without me."

"Have you been drinking?"

"I couldn't do this if I wasn't drunk or high on Meth or Cocaine, and I've had all of them in me all week."

"I'm glad to hear you say that."

"You are. What's that supposed to mean?"

Barbara noticed she teetered slightly and there was reaction from the crowd below.

"Do you really want to jump to your death in front of all these people? You just admitted you wouldn't do this if you were sober."

"I'm exhausted. I don't know what the hell I want to do anymore. This just seemed like the best thing to do and that's why I'm here."

Barbara walked closer until she was only a few feet from the woman.

"I hate this feeling I'm getting now." She said out loud to herself.

"What feeling?"

"I'm coming down and I feel like shit."

"Coming down?"

"Drugs."

"When did you sleep last?"

"I don't know. Delores help me off this ledge before I fall off."

The woman collapsed into Barbara's arms and they slowly sat on the roof. The woman passed out and Barbara grabbed her purse and started to call Delores, when she recognized Delores's voice beside her.

CHAPTER 32

"Thank God you were there when she succumbed to the drugs and passed out from lack of sleep. It hadn't occurred to me that I would be giving my name and then with all the reporters waiting, what I was opening myself up to, Delores. By the way I told her my name was Delores Rudolph."

Delores nodded, "Good thinking. I anticipated the bombardment of questions you would be deluged with from the reporters that would descend on you. When I told you to go up and see if you could help whoever was up there, I was strictly thinking from a police business point of view. I too, forgot your situation until you were already active on the roof. I left a Detective in charge and rushed up to assist you in any way I could, and help you exit the building no matter what the outcome would be. As it turns out you're a heroine and somehow we've got to keep it out of the papers. I'm not worried at this time, but I think I need to talk to Tom Wilson. He'll know what to do and give us some insight. It's getting late and we're both tired. Let's sleep on it and see what a difference a night makes."

"Good idea, thanks Delores."

"Barbara, I knew you'd make a good cop, but a super cop…wow!"

As I drove home I was thinking about the whole occurrence and I did have a warm spot in my heart about it and I was proud. Delores was a good friend and I believe that Tom Wilson would help us achieve a positive resolution to our current problem. I wasn't going to worry about it.

CHAPTER 33

"Oh mom, I'm so glad you're home. Mr. Salinger thinks he saw you on the evening news. He's stayed in the Sainte Claire Hotel and noticed there was some kind of activities going on at the hotel and discovered someone was threatening to jump from the top. The camera that was shooting the scene wasn't able to pick up the possible jumper or the person that was trying to prevent her jumping. But the distant image he saw made him think it was you. Was it?"

She sighed wearily, "Let me sit down honey."

"Of course mom. Sorry. I'm so excited. Would you like something to drink, coffee, tea, wine?"

"Coffee will be alright."

Katie rushed off to the kitchen, "It'll be ready in five minutes—"

"I changed my mind, I've had to much coffee already, I hope I can sleep tonight. Bring some red wine."

"You want me to fix you something to eat, a tuna sandwich, maybe?"

"I've already eaten. A glass of wine will be fine."

Barbara took a good swallow of the wine and looked at her anxious daughter.

"Yes it was me," she lamented, drained of energy. "Now we're trying to figure out how to make it *not me*, if that makes sense."

There was a brief knock on the door, and John rushed into the front room apprehensively wide eyed, where Barbara and Katie were talking.

Katie jumped up and gave John a big hug, "you were right, it was her. Sit down she's just about to tell us what happened today at the Sainte Claire Hotel. Would you like a glass of wine or a whiskey?"

"A whiskey would be great Katie."

She rushed off and was back in a few seconds with a whiskey.

"You must have had it poured already," he commented surprised.

"I did, I thought mom might have wanted something stronger, but she chose wine and I forgot to pour it back."

Grandma walked out of the bedroom. "What have I missed out on?"

Katie stood, brought her over to the divan and sat her down. "Would you like a cup of coffee Grams?"

"Yes, I believe I would. Thank you honey?"

"John did see mom up on the roof earlier," Katie hooted from the kitchen, then came bouncing into the living room with a cup of coffee.

They all sat staring at Barbara.

She smiled, "I love all this familial exuberance you're showering me with, but…it's not a good thing. There are negative ramifications from all this so called fame that I've imposed on myself, and indirectly on you."

John peered at Barbara and nodded mostly to himself in agreement.

Her mother appeared to be confused.

"What ramifications, Mom?" Katie queried, "You're a hero."

"Yes, and my picture will more than likely be plastered all over the front page of the Mercury News, and that *can't* be a good thing for me. I haven't forgotten I'm on someone's hit list and I'm sure my mug in the paper isn't going to be a deterrent."

"But Mom, you're a cop now, a Detective. You've got the whole police department covering your back. Doesn't that mean something? What nut would attempt to kill you when you're so directly involved with biggest police force in the Bay Area."

Barbara eyes went to John, who was now nodding with Katie's argument.

"John?" she said quietly.

"It's a viable notion, Barbara."

"Mom?"

"Honey, do whatever you should do," her mother added.

"What does Delores Rudolph think?" Katie asked, "Have you discussed this with her?"

"Yes, we did touch on it, but at no length because it was getting late and we both felt we should sleep on it."

Delores drove into the police parking lot earlier than usual because she couldn't sleep. She was still ruminating whether she should take this job permanently or going back to being a detective. The whole police department was short staffed, with no help in the immediate future, and the detective unit was especially short. Things were definitely getting out of hand, though she had been here before with the same problem as a detective. She lit the squad room with the flick of her hand and walked to the room where the pictures of possible perpetrators were displayed in the Mark Stevens murder case. *Why can't criminals just do the right thing?* She thought. *You know why Rudolph, you're just feeling sorry for yourself.*

The phone in her office began ringing.

"I'm not here yet," she yelled out and proceeded to her office.

"Rudolph," she answered, pushing the speakerphone.

"McDougal, I thought you might be there, now. Did you get a hold of Grevera?

"She's walking in as we speak. Are you still at the hospital?"

"Yeah, did you want to send her over here, or shut this thing down for now.

"Has Forensics' been there?"

"Everybody's been here. What do you want me to do, Rudolph?"

"Thank you Mac, I'll send her over?"

"I'm sorry for keeping you here longer than you should be," Barbara said as she approached Detective McDougal, sitting leisurely in a chair outside the door of the hospital room.

He stood, said nothing and walked inside the room and she followed.

"It all happened in o dark thirty, someone knew how to get into the hospital, was aware there was a skeleton crew and caught our vic in surprise. It was someone who knew what he was doing, just lift the head a quick jerk of the neck and bingo, it's over. Coroner thinks it was around midnight. Crime Scene Forensic believes it was a one man perp."

"Excuse me officer," a hospital guard said at the door, "I found these in the large dumpster behind the hospital."

McDougal scrutinized the items, fake glasses a grey man's wig, a necktie and a blue men's blazer.

"Yesterday must have been garbage day cause, there were only six trash bags in the large trash bin and this items sat alone on top of one of the bags," the guard stated.

"Thank you. Good work. I'll tag them and see what forensic comes up with. We believe that whoever did this wore gloves, but you never know, there might be a fingerprint on those items. At least we have something now."

"So what do you think, McDougal?"

He raised his shoulders. "We don't have anything. Those clothes might give us something, but no, we don't have anything. How well did you know this Carmen Llamas, Grevera?"

"We talked for fifteen minutes at a Safeway Starbucks about an accident that brought us together and we became fast friends. Maybe fifteen minutes at the most. The accident was incidental and caused no damage to either of our cars."

"Did you ever think the accident might have been planned and she was motivated to meeting you purposely?" he asked sincerely.

"Well yes, remotely. It did occur to me for a second that very day, but as you know my life has been a mess for so long…everything sounds like a threat on my life. I used to be in control of myself, a sound working Psychiatrist with a good practice. Now I'm a walking fragment of myself, suspicious, delusional, distrustful and sometimes irrational. Now…even self-patronizing, I have to blow my own horn to remember who I was."

There was a lull for a few seconds.

"Do you like what you're doing now?"

"I do, in some ways it's a lot like my old job, with some obvious differences. The police department has a camaraderie that is binding, almost familial and makes new hires like me feel like one of a large extended family."

She hadn't noticed before but Keith McDougal was a nice looking man. He was listening to every word I said.

"Do you have a family Keith?"

"I have a daughter. She's going to start going to San Jose State this fall."

"Really."

"Yup."

"You?"

"I too have a daughter that will be attending San Jose State."

"Does your wife work?"

"I lost my wife to Breast Cancer five years ago."

"I'm sorry."

"I think I heard your husband had been murdered."

"That's correct. He was murdered just a little over five years ago. How long have you been a policeman?"

"A little over ten years and if I pass the California Bar next week, I'll be a lawyer."

"I guess that means our little group of detectives will be even shorter."

"Sorry about that Barbara. I've been working for this advancement for the last four and a half years."

"I wonder if Delores would consider me working with you on the Llamas case."

"I already requested that she put you on as lead detective."

"Hum, wonder why she didn't say anything about your leaving."

"It has a negative connotation. Why make it worse by throwing it out there. She'll bring it up only when she has to."

"I guess congratulations are in order to you Detective McDougal."

"Thank you Dr. Grevera, it means something coming from you. Now if I can only pass the bar, I'll be set for what I want to do with my life. I've got somewhere to go right now, so I'll see you later in the squad room to bring you up to date where the Llamas case is. Okay?"

"Later."

CHAPTER 34

Grevera opened the folder on the Mark Stevens murder case and looked for the telephone number for the Holiday family. Something was not right about the .22 she had brought to Chief Rudolph from the Holiday household and she had always felt like things were a little off balanced in that small family, but she couldn't put her finger on the ambiguity of it all. By Susan's own admission, she and David had been out of sync for a while. Again she thought. *Could there have been a second .22 in the holiday family that was not disclosed? If David and Scott went hunting together, it could be possible that each would carry a .22 in a holster. It seemed logical to her that if Scott were to go on his own or with a friend, he would take his own pistol.*

"Barbara come into the office," Rudolph requested.

Barbara closed the folder and followed her boss into her office.

"Close the door," Delores requested flatly.

Barbara sat looking at her friend and boss and could feel her boss was in some kind of turmoil. Her body and facial screamed it overtly.

"The shit is about to hit the fan and I'm in charge of it all. You will be working more cases and we're losing McDougal and possibly another detective, though we might be getting a transfer from San

Francisco and I hear it's a woman. Meanwhile we're going to lose sleep and bitch a lot and we're going to kick ass. Okay? If McDougal passes the bar he'll be leaving us so, I'm making you lead detective on the Llamas murder case, starting tomorrow. Can you stick around? He'll be in soon and bring you up to date on the Carmen Llamas case."

"You want me to wait here in the Squad room."

"Yes, and about the lady that you saved last evening, she wants to talk to you. Guess who her father is?"

"Haven't the slightest idea, Delores."

"Do you know the names of the two Senators from California?"

"Come on Delores, I'm new here, I don't know the names of my neighbors on either side of me in Sunnyvale."

"Your right, you will know one of the senators pretty soon, cause he's coming here to *personally* meet you. Our mayor got a call from him and it was passed down to me."

"I thought we were going to sleep on this and then discuss it or when it was feasible. Does this mean that we're going to forget about the past and just shoot forward?"

"I'm sorry Barbara, everything is moving so fast, yesterday seems like a month ago. I called Tom Wilson last night and he brought up that your murderous psychopath had been assassinated in New York and that it would probably end any further efforts to have you pursued by a mercenary, and I for one, believe the same thing. Barbara the sociopath is dead. *We* know that and the chances of any retribution from those kooks in New York are over. I know it's easy for me to say that, cause it's not my life, but I'm right here for you and your family. There are no guarantees in life, we can take precautions, but we don't get any warrantees for a mistake."

"What's the ladies name that was on the roof top?"

"Penelope Lynn Peterson. Likes to be called Lynn. I guess you made quite an impression on her, because there's a short article by Lynn Peterson in the Mercury this morning, and she called me this morning for an interview with you that I couldn't okay because of our short staff. I knew you would be meeting with McDougal and then I would be making you the lead on the Llamas case…just to busy for an interview. Sorry."

"You don't have to apologize, I can't think of a thing I would say to her anyway. And her father is a California Senator?"

"Yup, and I like him. He's come to San Jose a couple of times on fund raising for his party. You'll get a chance to meet him cause he's coming to see *you, girl*. I just don't know when. Here comes McDougal."

"I'm ready whenever you are Barbara?"

"Let's do it."

"Like I said earlier, I don't have a lot on Carmen, though I did find out that the young man that put her in the hospital has a sister that lives in Hollister, California. I spoke briefly to her on the phone and then didn't follow up with a visit. Do you know where Hollister is?"

"I believe it's somewhere south of Gilroy and Morgan Hill. I've never been there. Isn't that where bikers from all over California meet once a year?"

"Not only California, but from Oregon, Utah, Nevada, and who know from where else. The town itself is very small and most of the time there are no problems from the overwhelming numbers of bikers that come there. Anyway, this is her address and you should to talk her. She may give you something that will help you solve the Llamas case. I hope you don't find out anything that points a bad light on Carmen Llamas, but I have a gut feeling that she wasn't what we saw. I've been wrong more than right, so it doesn't mean much. The only other case that I was working, Rudolph gave it to another detective. You know as much as me about the Llamas murder. I pretty much gave you all the info I got last night, which isn't much but it's all in the folder, which I will give you now. Do you have any questions, Barbara?" I don't now, but I'm sure I would like to stay in touch with you for a while until I get more involved with this case."

"No problem," and he extended his card to me, "this is my land line and cell number. You can call me anytime you want, in fact, I wish you would call me about the case and I will help you."

"Thank you Mac, I really appreciate that."

They both stood and he looked Barbara in the eyes and after a few seconds he extended his hand.

"I hope the best for you Barbara…and I just heard that you kept someone from jumping off the Sainte Claire Hotel. Delores thinks you're something special and I totally agree."

"Thank you. I hope I can live up to your expectations. Don't be a stranger."

"You can count on that, Detective Grevera."

She stood watching as he left the room.

"I think he likes you Barbara," Delores said as she approached her side.

"When does one find time to squeeze in friendship in this business."

"You catch it on the run honey," she winked and both laughed.

O' DARK THIRTY

CHAPTER 35

Detective Grevera arrived at the Eileen Dee Lynch home in Hollister, on Saturday morning at precisely nine a.m. and knocked on the door of the well-kept but older home. The door had glass at the top of the pea-green closure and the house was recently painted toothpaste white.

The door squeaked when it was opened and a voice asked who I was.

I took out my ID and displayed my picture and badge, "Detective Grevera with the San Jose Police Department, Ms. Lynch."

The door opened and exposed a woman in her thirties with black horned rimmed glasses, hair in a bun and a long plain blue cotton dress, and a white Nike running sneakers. She quickly assessed me and ushered me into a very conservative front room, where there were only kitchen chairs, intermittently surrounding a small wooden handmade coffee table. There were none of the amenities, one usually sees in front rooms. A single floor lamp stood at one corner of the small room. The floor was covered with fifties linoleum and displayed wear where the floor beneath rose and fell.

"My grandfather built this home, and passed it on to my father and he passed it on to me when he died six years ago. It appears crude in our contemporary times, but it's sufficient for me. Please sit, that chair you're standing in front of will sustain your weight well, Detective Grevera."

I sat. *She is obviously educated and leaves no illusion about herself or where she lives,* I thought. *She's a breath of fresh air and definitively direct. I like this woman.*

She sat in the chair directly across from me and placed both hands together in anticipation of my questions.

"Do you live here by yourself?"

Her eyes blinked several times behind the horned rimmed glasses.

"I thought your questions would be more directed about my deceased step brother."

"That's true, Ms. Lynch, and most of the time that would be the case, however, how well I know you has an influence on what you will be telling me from this point on."

"Yes, I live here alone."

"You're a professional of some sort?"

"I'm a high school teacher here in Hollister. I have credentials to teach, English, History and Political Science, from the University of California, Berkeley."

"I'm impressed Ms. Lynch."

"Thank you."

"I bet your students like you."

"Many do and then there's those who don't. Not that it's ever been said to my face, but some think I'm and odd ball."

"Why?"

Well, I don't look or dress like Mylie Cyrus and I've never been clothes conscious. I dress for myself and my clothes are clean and they meet with my approval, and the faculty has never reprimanded me for my attire."

"Tell me about you step brother."

"Well, first of all, he was not my stepbrother. My mother, God rest her soul, was unable to have any more children after she had me, but her only younger sister had a son and she insisted on calling him my brother, because I had no other family. Legally, he was not my brother, but my cousin. I would have been happy for him to be my cousin, but my mother felt otherwise."

"Would you say your cousin was a loner or recluse?"

She sighed. "He had friends that he associated with and to me, they seemed like good friends. But, I guess he was somewhat of a loner. In that regard, I am a lot like Michael, I don't have a lot of friends and the whispers I hear in the hallways, make me out to be some kind of weird nut. There have always been people like me in every class in the whole of the United States, and I suppose, the whole world."

I thought about my days in high school. Really not that much different, and I knew kids that colored their hair green and wore the baggy pants, and had pierced ears, nose, bellybuttons and other odd particulars, and now with the tattoos covering arms, necks backs. That stuff goes on all the time."

"Why do you think he tried to kill Carmen Llamas?"

"Was that her name?"

"Yes."

She threw up her open palms and said, "I haven't the faintest idea why he would want to kill anybody. I never felt that he had the moxie to do such an egregious thing like murder. Really Detective, I don't know where he conjured up that much anger or hate or whatever it was to do such a thing. I don't think he messed around with drugs. I admit I didn't talk intimately with Michael about his personal life, but we spoke openly about life. He loved animals, horses and dogs. His mother had given him a Scottish Retriever, as a young man and he loved that dog. It was a beautiful grey, black and white with a wispy fur pelt. He called it Zero." A tear formed in her eyes. "He was a gentle man and up to this moment. Where did the outrage come from a man that loved animals? Now he's dead and I'll never know."

"You said he had some friends. I need to contact them."

"I can give you the names of a couple of his friends, that I trust will not come back to bite me, and hope that they will assist you in getting the other names. Some of his acquaintances are from a different cut than Michael. I mean I never got good vibes, from our brief meetings. Michael was a smart man and had a good education. He was some kind of Engineer, and he had a soft spot for those less fortunate than him. I wasn't comfortable around a couple of his friends, even though it was only one time that we were all together."

"I hadn't considered bringing your name up to anyone, Ms. Lynch. We protect the names of people that help us, for obvious reasons."

"Good Detective Grevera. That's some consolation."

"You mentioned Michael's mother. Was she divorced from his father?"

"I'm glad you brought that up. No, they weren't divorced, Michael's father was murdered and there was never a resolution of his death. Time marches on so fast. I think it was two or three years ago. It was quite traumatic for both he and his mother. But like the phrase goes, time heals everything."

"How did the mother die?"

"She didn't. She lives in Monterey in one of the houses they owned.

Barbara was sure she had read in the report that McDougal had given her, that Alberta Rutledge was deceased.

"Were Michael and Mrs. Rutledge friends?"

"Michael loved his mother and as far as I know he would see and talk to her often."

Ms. Lynch excused herself and left the room and was back in a minute.

"This is her address and phone number, and you may say that I gave you this information."

"Thank you Ms. Lynch, you've been a great help and I hope that we can continue to find out what happened to Michael."

"One last question. Do you know if Michael was working when he was killed?"

"I'm almost certain that he was."

The drive to Monterey was beautiful and the countryside where vast fields of corn, strawberries, tomatoes and crops I couldn't distinguish grew in abundance, past the old Army Base a few miles from downtown Monterey.

My GPS took me into the small town, with its busy streets and along the ocean front and splashed itself against the rocky land mass and the wind shooed sprinklers of water drops on my windshield. I rolled my window down and smelled the salty breeze and the mist from the ocean waves hitting against the shore. My hair whirled as I smiled with the vim and vigor of teenager out for fun. The cool air was invigorating as I drove by a gold course. The sun was out and my car guide informed me I was close to my destination.

I checked the address and walked up to the front door, and it opened before I had a chance to ring it.

"Detective Grevera, I'm Alberta Rutledge and I'm happy to see you. Come in please," and she shook my hand ardently and walked me into the kitchen. "Have you eaten lunch Detective?"

"I had a cup of coffee this morning early and no, I haven't eaten lunch?

"Good, I hope you like Salmon, Broccoli and Pilaf rice and a cool glass white wine. Let me have your sweater, and she draped it on the back of one the kitchen chairs, "please sit down and we'll have some coffee. I put off my second cup for your arrival."

I was most impressed by her genuine hospitality and I felt like I had known this wonderful woman all my life. She was reminiscent of one my favorite actresses, now deceased, Ava Gardner. She was not only beautiful on the outside, but equally on the inside where it counts. Many have the wonderful God given beauty that is bestowed on them from birth, but nothing to back it up back from the inside.

"You drove all the way from San Jose and I want your brief stay in my home to be a cordial experience that I appreciate."

"Thank you Mrs. Rutledge and---

"My apologies for interrupting you. I realize you're here on official police business and I respect that, but would you mind calling by my first name, it doesn't sound so formal and it's more relaxing. My first name is Alberta."

"Then you can call me Barbara."

"Thank you Barbara."

The swinging door from the kitchen opened and a lady came in. "Are you ready for your lunch Alberta?"

"What do you think Barbara?"

"Yes, I'm hungry, I could eat a bear right now. Thank you."

"I love your candor, Barbara."

The maid brought the two plates of steaming Salmon.

"Dora this is Barbara Grevera from the San Jose Police Department."

"Nice to meet you ma'am."

"Like wise Dora."

"I'll bring your wine."

"We can discuss your business, after lunch with your approval, of course," Alberta stated flatly.

"That will be fine."

"I'm glad you got to meet Eileen. Isn't she just the sweetest and the most down to earth girl? Michael had very soft spot for my older sisters only daughter. I don't know why she chooses to live in the little house our grandpa built so many years ago. She could live anywhere she wants if she so chose, but that's just who she is. Her father owned half of the land in Hollister which he sold and became a millionaire many times and he stayed in the little house."

"Yes, she certainly is her own person, which is rare these days, especially with young people, and she is a special person, all right, and I have great respect for her."

The meal was eaten without further discussion and they moved to the front room.

"Tell me what you know about your husband's murder?"

"Yes, now where to start. I would like to briefly preface his life somewhat before he was…exterminated.

Barbara nodded and opened her pad and readied her pen.

"I don't think we ever really know all about the men that we marry and vice versus, and usually it doesn't matter. Originally, Gordon had been a good provider and a tireless employee for the company he helped found and nurture to what it became. He and the other two men who conceived the company became millionaires and that's when he began to change. At first, it was the late nights at the office, and then it was sleeping there, and then it was the trips to other states other countries, to sell the products they produced. The more successful the company became the less I saw of him or his partners. There were the usual complaints from the wives. We all had our problems with the husbands, but our voices were never heard, it was like a campfire getting out of control and burning hundreds of acres. We could only watch from a distance. Gordon tried in his feeble way to come back to me, but his life had become the company and it swallowed him whole. I tried to be understanding, at first, but then I felt like it was pulling me into this black fog with no direction." She stood and excused herself and then came back and seated herself, dabbed her eyes and continued. "The company purchased a condo and Gordon started living there off and on. I was miserable and it got to the point where we couldn't even talk. We each hired a lawyer and the attorney's became our voices. The next thing I found out was that he had a purchased a home in Palo Alto and my Michael had seem him with some beautiful blonde lady at a cocktail lounge we used to visit in better times. Essentially, Gordon had outgrown me and was living a different life. I felt bad for him and Michael began taking drugs with his friends. Down deep I knew Gordon still loved me because when we *did* get together with the lawyers, his eyes would say it. He just couldn't help himself." She paused and blew her nose.

"Did Michael like his father?"

A distinguishable smile emerged and she looked out blankly, "he loved his father, maybe idolized him would be the better word. His father had a great influence on Michael growing up and they were close. Not in the way some fathers with theirs sons, but it was more of respect for each other. Gordon thought Michael was the greatest son, and Michael thought his father a brilliant engineer and father. He was so proud when his father's company made him a millionaire. He even overlooked some of the things that were happening to him at his company, because he thought there was a price for such success. He gave his father more leeway than I, possibly because he was a man too…however as time went on he became quiet and distant and I knew Michael was also changing. Once he came here disheveled and incoherent and sat in the front room and sulked. I knew he was on something, because when I would ask him something he would blither about his father's behavior and he used the profane words to describe his relationship with the blonde woman. He never used expletives in my presence. Said he had snuck into his home and caught his drunken father beating on his mistress. Michael said that the women, in response had threatened to kill him if he ever laid another hand on her and that's when lead himself out of his father's new home.

"Were you aware no one had ever been held accountable for your husband's murder?"

"Yes, I was, but it was all meaningless. I no longer had a life that was good. Gordon was dead. Michael was dead, by the police doing their job and for a while I refused to let the whole miserable situation put me in a grave. It was like a real nightmare that just kept getting worse and I was immersed in it, and no matter what I did, it was there. It was a living thing that was clawing my life away. I couldn't eat, sleep or think about anything else. I don't suppose you've ever been in such gripping torment. For cowards like me, I did think about…well, I thought I didn't want to live, and that's when my astonishing eccentric niece showed up on my front door one Saturday morning and took me out for breakfast and changed all that by just being her sweet selfless person. She didn't talk about her uncle or Michael. She told me how young and beautiful I was and that I still had a lot of life in me. She told me that her mother always said that I had the Midas touch on life's gifts. She drove me down to the Monterey wharf and we walked, talked and laughed and we had a soft ice cream and she bought me a small porcelain bear; it was a Grizzly bear, she said it was ferocious and exempt from any kind of intimidation by anything in this man's earth. That evening, after she had ensconced me in my home, my mind was still pulsating from the day. My inconsolable life was fundamentally transformed by the presence of this wondrous young woman. Yet, it wasn't any particular thing that she did or said, it was her just being who she is. No pretense, no hypocrisy, no malarkey, Eileen Dee Lynch, my niece just being herself."

I was impressed with her story and proud for her. I knew what she had gone through. " I hate to bring this up, but…"

"I can handle it now Barbara. You're just doing your job."

"Thank you. Were you aware that someone had finished the job your son started on Carmen Llamas, the woman your son attempted to kill?"

Again I could see that she pondered my words and probed her memory.

"I never met all his friends, but a day or two before his grievous undertaking…to do harm to this woman, he came to see me. He was agonizing and wrought over something. He mentioned the names of two if his friends that wanted to do harm to someone and he wanted no part of their scheme."

"Was he lucid?"

"I believe he had been drinking and maybe under the influence of some kind of drugs. My regular

Michael was a gentleman, respectful and looked at me when he spoke. That day he walked back and forth and talked in fragment sentences. He kept saying that Chip and Chet would take someone out and leave him out of it. He kept saying that he didn't want any part in their bizarre plan."

Chip and Chet were two of the names Ms. Lynch had mentioned, she thought.

"Alberta it has been a pleasure meeting you and you've been very helpful. I have a better understanding of what transpired in your husband's murder now. Thank you for your kindness and I will try to keep you abreast of all that I find out, though it may be a while. Our department is understaffed at this time as is the whole police department because of the slow economy."

"I know, the Mercury News has reported as much. You get some rest and good luck."

At the door, Alberta gave her a big hug and smiled broadly.

It was nice to know there are good people like Alberta Rutledge and that they can bounce back from a living nightmare like her life was for so long, Barbara reminisced as she drove back to San Jose. She could here her phone vibrating in her purse as she drove onto Monterey Road in San Jose.

"It's your dime Delores," Barbara said.

"Where are you?" She asked with excitement in her voice.

"Close to the station?"

"I was just going to call you, because Senator Peterson will be here at the Police Station in a half hour."

"Isn't today Saturday?"

"And your point is?"

"I guess no one has a life anymore."

Barbara arrived in the squad room looking a little down.

"Why the gloomy face, girl?"

"I don't know a thing about Senator Peterson. I just feel some discomfort from all this hoopla. I've never been at ease in situations similar to this, especially now. I've been hiding for the last few years and now here I am, exposed by doing my job; to put it lightly, I'm nervous as hell about it, Delores. It just doesn't seem right."

"I get it. Some people would be happy about a situation like this. They would feel proud and---"

"Sorry to interrupt…last night I was proud and happy because I did my job well. I was glad that you were proud of me and that I had managed to help someone that might have killed herself. Does there have to be more than that?"

Delores smiled at her friend. "I wish there was some way I could get you out if this thing now, but this is bigger than me, bigger than the department. He's a Senator. If it had been a homeless person, it would have got some ink from the Mercury and that would have been it. But you helped the daughter of a well known powerful politician and you're just going to have to smile through it all and know this will also fade away one day."

Barbara's desk phone rang and she picked it up.

"Grevera…slow down, who is this?"

Delores pushed the speaker button on Grevera's phone.

"He's got a gun and I think he's going to kill himself," she cried hysterically, "you've got to come over here, now…please. "Put the phone down Susan," David yelled.

"Please Detective. Hurry!"

The line went dead.

"That was Susan Holliday and her husband David. I've got to go Delores. I'm sorry," and she was halfway to the door before Delores shouted, "Good luck."

Grevera was happy to be leaving all the ballyhoo and she was certain Rudolph could handle the situation. We were, in fact short handed and I was working on Saturday. Surely the Senator could understand that. She was in her car and started for the exit of the parking lot, and suddenly surrounded by four men raising their hands for her to stop. She lowered her window.

"Are you Detective Barbara Grevera?" The man asked officially.

"I am."

He turned and waved and a tall blonde man came jogging over.

Detective Grevera, this is Senator Tony Peterson."

"Hi Detective, I'll take it from here, George" and he jogged to the passenger side of Grevera's car.

She unlocked the door and he slid into the seat beside her.

"Sir, I don't know how this fits into police protocol but---

"Well, Detective Grevera, since I'm one of the Senators of this great state, I wouldn't worry about it. I think it will be all right and I understand this is an emergency, so I suggest we rock and roll, Detective."

"Yes sir," and she stepped on the gas.

"Do you usually work on Saturday Detective?"

"We're short staffed currently and everyone works overtime."

"I see, how short are you in your division?"

"You would be better informed asking our chief Delores Rudolph. Normally, I would be working with a partner today."

"Well, for today, I hope I can fill in until you get someone permanently."

"Sir, you realize there might be some gun play in this home where were going."

"Put your mind at ease Detective, I'm a veteran Marine Corps Colonel and I know more than a little about gun fire."

"This is the place Senator and if you don't mind I'll take the lead here."

"I'm right behind you Detective Grevera."

They walked cautiously to the door and discovered it was slightly open. She pushed the door open and stepped into the short foyer, "Susan, it's Detective Grevera. Are you all right Susan? Hello David, I'm coming in."

They could hear someone whimpering.

"Where are you Susan?"

She could see there was no one in the front room. The low moaning was coming from the kitchen.

She peaked into breakfast room and saw David Holliday sitting at the table, head down and groaning inarticulate words and sounds, a pistol in his right hand his white polo shirt had splotches of blood.

"Mr. Holliday, it's Detective Grevera and Senator Tony Peterson."

"Oh my God, Barbara," and he stood, "you're finally here, I think I killed Susan," he lamented, waving the pistol in the air.

"Where is she?"

"I think she's in the basement. Who's this man? Is he with you? Stay where…or I'll shoot you," and he raised the gun and fired a shot into the ceiling.

"Calm down David." Barbara asked calmly. "This man is Senator Peterson. You may have even voted for him. Put the gun down and let me go look at Susan in the basement. Okay?"

"It was an accident. I didn't mean to shoot her," he sobbed the pistol still in his hand, and he fired another shot that broke the window on the side of the house. He looked confused and dropped the gun to the floor; still standing he became momentarily catatonic staring blankly into space.

Barbara walked over and picked up the pistol and the Senator maneuvered himself to David's side.

"I voted for you Senator."

"Good."

"Is everything all right in there," an aide yelled from the doorway. "The Mercury News is out here Senator."

"Keep them out George. Don't let anyone in here and call an ambulance."

"I wasn't going to kill myself, Senator, but Susan didn't believe me. We argued and she reached for the gun and my finger was on the trigger and it went off and the bullet hit her in the head. It was an accident and now I don't have anyone left in my family. I didn't mean to shoot her. Oh my God, what have I done?"

"The paramedics are here. Do you want them to come in sir?"

Barbara walked into the kitchen aiding a blood soaked Susan who collapsed into the waiting arms of the Senator.

"Yes, send them in."

There was a flash of a photographer's camera just as the Senator turned.

"No one except the Medic's should be here. Please wait outside ma'am," he reprimanded the female paparazzo."

Grevera's phone was ringing and Barbara pawed through her purse to retrieve it,"Grevera."

"I've sent Forensic's out there Barbara and they should be there soon. Don't be surprised if the press is there, this guys a magnet to the Mercury News.

"Thanks Delores, this Senator is all right. Did you know he was a retired Marine Colonel? Barbara peaked out the front window, "Oh my God Delores, there must be two hundred people, two fire trucks, police and what appeared to be Mercury News cars blocking the street as far as I can see."

"I should be there in about ten minutes and try to help you and the Senator with all the privy throng."

When I turned around the Medic's had bandaged Susan's head and she was being ushered out toward the front of the house.

"Hold up guys, I need to talk to her for a second? And she displayed her badge. I'll come and see you tomorrow Susan. You're going to be all right. I'm a little worried about David, but I'm sure he'll be all right, too." Barbara gripped Susan's hand and she and the Medics escorted her through the cameras and microphones to the ambulance just as Chief Rudolph arrived.

"Thank you Delores," a pause, "there is a God!"

"I've been called a lot of things Barbara…but never a God."

They stopped and eyed each other and they both smiled. They dared not laugh out loud with all the eyes pointed at the two women.

CHAPTER 36

Two days later, Delores had agreed to meet Barbara in the squad room at 5:00 a.m. for their morning briefing.

"I've never been comfortable in the limelight Delores."

"I think I'm finally starting to get that about you Barbara. Those aren't idle words you're stating. That's part of your Bible. The thing that some in Hollywood people rush to stand in...the *spotlight*, is your nightmare."

"I'm not sure I would elevate it to nightmare stature; more at painful or troublesome. It creates a faux impression of who I am, a counterfeit perception. I always think of James Stewart, the actor who seemed to be a person that had this great talent for acting but was more comfortable at just being Jimmy Stewart, the man, without all the movie star accolades. Yet, he became quite adept at overcoming any unfortunate confrontations with those that imposed this star mask on him and was always polite and cordial with his responses."

Delores nodded, "that seems to fit Mr. Stewart quite well."

"I have a lead on one of the people that might know who killed Carmen Llamas on the East side of San Jose," Barbara stated looking at her daily planner, "but first I'm going to stop at O'Conner Hospital in San Jose, and see Susan Holliday."

"You're like a blood hound. You've got the scent and it's off you go. I hope Susan is going to be all right and you *solved* the pistol mystery. Poor David carried that secret around with him until it made him crazy. You did good girl."

"Yes," and Barbara eased herself into a contemplative stare.

Delores eyed her friend, "Where did you go Barbara?"

Barbara smiled and looked up at her friend. "We love our kids so much that we overcompensate for their frailties. Everyone makes mistakes. We've all fallen down; bruised our egos. It's what makes us stronger and smarter. Can you imagine going through life without ever making a mistake or never breaking a toe, arm or finger or worse? David would have been better off telling me what really happened from our first meeting and saved all the self-imposed mental anguish he and Susan went through." She sighed. "Yet I understand his motivation. Scott made one critical mistake that his father had trouble forgiving. He was decorated for what he did on the battlefield…killing many of the enemy. Presumably, Mark Stevens made the mistake of giving his friend a drug that killed her and he became the enemy in Scott's eyes. Scott in turn, did the only thing he had been doing for the last year and because he was honest and had integrity, he confessed to his father. Never thinking it would encumber this nightmare on his best friend and father, and that it would proliferate to his mother. Then Scott went back to his unit in Afghanistan, probably never giving it a second thought. The burn here is, David was very much like his son, with all the wonderful attributes Scott possessed, but with a conscious that slowly began festering with the terrible awareness his son had committed."

Delores shook her head. "How do you rat your son out to the police?"

"Wow, that was quite a story ma'am, sorry for eavesdropping but I got caught up in it as I entered the squad room. I'm Detective Edward Talbot, from the Los Angeles PD. Which one of you is Chief Rudolph?"

"That would be me, Detective Talbot, and this is Detective Barbara Grevera."

"I'm supposed to report to you for duty, ma'am."

"I was aware that our Senator Peterson was a fast mover," Delores said aghast. "But can you *really* be our new replacement."

"Thanks to you Chief, and Detective Grevera, I got to meet and talk to our Senator. He personally approached me, because he found out through my boss that I had lived in Redwood City a few years ago. He thought since I was at least familiar with the Bay Area I could be of help right away. Incidentally, Detective," he was addressing Grevera, you must have been wearing a dress on the day he assisted you to the Holliday home.

"Yes, I believe I was."

"He was very complimentary of your legs."

"How so?" Delores quizzed, "Is he a dirty old man?"

"No ma'am, I don't know that for a fact, but I've never read anything bad about the Senator. I've only seen pictures of his wife, and she appears to be a beautiful woman. He told me that Detective Grevera had saved his daughter's life and that's the reason he was here in San Jose."

"And the legs?"

"Ma'am?"

"How did he phrase the compliment to 'Barbara's legs?" Delores asked cynically."

"Let's see now," he said, 'she appeared to be in very good shape and her legs were well defined,' I believe that's how he put it ma'am."

"Would it be all right with you if I went to work now Chief?" Barbara asked as she stood.

"Wait for just a minute and let me talk to Detective Talbot and get him on our roster. Okay? I'd like him to go with you to the East side. Isn't that where you're going, to the East side of San Jose?"

"It is, and that would be fine, Delores."

"Is that still the rough side of the city? Edward asked.

"It is and I guess it hasn't changed much since you lived in Redwood City," Delores responded.

"Did you want to start today, Edward?"

"Sure. Is that all right with you, Detective Grevera?"

"Absolutely!"

"Give me five minutes with Edward, Barbara and you can be on your way."

Delores opened up her note pad and checked the names she had written down beside the names she already had there and placed them on the chalkboard.

Edward entered and saw the names on the chalkboard. "We're going to be working on a homicide case that is taking us to the East side to talk to someone that knew Michael Rutledge. Right?"

"Right, and on the way, I'll fill you in on the why, Okay?"

"I think I can see why Delores and you referred to the East side as the rough part of San Jose." Barbara commented as they stopped at the address listed on her note pad. The yards on this block were not maintained and were scruffy with weeds and discarded soft drink cans, bike tires, and car seats.

"Let me get this straight now, the unsub we're going to see here was a friend of Michael Rutledge, who was killed in a shootout with the SJPD after he was caught trying to kill a woman by the name of Llamas."

"Right."

"And you think that this person might be the person that finished her off while she was in Stanford Hospital recuperating from the gun shots.

"Right again. However, I'm not saying definitively that this is our man, because we have another name that we still need to check out."

"And this guy's name is Chip Puzzo."

She nodded as they stepped to the front door and knocked. Ed moved close to the door when no one came. "Did you call first?"

"No, I didn't want him to know I was coming for the obvious reason."

"But the address is good. Right?"

"I don't know that for sure."

Ed started to knock again when the door opened an inch and a woman's voice asked, "Who are you, and what do you want?"

"Are you Mrs. Puzzo?"

"Who wants to know?"

"We're police officers with the San Jose Police Department.

"Can I see your badges or ID's please?"

The door opened and she allowed them to come into the front room.

"I'll get my robe."

She came waddling back a few minutes later, tying her robe.

"Mrs. Puzzo?"

She nodded. "Is Chip in some kind of trouble?"

"I'm Detective Grevera and this is Detective Edward Talbot. Does Chip live with you ma'am? Is he here now?

"No. I hope he's working."

"Where does he work?"

"Huey Dieb Inc, in Sunnyvale."

"Did we wake you up, Mrs. Puzzo?" Ed asked politely.

"I work the night shift at Lockheed. I had just lain down when you knocked. I only sleep a few hours during the day."

"We'd like to talk to Chip, Mrs. Puzzo." She extended her card, "would you have him call us as soon as possible or have him come in and see us at the station. It's important that we talk. We'll let you get back to bed ma'am."

"He's a good boy, I hope he's not in some kind of trouble."

"So far he's not in any kind trouble Mrs. Puzzo, but we do need to talk to him."

"I'll have him call you as soon as he gets home, Detective."

"Thank you," and they walked to the front door. "Does Chip have a friend by the name of Chester Roberts," Barbara asked.

"Yes, he's Chip's best friend. He works at Huey, too."

"Sorry we encroached on your sleeping time, Mrs. Puzzo," Ed apologized.

"Well, I wasn't asleep yet."

The two detectives sat in Barbara's car for a minute.

"Would it be all right to call you Barbara, Detective, while we're working?"

"Yes, that would be fine."

"I know it's only eleven in the morning, but I never ate breakfast and I'm starving."

"Where would you like to eat?"

"Do you have any Chili"s Restaurants here in San Jose?"

As they sat, the waitress introduced herself and brought two menus. Edward spoke first.

"You look like you take pretty good care of yourself Barbara."

"I try to get to the fitness center at least five days a week, but lately, I'm lucky to go three, and once a week I participate in martial arts training at a little place on El Camino in Sunnyvale."

"Martial arts. Wow! So what's your story, Barbara?"

"So what do you know about me, Edward?"

"I didn't get a chance to talk to the Chief about you. The only thing I learned from my conversation with Senator Peterson was that you saved his daughter's life, and that you were a trained Psychiatrist, which is very unusual for a someone in your profession to become a cop."

"Well, it's a long story Detective and---"

"Excuse me folks. Are you ready to order?" the waitress interrupted.

"I'd like the Salmon steak, Broccoli, Rice Pilaf and a cup of coffee."

"I'll have the same," Barbara nodded.

"Look Barbara, I can see you're really not into talking about yourself, and I can appreciate that."

They sipped their coffee and Ed finally spoke.

"This is just a hunch, but I believe this guy Puzzo will be calling us soon."

"Really?"

"Mrs. Puzzo is a stand-up mother and she loves that kid and has probably already called him at work to tell him that we want to talk to him."

"And you think she told him that it would be better if he came to us as soon as possible."

He nodded as he took a bite of his Salmon and she thought about what he said. She also was hungry and they hurried through their lunch.

"How long have you been a policeman?"

"In January, it will be twenty years. But who's counting?" he said with a grin.

"May I ask you a question that might be personal?"

"Fire away!"

"How is it you were able to get here so fast, and what about your family? Surely you have some family or someone that means something to you."

"I have to admit, coming here had to be some kind of record, even for me. I had a wife, but after she endured the crazy hours and the late nights, the all night stakeouts, and the short staffing periods, for nine years, she bailed out. Never blamed her. Being a cop is harder on the wives and kids than on the officer. We're still friends, but she met and married someone who comes home every night and goes on vacations. She has two kids now and I'm happy for her. My dad was a cop and his dad was a cop. I knew what I was doing when I graduated from college and told my mother I wanted to follow in my father's footsteps. She warned me many times of all the pitfalls. I'm not feeling sorry for myself, Barbara. I like what I'm doing. I have no regrets."

I had a lot respect for Edward Talbot. He was honest with his choice of profession and had respect for his wife's choice to leave the marriage and find someone else more suitable to her needs. I'm sure he still loves his wife, but honors her decision. He would make a good partner.

Her phone buzzed in her purse.

"Grevera. Yes, we should be there in about ten minutes. You were right Ed about them contacting us ASAP," she said as they hurried out, leaving cash on the table to cover their meals.

They sat in Delores's office determining who would go with whom to each Interview room.

"Barbara, would you and Ed go with into Interview I, where Chet Roberts is now waiting and I'll go into room 2, to talk to Chip Puzzo.

"We'll be recording our conversation with you Mr. Roberts, and I'll need for you to recite your name and address and where you work, please."

"Thank you, and I'm Chief Rudolph and the officer sitting with me is officer Deen."

"When did you meet Michael Rutledge?"

"We were friends of the daughter of the man and woman that worked at Huey, and it was their party. I had dated her off and on. We were there briefly to pick her up, and Michael was there when we arrived and we were introduced."

"How old are you, Mr. Roberts?"

"Twenty six."

"How old was Michael Rutledge?"

"I don't know. Is that important? He balked.

"You said he was a good friend."

"That's right. I'm not gay if that's where you're going with this Detective."

"I'm sorry Chet. I wasn't going there with that question. How did you become friends with Michael Rutledge?"

"The people that worked at Huey knew and liked Michael and they mentioned that Chip and I were looking for work. He checked around his department, found out they needed help in the mailroom and he called us in for an interview. Well, since he put in a good word for us, we got the jobs and that's how we became friends. He was single and we would get together and smoke pot. We really liked the man. He was real. He wasn't phony and he genuinely liked us for who we were, which was nobody. He dated girls and he even introduced us to a couple of the beautiful ladies he dated. He was a good-looking classy guy. We even got to meet his sister, who was really his cousin."

"You mean Eileen Dee Lynch?"

"Michael referred to her as Miss Lynch and told us she had enough education for three people. He loved his sister and had a lot of respect for her."

There was a bond between these boys and Michael Rutledge, for sure, she thought.

"What did you think about Michael when you heard he had been killed in a shoot out with the SJPD"

" We were saddened. We lost a good friend. We knew he was having a rough time with his father's death, but had no idea what he was planning."

"We?

"Chip Puzzo and I."

Interview room 2

"Hello Mr. Puzzo, I'm Detective Barbara Grevera and this is police officer Edward Talbot. We're going to be recording our conversations. I'll need your name, address and where you work Mr. Puzzo, and thank you for coming in so quickly."

"My mother was responsible for that. Now, I'm not under arrest am I?"

"No, you're not. May I call you Chip?" He nodded and gave his full name, address, and where he worked.

"Did you know a man by the name of Michael Rutledge?"

Chip looked over at Officer Talbot then back to Grevera.

"Yes, he was a good friend."

"How long did you know Mr. Rutledge?"
"I guess around six years."
"How did you meet him?"
"At a party given by one of workers who was an employee at the Huey Company.

"He never mentioned anything about wanting to kill someone."

"No ma'am. I don't believe he ever would have brought that up with us. He was a very private man about things like that. He did talk a lot about his mother. He wasn't the kind of guy that talked negatively."

"You said he would smoke pot with you. Did he ever ask you for other drugs?"

He stood, without thinking, then, realized he shouldn't have, and sat back down. "He wasn't a bad person. Yes, he did ask us if we could get him some cocaine, which we did. We didn't use the stuff, but we knew where we could get some for Michael. I think we got it twice for him. He was having a bad time of it because of his father's death. He just wasn't the man we liked and respected at the end. He was being swept away by something we never knew or understood and I don't think he wanted us to be involved. He couldn't talk about it. We knew it was eating him alive, but---." He stopped talking.

"Did you kill Carmen Llamas?"

"What! What do you mean? We didn't even know Miss Llamas. The only reason we knew who she was because of her picture in the Mercury and what we read."

"Somebody knew who she was because they killed her. I think you might know that person, Chip."

He hesitated and moved his position in his chair, and shook his head. "No, we don't know who killed her."

"I hope you're right, because if you know something *now* and don't tell us, you could be an accessory.

"What do you mean an accessory?"

"If you're impeding our investigation, by withholding information that could be critical to our inquiry you could be held as a material witness."

"You mean I could go to jail?"

"The court could hold you in contempt for failing to comply with its lawful orders. Yes, you could go to jail."

"But I didn't kill anyone?"

"That could be true, but *if* you know something about the murder of Carmen Llamas, and you don't tell us, you could do some jail time."

There was a knock on the door and a police officer motioned Grevera over. He whispered something in her ear and left.

"Your partner has given us the name of someone you both know that *might* be able to tell us who killed Llamas."

Chip lowered his head to his chest and shook his head.

"Are you worried about retribution from this person?" Grevera queried.

"Some, but what about my mom and Chet's family."

"We'll see what we can do for your mother and Chet's family before we make contact with this person. Was this the reason you couldn't give me his name?"

"Well, yes, but there's more. But right now I don't know how much Chet has told you."

"The man gave us a name and a telephone number to contact this person, which we did. Then Chet thought we should memorize the name and number because all of this was so mysterious."

Grevera thought she should be talking to Chet at this point and excused herself and went to talk to Delores and Deen.

After a brief discussion, Delores suggested Grevera bring Chip Puzzo into Interview 2 and they would talk to both young men at the same time.

"So you two had received some kind of instructions with the name of a man you were to call on a throw away phone that was provided with the instructions."

"That's right."

"Did Michael Rutledge give you these directives?"

"No, but the person that called knew Michael. He said he was a distant friend of Michael and David, and that he would see that we received instructions. Right Chet."

He nodded, "that's right."

"How did you get this information?"

"Chip found the package on his front porch one morning and then called me."

"How big was the package?"

Chet spoke, "It was about 6 by 6 inches and about four or five inches high."

"Did the package have any instructions on the outside?" Ed asked.

"No, the caller said all the information would be inside the package. There was brief note, a bulging manila envelope, with the name Rio Martin, and a note with what to do with the contents, as well as instructions to smash the phone to pieces."

"What did the note say?"

"Chip has a better memory?"

The detectives turned their eyes to Chip.

"After we read the instructions for delivering the manila folder, you are to throw away everything except the phone. Call the number, at three p.m. Tuesday afternoon and ask for Rio Martin and when he came to the phone, I was to inform him that someone would be calling him at three thirty. The caller would call me on the phone and give me directions for the placing of the manila folder, and *when*, and I would never hear from him again."

"That was it?" Edward responded.

"Except for the warning at the end," Chip added, "that it was in our best interest not to speak to anyone about it. The truth is, we did think about calling the police, but whoever did this knows a lot about us. Don't you think? We were very reluctant to come to the police station to talk to you today, but Chet thought since we didn't know *that* much, they wouldn't bother with us. That's all we know. Can we go now?"

"Where did you deliver the Manila folder?" Grevera asked.

"To an all night fitness center on Lawrence Expressway. Locker number 2212 had a combination lock that the caller had given us the combination to. We placed the folder in the locker and then hurried out of the place."

"What was the name of the fitness center?"

Chet said, "Fitness 19."

"No, it was Fitness 24," Chip corrected.

"Do you remember if you placed the manila folder in the locker *before* or *after* Carmen had been murdered?" Grevera asked.

"After. We saw the article in the Mercury News about the Llamas murder and Chip wondered if that was the purpose of the thirty thousand dollars in the manila envelope. You see, the caller had phoned earlier that day and told us to place the folder in locker 2212 ASAP, and to dismantle the throwaway phone."

"So you knew how much money was in the folder."

"Yes," Chip replied, "and we counted it, but we knew better than to keep a dollar of it."

There was a pause in the room.

"And you're sure this man that you called on the throw away phone is the killer?"

"No. Right now we don't know who the killer is. We thought we knew, but when the note in the package told us ask for Rio Martin, it confused us.

"But Martin is the name that Chet gave us. Why would you think he was the man that killed Carmen Llamas?"

"Chip can tell you better."

"We invited Rio Martin to one of our parties at the request of Michael Rutledge."

"Are you saying you didn't know this Martin fellow before Michael requested him?"

"Yes, that's what we're saying. We didn't know Rio Martin. We were going to have a party for Michael and he asked if he could invite a man by the name of

Rio Martin. Of course we agreed. Michael said he would call Rio personally for the time and place."

"Did you think this an unusual request?"

"Not really, Michael was our friend," Chip responded, "and I assumed the guy that said he knew Michael was Rio Martin. He seemed different, greasy hair, dark skin, brooding eyes, tattoos, and he spoke very little. Creepy, know what I mean? Like in some of those movies with characters that kill people."

"Who used the phone to call and ask for Rio Martin?"

"I did," Chet spoke up.

"Did he sound like Rio Martin?"

"We never got to speak to Rio long enough to tell whether it was his voice."

"All right you two. Unless someone has a question we're going to let you go. Call us if you remember anything more and don't leave town," Delores said as they all stood. "Thanks for coming in and I'm sure we're going to be talking to you in the near future."

The two men hurried to the exit and the detectives ambled to Delores's office.

"What do you think, Ed?"

"I think they're on the up and up. I think they'll be calling us with more information as they remember more of what transpired. They don't want any trouble."

"Barbara?"

"I think there's a possibility Martin is an alias."

"Officer Deen?"

"All of the above Chief, and thanks for the opportunity to sit in on the interviews."

CHAPTER 37

On the way home Barbara thought of a question she had for Chip and Chet. She pulled to the side of El Camino and reached in her purse, found her note pad and scribbled the question down. Now she was sure she wouldn't forget to bring it up at the next session with the two men. She was feeling fatigued. *Police work is mentally tiring and stressful,* she thought, and at the same time, it had to be left at front door when you get home. She was lucky to have Katie and her mother there. They understood her. Her treasured friend, John Salinger was a peach of a man. I'm surrounded by the best family and friend anyone could have. My, it's barely five in the evening and it's already getting dark and soon we'll be setting our clocks back. Time flies when you're having…well, when you're busy. She should go work out tonight for an hour before she ate anything. She could see her daughter waving excitedly to her from the front window. Barbara hurried out of the car and up to the front door where Katie met her smiling with a secret.

"You have a special guest here, Mom."

They walked arm in arm into the kitchen where her friend Michelle Danese stood. Barbara's mother and John also stood and Katie joined them as they walked off to the front room, leaving the two friends sobbing with tears of friendship as they hugged and inspected each other.

"Where's Peter?" Barbara finally asked.

"He didn't come. He thought the reunion was more for you and me, and as I tried to coerce him to come, he just got more adamant. He wanted me to see you, and find out how you're doing. In fact, I brought your name up one time too many and then he insisted that I go. So how do you like being a *cop*, as Katie puts it?"

"I don't know if I could do this for the rest of my life, but I have found it to be stimulating and it has given me a certain sense of security. Though I suppose if someone really wanted to kill me, it wouldn't matter."

"And has someone tried to kill you lately?"

Barbara looked into her friend's eyes, "Would you like a glass of whiskey?"

"Just like old times, Barbara. I would love a glass of whiskey."

She brought them each a half glass of Jack Daniels and sat down. They toasted and downed the shot.

"I purposely didn't write to you for all this time because I wanted you to remain safe in France."

"I know. We had agreed that there would be no communication when I left, for that reason."

"By the way, you must be working out, because you look great…in shape."

"Thank you. I have, but not as much as I would like."

There was a pause.

"I need to tell you something because we have always been honest with each other and you deserve the truth, however I need to find out if my family is in ear shot."

Barbara came back in less than a minute.

"Does this mean you haven't shared this information with Katie and your mother?"

She nodded and sat.

"My friend, boss, and now accomplice, and I took a trip recently to New York at her request and specifically to Samson and there we eliminated the person that was putting the contracts on our lives. We think that there will never be anyone else looking for us."

"Your friend, the Chief Detective, requested that you go to Samson?" Michelle looked at Barbara and a tear appeared in Barbara's eyes as they met. Michelle stood, walked to her friend and held her. She too began to sob.

"It was the Chief's idea to go to Samson and do this thing?"

"She insisted that we go and get this monkey off my back. I'm telling you this because you're my closest friend, I'm confidant and you'll be leaving soon again. I need to tell someone that I know well. Plus now, you too can be relieved of the worry that someone might come for you one day."

"I don't know what to say, Barbara."

"Am I becoming someone else? She lamented, am I the same person you knew just a little over a year ago?"

"Of course you are. Remember, just because men go to war and kill people by dropping bombs on them and shooting them with bullets, and use those huge guns that pepper towns and cities miles from their location, they don't change. Well, some do, but most don't. We're just trying to stay alive and sometimes by hard measures that are thrust on us. Things we wouldn't do if we had a choice. That's what we did in Washington State Barbara, and what you did in New York. You've been injected into a war you had no right to be in, nearly *dying* and you've done everything from changing your name and moving to a different state, to prevent more harm and still they wouldn't leave it be. Because you're intelligent and have good friends, you have endured. You stopped running and instead went to the source of your predicament, looked it in the eye and resolved the issue. You have nothing to be ashamed of. In this world of survival, everyone in your place either faced the terrible dilemma or succumbed to the enemy. Haven't you always been the person that took on problems face to face and prevailed? That's who you are."

Michelle stopped her dialogue and scrutinized her friend's eyes. She had completely held her attention through the speech. That's why you're my best friend, Barbara. And you're still that wonderful person. You haven't changed your core values. I don't need to be around you for days, weeks or months to see that. You can still cry and that says millions."

Katie began clapping quietly from the hallway as she entered the kitchen.

"I'm sorry, I wasn't eve dropping and I *only* heard the end of your speech Aunt Denese."

"Come on in sweetie, and join us," Michelle requested.

"Did mom tell you she was a heroine?"

"A heroine?" Michelle responded lifting her eyebrows and peering at her friend in anticipation of a story.

"Oh poof, I did nothing that you or any psychiatrist would have done under the same circumstances."

Katie left the room and was gone for only a short time with a copy of the story in the Mercury Newspaper. She extended the paper to Michelle and she was staring at the front-page picture of Barbara and a handsome man beside her.

"He's one of California's Senator," Katie said proudly.

"Do you have an extra copy?"

"I sure do Michelle. Please take this copy with you."

"I wouldn't dare put your mother through the trouble of giving me the high light of this remarkable story, Katie. She eschews attention," and winks at Katie. "Would you give me a synopsis and I'll read it in its entirety on the plane home? I would also like Peter and some of my new friends in France to be able to read this special anecdote and that she is my *best* friend of course."

After Katie finished, Michelle looked over to her friend.

"All in a cop's day's work Michelle," Barbara said modestly.

"Of course, Mrs. Humble Pie. All in a cop's day's work. You have not changed one little iota, my sweet, dear friend and you never will. I love you Barbara and before I forget, I am inviting all of you to come and visit Peter and I. Please come as a unit or by yourselves."

"Me too, John Salinger said walking in."

"You too John."

"Why did Aunt Michelle leave so soon Mom?"

"She was here in the states longer than one night, honey. She had other stops. Her family in New York and she also stopped at Peter's family home, and the only reason she was here only one night was because of our circumstances."

"She seemed like the same person now and very happy living in France."

Barbara turned away and walked to the front room.

"I'm sorry Mom, I didn't mean to make you sad. I know how you feel about---"

"Honey, you don't need to apologize, Michelle and I have a very strong bond, very much like ours and my mother. Life has its ups and downs. We must adapt and change where we have to in order to keep going. That's what we're doing now. You're here because of what happened to me. You've adjusted well because you love me, with all my negative baggage and the same with my mom. I'm very fortunate to have two wonderful people that go along without the shouting and disagreeing with all the pitfalls that have monopolized us. We have adjusted well and I'm happy with my job and that you're going to be going to a fine university."

Katie looked at her mother with a daughters love, and then hugged her. "Are you really Mrs. Humble Pie?"

"Excuse me."

O' DARK THIRTY

CHAPTER 38

"Someone has been trying to contact you from O'Conner Hospital, but no name. Prepaid would be my guess. Know anyone at that hospital, Barbara? I got the same number day before yesterday, now that I think of it. If I had to guess I would say it's a patient. If it was an employee, they would probably use a house phone, certainly not a prepaid unless- -."

"I think I'll go to O'Conner and check it out. It might be important, Delores.

"Good idea. I see that Ed's not here yet. I'll have him wait for you."

"I'm Detective Grevera from SJPD and I'd like to speak to someone in charge."

"One moment Detective and I'll ring someone for you. Would you like to sit down Detective Grevera?"

"No, thank you."

She stood for a few minutes and then a woman approached her.

"Detective Grevera, I'm Katherine Merritt, the assistant administrator. What can I do for the San Jose Police Department?"

I explained the message I had received at the department and that I thought it might have been a patient on one of the wards here.

"Let's go to my office and I'll call each floor supervisor and see if anyone called the police department."

"It may have been a patient that called, Ms. Merritt."

"I understand. Would you like a cup of coffee Detective?"

"No thank you."

After receiving negative responses from the first two floor sups, the third floor sup was holding a letter for Detective Grevera.

"We have a hit on the third floor detective. I'll go with you."

"This is head nurse Judy Tyler and Gwen Wilgus, floor supervisor."

Wilgus spoke up. "I found the letter yesterday after Mr. Taylor had passed and brought it to the attention of Ms. Tyler."

"Has it been opened?"

"No ma'am, as you can see it's addressed to you Detective."

"Thank you. What can you tell me about the man who left the letter."

"Mrs. Wilgus again spoke up. "He was polite, but reserved and the only man that came to see him appeared to be gay."

"Why would you say that?"

"When the man left, they kissed on the lips, like married people."

"This man that came to see Mr. Taylor. Did he have a name?"

"He did, and she reached into her sweater. Oh shoot, I wore a different sweater yesterday and I believe I left my note pad in it. I remember his first name, because I dated a young man in my youth, but right this moment I don't recall his last name."

"What was his first name?"

"Ari."

"A-r-i?"

"Yes."

"I would appreciate his last name as soon as you can get it to me Ms. Wilgus. I'll leave you my card."

"Do you know if Mr. Taylor was married?"

"I don't know," Nurse Tyler responded.

"Do you have an address for the man," Barbara queried.

"What has Mr. Taylor done to bring you here, Detective?" the administrator asked. "Because the information in the medical file is only for the family of Mr. Taylor."

Barbara opened the letter and began reading and after a couple minutes she stopped. "According to this note Mr. Taylor was an accomplice in a recent murder. So I will be needing his address." Barbara's attention was directed to Nurse Wilgus.

"Can you describe the man that came to see Mr. Taylor?"

"Well, he was tall and handsome, wore a suit the only time I saw him; looked prosperous and was quiet if not reserved, but polite and engaging if pursued."

"How so?"

"Well before I realized he was gay, he was friendly if not coquettish."

"Coquettish?"

"He flirted with his eyes and manner, like most guys that come in here."

Barbara looked closely at Ms. Wilgus, she *was* pleasant to the eyes.

"Was he overweight? Did he have dark hair or was he bespectacled? Did he have an accent when he spoke to you or carry an attach case?"

"Well, he looked good in his suit, not overweight, he did have dark hair with just a little gray on the temple, was not carrying anything and he spoke English without an accent."

Barbara nodded. "Why was Mr. Taylor here in the hospital?

"He had Pancreatic Cancer and was on a short leash on life."

"Had he been here before?"

"I believe he had, but let me check that out for sure." She opened the chart and scanned it. Yes, he did spend a night three months ago. He was receiving Chemotherapy at our clinic."

"Thank you Ms. Wilgus, if you think of anything more about Mr. Taylor or our handsome visitor, would you let me know?"

"Absolutely Detective," and she accepted the card from the officer.

"I think I can find my way out if you need to remain here, Ms. Merritt."

"I'll walk down with you Detective. I hope the letter he left for you will be helpful."

"Thank you Ms. Merritt, I believe it will be and thank you for your assistance.

In her car she read the note again and then drove to the station. She walked over to Edward's desk where he was busy studying something and apologized for being late and asked him to follow her to the Chief's office. Rudolph was with another detective so Barbara extended the note to Edward.

"Sorry I missed you this morning Barbara. I should have been with you."

"Sometimes I come in early because I know that Rudolph comes an hour early just to talk to her about personal stuff. You don't have to apologize Ed."

"Sounds like this Taylor guy had a change of heart on his death bed?" Ed commented as he returned the letter to Barbara.

Barbara nodded and the door to Rudolph office opened and she waved them in.

"Any luck at the hospital Barb?"

Barbara offered the letter to her boss.

"Wow! A bombshell," she said excitedly and returned the letter to Grevera. "We need to bring the two young men that work at Huey's in for further questioning or if it would be faster you two should go see them at their residence ASAP."

They stood, almost in unison and looked at each other and began laughing.

"Maybe we could meet them at Huey's on their lunch hour, if that's possible or arrange to meet them tonight."

"What's your take on the letter?"

"Taylor was verifying that Chip and Chet were innocent of any crime except that they were the go between Taylor's contract with the unknown subject."

"Does that mean that he knew the two young men?"

"I think I would have to say I don't know. Strange to think that a man who puts out a contract to kill someone would have the ethical conscious of making sure Chip and Chet were innocent, even though he may not have known either man personally, yet he didn't give us a name of the unsub that did the actual killing. Too bad we don't have the help of 'Criminal Minds,' and the profile experts."

"You want me to call Chip and Chet and set up something?" She asked.

He nodded, "I think you should do the calling Barbara. They liked you."

"Oh poof, I'm just a mother figure to those young men, that's all."

He smiled. "What about Taylor's family or visitors?"

"According to the floor nurse, Gwen Wilgus, he had no family and only one visitor that was more than just a friend, but no one got his full name."

"Gotta make a head call, Barbara and you need to get us an appointment with Chet and Chip."

"TMI Ed."

"Sorry," and he waved going away.

"Men." She said quietly to herself.

"What's the word," Ed asked as he returned

"We're going to meet them at Huey's at ten forty-five this morning. All right?"

He nodded, "whatever you say."

"I would like to go and see the family of the last case I worked on. You're welcome to come along unless you have something you'd rather do until we meet the boys at Huey."

"I'll tag along."

"San Jose has grown a lot since I lived in Redwood City," Ed commented as they drove to the Holliday family residence.

"I think I read recently that there are a million people living in San Jose now."

"Wow, so the farm town now has more population than San Francisco," Barbara responded.

Grevera parked. "This is the family that Senator Peterson assisted me with and he was able to talk David Holliday into surrendering the hand gun he was waving around and finally dropped to the floor."

"I never did hear the whole story on this family. The Senator only mentioned that the son that committed the crime locally had been killed after returning to Afghanistan."

"It's a long story because the father was aware the son had killed the person, and he refused to accept it. He became deceptive and the mother had health issues that resulted in the lack of trust and transparency. The son's abrupt death in the military resulted in their lives spinning out of control. The father began losing it at the end, and the wife thought he was going to kill himself, that's when the good Senator came along with me. I'm sure it was against all of the Senator's diplomatic code to assist some local detective on a mission where there might be shots fired. He was fearless and gave it very little thought. Did you know he was a Colonel in the Marine Reserves and had seen duty in Desert Storm?"

Susan Holliday opened the door and greeted Detective Grevera with a wide, teary smile.

"Thank you for coming, Detective Grevera. I think we're back to the living. Is this your new partner?"

"Yes, this is Detective Ed Talbot, and the man approaching us is David Holliday."

"Come on in Barbara, Ed" he beckoned and they moved into the kitchen. As they sat at the table, Susan busied herself at the counter with coffee and some kind of special treat.

"I'm surprised you still consider us friends after all we put you through, Detective Grevera?"

"She nodded, "we did go through some trying times, but like Susan said, you're back to the living."

David smiled, "The judge was very kind to me, for what I did in trying to mislead you by giving you the wrong pistol. A slap on the hand was about all I got."

"Judges are people too. They are able to understand that human tragedies make for odd reactions."

Susan put a small piece of Apricot Strudel on four small plates and brought along freshly ground coffee. They imbibed in the delightful tidbit and all were quiet as they enjoyed the impromptu delicacy.

"I'm glad it's all behind us now," Susan spoke, "it seemed like a living nightmare for so long. I guess, from the words of our therapist, good people do bad things sometimes and it isn't the end of the world."

The words invaded Barbara's consciousness and she stood, abruptly. "May I use your bathroom, Mrs. Holliday?"

"Of course. Down the hallway and to the right."

She stood in front of the mirror and peered into her eyes. 'Good people do bad things and it isn't the end of the world,' and she was instantly back in New York in front Dimitre Aristotle in all his arrogance, even as she held the pistol to his head. Now, it seemed to her, that he thought she would never pull the trigger.

Aristotle was defiant to the very end. She sat on the commode and labored the thought. Would it always pop up bringing this apprehension…guilt, if that's what it is? She stood, powdered her face, and walked back to the kitchen.

"Are you alright Detective Grevera?" Susan asked, concern in her voice.

"I'm fine Susan. It might have been the first cup of coffee of the day and the wonderful Strudel. I assure you I'm fine, however Detective Talbot and I have another appointment."

"He was telling us you're already working on another case. I wish I could say I remember Senator Peterson's visit here, and that it had been more friendly, but I don't remember a thing about what happened that day."

They stood and walked to the front door. "Sometimes the mind saves us from remembering an unpleasant situation, and I think that's good thing, Mrs. Holliday."

"Yes, I suppose you're right Detective. Well, don't be a stranger and Detective Talbot, please feel free to come and visit anytime."

They were on their way to meet with Chip and Chet at Huey's in Sunnyvale.

"The Holliday's are a nice family, Barbara." Ed commented as they drove up Highway 101.

"We met you at the front doors because we weren't sure you would be allowed in, Detective."

"Good foresight Chip and this is Detective Talbot."

"We remember him. The company allowed us to use one of the conference rooms on the main floor, which has all the amenities of a small restaurant."

They declined the coffee and sat.

"I know we asked you most of these questions at our last meeting, but we thought you might remember more with a little time. How many parties did you have where your friend Michael was in attendance?"

Chip glanced at Chet. "Maybe a half dozen?" Chip nodded.

"Did Michael ever bring anyone, besides the girls you mentioned before? Did he ever bring any men to your events?"

Chet spoke up, "You mean like a date?"

"No, maybe a friend or buddy. We know he *liked* girls."

Chet shook his head and eyed Chip.

Chip ruminated briefly, "not that I remember."

"Were there ever people at your get together, that weren't invited?"

They both nodded, "some were friends of the friends that we did invite. If someone did come without an invitation, they would usually introduce themselves and offer something in the way of drinks or food, but that was very unusual. I only recall one time when someone came who wasn't invited, and he heard about it at the place where Chip works out, in Sunnyvale. Chip didn't know the young man, but he was one of the instructors there."

"Did you ever see someone that might have come in alone and spoken to your friend Michael Rutledge?"

"Michael spoke to a lot of people. He was friendly, polite and very smart. He had an endearing personality that was easy to like."

Now, I do remember a man that had Michael's ear in a corner that I had never seen here before. He was tall, maybe six-one or two and did wear a suit. I think that's what caught my eye. I could see that Michael was quite engrossed in their conversation. It seemed like a serious subject, because no one was laughing. However, I mingled with the few that were gathered in the front room and when I went back to see if they were still engrossed, neither was there, but a few minutes later Michael came walking through the front door by himself. I approached him and asked him if everything was all right, and he simply nodded. I was not comfortable questioning him."

"What made you think he was six-one or two?"

"Both were standing, not leaning on the wall, but standing, and he was just slightly taller than Michael, which I knew was six-one, the same as me?"

"Now Chip, I want you to close your eyes and see Michael and this man in the suit talking. You said he was wearing a suit, what color was it?"

"It looks dark, maybe black or dark brown."

"What color is his hair?"

"Dark."

"Is he Caucasian?"

"I can't tell. He has dark skin. It could be a suntan or he could be Italian, or East Indian. I really don't know."

"How old is the man?"

"He looks older than Michael."

"Much older?"

"No, maybe fifty or fifty two. He's also in good shape. I would think he works out somewhere."

"And you don't remember his name?"

" I never met the man."

"How about you, Chet?"

"I had to pick up one of the young ladies and had just walked out the front door when this man arrived. I just said, hi to him, but I turned around and heard Michael call him something. I don't know if it was a name or a greeting of some sort. Is knowing his name important?"

"It could be, guys."

"It could have been Harry, Barry or Kerry, something like that. Let it stew in my pea brain and I'll see if something will materialize." Chet said trying to remember the name.

"All right fellas, thanks again for your assistance and Chet try to think of that name. Ed do you have any more questions at this time?"

"We need to find the place that you two called for Rio Martin, or whoever he is. I know one of you said the directions you received anonymously required that you forget all the information on that note. It would be a great help, so please give it some thought."

"A Gwen Wilgus called for you from O'Connor Hospital and wants you to call her when you get the chance," Chief Rudolph said approaching Grevera.

"I think we're starting get somewhere Chief. She has a name of a man that might have sent the package to Chip and Chet. If not then at least there might be a connection between this name and Milton W. Taylor. Ed and I need to talk to the this man ASAP."

"Wilgus said you could call her anytime because the number she gave you was her cell phone."

"Good, I think I'll call her now."

"Mrs. Wilgus, this is Detective Grevera. Do you have a name for me?"

"Ari Maggio, hopefully it will help you, Detective."

"It will Ms. Wilgus, and I want to thank for calling me so quickly."

Grevera stood from her chair, walked the board and wrote the name, "Ari Maggio, friend of Milton Wayne Taylor."

"So how are you and Ed doing with the Carmen Llamas murder?"

"We've accumulated three unsub names and next we need to find them.

"Is that your cell ringing?"

Grevera checked the name. "This might be good news, Delores."

"Grevera. What do you have Chet?"

While I was making my rounds today at Huey, I heard someone in an office mention the name Maggie and it kicked loose the name that was eluding me. Ari Maggio arrived at the door just as I was leaving. Michael had greeted him by his full name. Ari Maggio. Weird don't you think?"

"Well, I have a different perspective, Chet, I think our minds are quite extraordinary. The first time we asked you about the name, you thought it was Harry or Kerry and just two days later, you come up with what you actually heard. Don't you think it's remarkable that we are able to transform information that was uncertain to cocksure?"

"I like that Detective Grevera, Maybe weird was the wrong word for me to use."

"Have you given any more thought to what kind of establishment you might have called for Rio Martin?"

"Again, and as you said Detective, both of us had read the numbers, but we disagreed on the last digit. We were able to come up with the number, except, I thought it was nine and Chip thought six. The nine got us a residence and then we thought about giving you the six, because we were sure one of us was right about he last digit, and let you call. We thought we might be putting our lives in danger."

"Good thinking, Chet."

"When Chip called that day, he could hear music in the background and he knows some Spanish. Someone, in the background had asked in Spanish about the El Cantina hours. Anyway, that's when we decided we should let you do the calling. But since Chip lives in the area, we looked up El Cantina and drove by the establishment. We think it could be the place."

"Wow, you two must have felt like you experienced an epiphany. Initially, you were not supposed to remember all that transpired but your mind did just that. It was essential that you remember everything and like a miracle you did. Now that is truly remarkable, Chet."

"When you put it like that Detective, I guess it is special. Do you have a paper and pencil and I'll give you the number and address of the El Cantina in East San Jose."

"I'm ready." Grevera wrote it down.

"Are you still allowing the police to drive you back and forth to work?"

"Chip is still doing it, but I'm not. I don't have a good reason I just don't feel right with the police car and all. It's uncomfortable Detective."

I think I understand his discomfort. I would probably feel the same. "I can't make you do this Chet, but I think I understand why you don't want to."

Now if he just doesn't get himself killed, I'll be able to sleep at night, she thought.

"Ed, you probably have more experience than me in confronting people in places like El Cantina. Do you think this would be a bad time to go and talk to someone there?"

"Hey, you're the one with a family. We can do this tomorrow at an earlier time, Barbara."

"In regard to my family, as long as I'm home by eight or nine, it will not be a problem. Would this be a better time?"

"Let's do it, Detective."

"Wow, it looks like they do a thriving business," Barbara observed. "The parking lot is full."

"I don't know you well enough to make this comment, but there are a lot of drugs, military hardware, and money circulated in and out, and a lot of valuable information bought and sold in these putrid dives. Lives terminated for as little as five hundred dollars, and some for thousands. I'll lead here if it's all right with you, Barbara."

Ed pushed the door open and could smell cigarette smoke. He observed a man at a small table resting his head on his forearms, a fresh beer directly in front him. He looked around the room and saw some heads turn toward the two Detectives. When his eyes met with the bartender's, who quickly looked away and busied himself. Ed ambled to the end of the bar and waited for the mixmaster to come to them."

"What can I get for you officers?"

"Looks like you have a busy place tonight. Are you a full time tender here?"

"Practically a slave."

"Sorry to hear that. But for us, it might be a good thing. You probably know most of the regulars here."

"I know some of them. We have a large clientele."

Ed turned and walked to the man whose head was on the table and nudged him, "you all right fella?"

The man raised his head and tried to focus on the police officer. "Yes, I'm just trying to get a little shut eye before I go home."

"Don't let me keep you up," and Ed walked back to bar.

"Okay, what do you want?" the bartender asked defensively.

"Ever hear of man by the name of Rio Martin?"

He stared hard at Ed. "What's he done."

"Nothing so far, we just want to talk to him."

"He's a pretty serious guy. He would be very angry if he was to find out that I talked to San Jose's finest."

"Is he in here tonight?"

"We have two other names of people that might know him. But you're the first one we've talked to, and we're not going to tell him that we spoke to you."

"He's a crazy bastard. He doesn't need an excuse to kill someone. If he just thinks I talked to you, he wouldn't hesitate to kill me.

"Like I said, we have two others that we're going to talk with. We picked you first because you were nearest the station. Are you saying he would kill everyone that he's made contact with and that might have talked to him?"

"From what I hear about him, he *is* that crazy?"

"Do you have an address or know where we could find this man?"

"No, you might want to talk to one of his friends, but you *can't* mention that I put you on to him."

"So this fellow is Rio Martin. Is that what you're saying? Barbara interjected, "And his friend's name is?"

"You gotta promise me that my name will not be mentioned."

"We don't know your name and we won't tell anyone where we got this information."

"Good enough.

"Can you describe Rio Martin?"

"Are you saying Rio or Leo Martin?" the tender asked confused.

The officers looked at each other, also confused.

Barbara said, "Rio."

"I don't know any Rio. All this time I thought you meant Leo Martin."

"It could have been Leo Martin. Describe him." Ed interjected.

"He's around six-four or five, long hair, dark and interspersed with gray and weighs about two sixty. He has tattoos on his arms and most of his body. The first time I saw him he reminded me of a movie that I saw a long time ago that had the Indian Cochise in it. He looks like the real Cochise."

The officers looked at each other.

"Do you know of any other place that…'Cochise' might hang out?"

"Some sports bar in uptown San Jose, though I don't know which one."

"All right. Thanks for your help."

"What help?"

The officers turned and started for the door and Ed noticed the man still sleeping at the table. He walked back to bartender.

"The License Commissioner would not like to see that man sleeping it off in you establishment."

"I'll call a cab," the bartender responded.

They both agreed that Rio and Leo were probably the same person and that someone had mistakenly injected the letter 'R' for 'L," because the description seemed to fit the Leo character.

They walked out to the car and were about to leave when a man tapped on Ed's passenger window.

"Ed rolled the window down. "I heard you ask about Leo Martin."

"That's right. What can you tell us about them?"

"What's it worth to you?"

"That depends on your information."

"Would you mind if I stepped into the back seat of your car? I don't want anyone to see me talking to you - - if you know what I mean."

Barbara unlocked the back door.

He climbed in.

She rolled the windows down.

"It's been a while since I showered and I'm sure I must carry a bad odor," he volunteered a weak apology for his odorous stench. "I know where his mother lives."

"Here in San Jose?" Ed inquired.

"Not too far from here. I can take you there, but I'd like a hundred dollars, first."

Barbara turned her head toward Ed for approval.

He responded with a positive nod.

She reached into her purse and retrieved a hundred dollar bill, which she extended to Ed.

He displayed the bill to the man. "Show us where she lives."

"Drive down Alum Rock and turn right on Denim Drive, which is about a mile away."

"Okay, the next right is Denim, then go down to the yellow apartment house on the right."

Barbara parked in front of an old run down, yellow, three storied tenement.

"She lives on the third floor, apartment twelve. Her name is Rose Garden."

"Rose Garden?" Ed repeated.

"How do know all this?"

"I grew up three tenements down from here, and Leo lived with his mother in this place. I knew who he was, but I was practically invisible to him."

"How so?"

"Leo was always big for his age, his friends were older and he drank beer openly when he was barely a teenager, and was always in trouble. The cops were forever at his apartment and his poor mother was always trying to keep him out of jail."

"I'll go check it out Ed, and give you a call if she still lives there."

As she walked up the stairs of the aging building she could see that it wasn't kept well. There were litters of paper, strewn about the wooden stairs that creaked with each step. She didn't hear any sounds, like loud radios or TV's. It was remarkably quiet and she wondered how many people lived in the run down domicile. Climbing these stairs on a daily basis would certainly keep your heart rate up, unless you're old. Finally Barbara reached the third floor and located apartment twelve. She knocked on the door.

"Who is it? A gruff woman's voice responded from the other side.

"Detective Grevera Mrs. Garden."

"What do you want?"

"I'd like to talk to you."

"I ain't done nothing wrong."

"I know that, please open the door. I need to talk to you."

I texted Ed while she unlocked the door.

"You alone?"

"My partner will be arriving soon."

"Can I see a badge or sompen that says you're a cop?"

I placed my picture and badge up to where she could see them. She squinted at the ID and allowed me to come in.

"Leo in some kind of trouble?"

There was a light rap on the door.

"We'd like to talk to him. That's probably my partner."

"Let him in," she ordered. "He ain't lived here for a long time."

"This is Detective Ed Talbot."

She glanced over to him. "I was kinda hopen he'd out growd all that nonsense by now. What's he done now?"

"That's why we want to talk to him. Right now he isn't accused of anything."

She walked to her lazy boy chair and sat.

"May we sit down, Mrs. Garden?"

"Sure. Sorry I ain't lost my manners, jus thought all this was behind me. The boy don't seem to have a good bone in that big body of his. Trouble finds him no matter what he does or where he is. His daddy was pretty much the same, losing jobs and fighting with people and never getting along with nobody. I dun what I could, but when his daddy was killed, it was hard. I got a good job at the County Hospital and worked for thirty-two years in the laundry service. No one to watch what he was doen while I worked. It was hard, him skipping school and hangen with his good friend Dino Tercero and with the older boys and all. But I thought he got a good job at that motorcycle shop on Fourth Street. Said he liked working there. Is he still working there?

"What's the name of the shop?"

"Harold's. The reason I remember the name is 'cause it was his daddy's first name," she smiled.

Barbara wrote the name down.

"So you don't know if he is still working at Harold's Motorcycle Shop on Fourth Street?" Ed asked.

She stood, walked into her kitchen and came back carrying a small geranium plant. "He brung me this plant for my birthday, and that was on September 23rd. He was still working at Harold's then."

"So that was about two months ago," Barbara speculated, "Good, I think we'll go to Harold's and see if he's still there. Please don't get up, Mrs. Garden, we'll show ourselves out, and I left a business card on your coffee table, Mrs. Garden."

At the door Barbara turned, "Does your roof leak when it rains, ma'am?"

Rose nodded.

"I'll see what I can do for you," Barbara said as she closed the door behind her.

"That looks like Harold's Motorcycle Shop, Ed. Would you mind taking the lead."

Inside the shop, owner Julio Territo was looking out the front window.

"Looks like the fuzz coming guys," he announced through the PA speaker. "Who's done something bad?"

Leo Martin looked out the window and walked to the bathroom.

The officers walked to the large garage entrance, where all of a sudden everyone was working.

"Hi there, I'm Julio Territo, the owner of this establishment. What can I do for the San Jose Police Department?"

Ed spoke up, showing his badge and ID, "I'm Detective Ed Talbot and this Detective Barbara

Grevera. Do you have a man by the name of Leo Martin working here?"

"I do. Can I ask why you want to see Leo?"

"Well, it's personal and we'd like to keep that between Mr. Martin and us."

"I see. Roy would you go to the head and tell Martin that he has two guests that want to speak to him."

"I see an old Indian in the corner over there," Ed said pointing to a beautiful refurbished Indian Motorcycle."

"You've got a good eye, Ed," Julio smiled, "you a biker?"

"I was once, but that was a long time ago. After a broken foot, leg, arm and twenty two stiches on my right buttock, I stopped riding bikes."

Barbara was watching in the direction that Roy had gone to retrieve Leo Martin, and when she saw the man walking toward them, she almost gasped. He really was big. Six-four or taller, and he really did look like an American Indian, with long flowing hair. The Indian nickel came to mind. The man that described him shortchanged Leo Martin. In real life, Martin seemed bigger and more intimidating, Dick Butkus, Lawrence Taylor and Ray Nietzsche came to mind. How would you handle someone like Martin if he got mad at you? He looked fierce."

"Ah, here is our man Leo Martin, Detectives, Julio announced, "you can use our small conference room and I'll walk you there."

Barbara looked up at the man and he purposely kept from returning her gaze. He seemed unconcerned that we were police officers and that he might be in some kind of trouble, however our informant had said police were part of this man's life. She was awed by his size and yet there was something about the man that gave the impression he was almost…delicate? She was honestly confused by her perception of the behemoth before her. There was *no* arrogance in his gait as we moved into the conference room. He still hadn't said a word.

"Would you like some coffee officers, Leo?" Julio inquired politely.

Barbara shook her head, and Ed responded, "I'm okay."

"Leo?"

"No thank you, Mr. Territo."

Barbara was astonished by the refined response from Leo Martin. She pondered his words and how they were presented. They had never spoken to Leo Martin to know if this was his normal manner of speaking or if…could it be that he….

"I'm sorry Ed. What was your question," she replied awkwardly.

"I think we should talk to Mr. Martin, at the station, where we are be able to record, save our conference, and all relevant information given by Mr. Martin."

"Your absolutely right. Would you have any objections to that, Mr. Martin?"

"And if I did."

"We would have to take you into custody as a material witness, but if you voluntarily to go to the station, we would only be questioning you."

"When could I come in to do this?"

"Sounds like you've got a good boss, in Julio Territo. Sometime this week would be alright."

He stood, "I'll go ask him if I can come to the station tomorrow."

The door closed behind him.

"What do you think Ed?"

"I was thinking, if he decided he *didn't* want to go to the station that we might have needed backup."

She nodded, "When I saw him walking toward us from the bathroom, it did occur to me, but then when he responded to his boss about the coffee, instantly I felt he was civilized. Do you think our informant's description of Leo Martin was accurate?"

"Not exactly. You're the people profiler. What's your assessment?"

The door opened and Leo stepped in.

"Well, today is Tuesday and Julio has two bikes coming in tomorrow in the morning with incidental problems, that Julio thinks I can handle by the end of the day. Would Thursday be all right with you?"

"Thursday it is, Leo," and he extended his card to the man.

He checked the address on the card, "Did you folks move the police station?"

"Yes, as a matter of fact, this is a new location for the last three years." Barbara interjected.

He nodded, "What time would you like me to be there?"

"How about nine in the morning?"

"I'll be there," and he gave us what I think was a possible smile.

CHAPTER 39

It was four-thirty in the morning as Barbara entered the large detective quarters. This was early even for her. She had already stretched for fifteen minutes, run two miles, a hundred sit ups and used the dumb bells for fifteen minutes. There was something in the back of her mind that wasn't transparent to her. Was she purposely avoiding bringing it to light? Barbara sat and began looking over her notes. She had Ari Maggio's phone number, which Ms. Wilgus had been able to obtain from the man at their last meeting. She hadn't written why it was important to know that. She finally decided it wasn't essential to know why. Lately there was so much info passing through her brain that she had to sit quietly in the morning to organize into its proper sequence. Leo Martin tomorrow morning at nine and an eight o'clock meeting with Ari Maggio this morning.

I haven't had any coffee yet, she thought, and stood, walked over to the coffee area. She emptied the little coffee that was in the pot and washed it with water, emptied the coffee grounds and made a full pot of San Francisco Bay French Roast coffee. She ambled over to the window that showed the parking lot. Soon it would be full. What was she doing here so early? She thought she knew herself well enough, that she couldn't fool herself, but this morning was a little different, and then she roamed back to the coffee pot and watched as it terminated its boiling. She poured a cup and went back to her chair, and realized why she had arrived earlier today. Sipping her very hot coffee then, placing both hands around the cup she allowed herself to go off in her thoughts.

How long am I going to be able to do this job, and do I really want to? It seemed like a good idea at first, but lately. Or am I thinking about it now because I have the time to do so? Is this really who I am, doing this or is it that I like the protective armor of the police department. Besides, I think I took care of the problem, with the help of Delores Rudolph, of course. I still can't believe we did what we did. Delores is a real tough cop and I have the highest regard for her kind, but does it affect her very being? I don't think so. Is it really that simple? Delores thought nothing of…eliminating Dimitre Aristotle, like a rotting apple in a box full of good apples. That's all he was. Take out the rotting apple and throwing it away. Her temerity had emboldened me. The chief is so police oriented. Maybe that's the answer. You do the time as a homicide detective and over time one builds this impenetrable shell around oneself and it's all in a day's work. Can it really be that simple?

"Hey girl."

I jumped and the coffee splashed onto the table.

"Sorry Barbara, I didn't mean to startle you."

"No problem, I was somewhere else."

"Is that fresh coffee?"

"Made it myself a few minutes ago."

"Want to talk about it Barb?"

"It was nothing new?"

"New York?"

"Only in part."

"Family?"

"No, my family thinks I like what I'm doing."

"And do you?"

I sipped my cooling coffee, "I think I do."

"You're a natural. You stepped in just like you'd been doing this all your life. I know you don't like all the fuss made about what you did with the Senators daughter, but without any training you brought her down and in her own words you were a hero. I'd hate to lose you, but if it ever comes to that, I want you to know I would understand."

Barbara sighed. "You're really a good friend, Delores," and she reached across the table and squeezed her hand. "I don't really want to talk about it."

"Good, so what does your day look like?"

"I made an appointment for Ed and I to talk to an unsub at this morning at eight, and we have Leo Martin coming in tomorrow at nine AM, hopefully. So we're going to be busy for the next few days."

"Tell me about the unsub at the hospital."

"Most of it is speculation. Ed and I still think Mr. Taylor was most, if not all of the inspiration for the murder of Carmen Llamas. We think Taylor somehow obtained enough information on Leo Martin to secure his service. Right now. How he did this is unknown."

"What's the connection to Michael Rutledge? I thought he was the initial perpetrator."

"Right, and Michael was killed in a shootout with the local police. According to his mother. Barbara stood and walked to the board, and pointed to the picture of Alberta Rutledge.

"Michael actually witnessed his father's death by one Carmen Llamas," she pointed to the beautiful, now deceased woman. At this time, Ed and I don't know how Michael Rutledge and Milton Taylor were acquainted or even how our man Ari Maggio, the man we're going to see today fits into our ambiguous scenario."

"Let me see if I got this right. Milton Wayne Taylor, initiates the murder of Carmen Llamas, *after* Michael Rutledge had witnessed his father death by Carmen Llamas who was later determined to be an assassin, and he is killed in a shoot out with the local police.

Barbara nodded her approval.

"So, Taylor hired Leo Martin to finish the job that Rutledge started. Do we have a picture of him yet?"

"Yes, to your first statement, and we'll get a photo of Martin tomorrow," Barbara assured her.

"We don't have any proof yet, that Leo Martin *is* our murderer. All we know is that our informants, Chip Puzzo and Chet Roberts believe he might be the man that they called via a message they received anonymously from Taylor, though it could have come from the man we're going to see this morning…maybe."

"And what's his name?"

"The name we have is Ari Maggio. Taylor died on a Wednesday, and Maggio came to see him on a Tuesday. One of the nurses told me she thought they were very good friends, because they kissed like lovers."

"Taylor and this Maggio are gay?"

"I guess so, though that hasn't been verified, and it' not significant to our investigation."

"And the letter you obtained from the nurse at the hospital was written by Milton Taylor, who you think was responsible for the whole thing. Why are you meeting with Maggio today?"

"We want to know how much Ari Maggio knew about the box of directions that was sent by Taylor to Chet and Chip, or if Maggio sent the package. At this juncture, he may be innocent of all this mulling."

"Well, it sounds like you're getting close. Don't you think Ed?"

"Yes, by the way, does the San Jose police department have a swat team?

"We sure do Ed, and they're great. Why?"

"Leo Martin is a mountain of a man and I was thinking if he decides to be a problem, we might need them, if no other reason but to demonstrate some power."

"Let me know if you need them, and I see you two should probably heading for your appointment with this Maggio character," the Chief said checking the big clock on the wall.

"I wonder what kind of rent he pays for this high rise suite he rents here in Palo Alto?" Ed asked rhetorically.

"Is the rent high here in Palo Alto?"

"Tall Tree has always been high in rent."

"Tall Tree?" Barbara questioned

"Palo Alto, Tall Tree. You wouldn't know that because you're from New York."

"In the recesses of this screwed up mind, I think I did know that Palo Alto was Tall Tree, I read it somewhere."

"Hey they even have a doorman at this joint," Ed laughed, "this guys a high roller."

"Can I help you folks," he asked politely.

"We have an appointment with Mr. Maggio."

"May I tell him you're coming Ms...."

"Detective Grevera and Talbot," and they displayed their ID's.

"He walked to the phone and dialed, " there are two police officers here to see you, sir."

He ushered them to the elevator and they all climbed in.

"He lives on the ninth floor, suite E. I hope he's not in some king of trouble," he asked politely.

"We just need to talk to him. He's not in any kind of trouble," Barbara responded courteously.

The elevator stopped and he allowed them out first and then he stepped out. "He's the last door on the left, Suite E."

They rang the doorbell, and a pretty Chinese lady opened the door.

"Please come in, Mr. Maggio is in the study and I'll take you there. She tapped on the door and opened it.

"Come in Detectives, I was just finishing up some loose ends. I'll be with you in four minutes. Holly, would you get them some orange juice or coffee, please?"

Ed looked around, the place was meticulously clean and organized and the man was very good looking and appeared to be in excellent health. Other than living in a very expensive pent house in Palo Alto, the rooms were very simply decorated. This man appeared to be the real thing, Ed thought. He liked him.

"I apologize for keeping you waiting. I really needed to finish this small, but essential project. Thank you for waiting. What can I do for you two?

"How well did you know Mr. Milton Taylor," Barbara asked taking her note pad out of her purse.

"We first met in college. In the early eighties, specifically nineteen eight-two, and then later on, he went to graduate school at Brown University and I went to Princeton University. We would try to meet at least once a year, primarily to see where life was taking us. I had always liked Technology and he liked business courses. Milton was a very bright man. He really did know business. He started a company here in the Bay Area, and it is doing very well. About fifteen months ago he developed the same illness that the founder of Apple Computer had. Pancreatic Cancer, a terrible disease. I wasn't informed of this deadly affliction for the first three months, well, until I came to visit him and saw that he was losing weight. He reluctantly confessed that he was dying. I was living in Boston, Massachusetts, where technology is alive and doing well, but the weather here is a little easier to take, so with some friendly coercion from Milton, I moved here to Palo Alto, to be near the man I had fallen in love with years ago, but only realized recently, Milton felt the same."

"Does the name Michael Rutledge mean anything to you?" Ed queried.

He nodded, "Yes, he was Milton's friend, via Michael's father, Davie Rutledge. I attended a small gathering of Michael's friends with the intention that Milton would be there, but something came up at the last minute and he didn't show, but he did call Michael and informed he wouldn't be able to attend, and for me to come to his apartment from there. I didn't want to be rude, so I stayed a few minutes longer and then left for Milton's apartment."

"What about the names, Leo Martin and Dino Tercero?"

Ari thought for a few seconds, shook his head, "no I don't recall either name."

"Do you recall anything about a package that Mr. Taylor had sent to someone?"

He pursed his lips and again shook his head. "No, but I wasn't privy to a lot of Milton's personal, day to day life. You're starting to create some doubt about Milton Taylor. The man died only recently and I'm getting the feeling, you're probing for something more sinister than curiosity. I don't believe he would intentionally hurt anyone," and he stood, "but I *really* didn't know much about his personal life. I don't suppose you can tell me where you're leading with these questions?"

"We honestly don't know ourselves, and that's what we're doing now Mr. Maggio. Speculating is a big part of our job; you might say a *puzzle*, without all the parts to the end picture. You seem to be sincere about all your answers that we've asked you."

"Obviously I didn't ask enough question about Milton, nor did he ever probe me about anything personal. Now that I think about it, we were pretty much the same person. I wish now I had been a little more inquisitive, but that's not who I am and I really believe he felt the same. I wish I could help you clear up this fog you folks appear to be in. I'm certainly at your service and of course you know where I live."

The Detectives stood.

"If something comes up that would help us clear up your, Milton Taylor, please call us. We need all the help we can get."

"What do you think Ed?" Barbara asked as they walked to the car.

"We don't get to meet people like Ari Maggio in our business very often. I think he's a straight shooter. He never paused about anything he said today. Every word flowed out without hesitation. I believed every word he uttered. What about you?"

"If he lied, he also sold me on the lie, but I agree, he is a straight shooter."

Ari buzzed his maid and ordered a cup of coffee with cream and waited for the coffee thinking thoughtfully about what had just transpired. He picked up a disposable phone and it rang once.

"I was just about to call you Mr. Maggio. You were right those cops were followed here. One of the two men walked up to the door of your building, looked in and then went back to his car. After the officers left the building, they left too."

"Did you get a picture?"

"Yes sir, three good photos."

"Come on up Sal."

Dino looked around the tavern looking for his friend, Leo. He finally saw him sitting by a window at the back of the noisy pub.

He walked up and stared down at his friend, "What ya drinking, Leo?"

"JD doubles," without looking up.

"What can I get you Dino," the bartender asked approaching the two on a busy night.

"Four double JD's."

Dino sat down, "What's eaten you?"

"Two homicide cops tomorrow at nine in the morning."

"Leo, your sounding like you've done something wrong. What's wrong with you, man. Loosen up. This isn't a firing squad you're going to in the morning. They just want to talk to you."

"Here you go guys," the female bartender said, setting the four drinks down and picking up two twenties. Would you like to order a sandwich from the kitchen?"

They shook their heads.

She laid the change on the table and scurried off.

Leo downed the drinks one after the other and looked out the window.

"You holding out on me, Leo?"

"What? What are you talking about?"

"You just paid for our drinks again and you seem to be off somewhere. Like there's something else bothering you."

"I paid for some drinks and I'm holding out on you. Is that what you think?"

"Yeah, and yesterday you paid for our dinners at Chili's".

"Screw you Dino."

"You've been acting strange lately, Leo."

" So. I'm a little nervous, I guess, yeah I'm just nervous. What time is it?"

Dino checked his watch. It's eight-thirty."

He took the shot glass and poured it down, "I going home and get ready for tomorrow."

"Your just spooked---"

"Can it Dino, it's not *you* having to face those cops." and he dropped two twenty on the table.

Dino picked up the twenty's and put them in his shirt pocket. Leo didn't realize he's already paid for the drinks. He sipped on his drink and thought about Leo. He was changing as a person. Things like talking to the cops didn't use to scare the big bastard. Now he was like a little boy. I gotta go home and get ready for tomorrow. What kind of shit was that? That was the other thing. Where did he get the money to lay down a twenty every time they had a drink or ate somewhere? Something was not all right with Leo. Whatever he was doing, it was behind my back.

"Barbara, I'm glad you're here, Detective Romero wants to talk to you ASAP. Here's his number. She sat and called. They spoke briefly. If you don't need Ed and I, this morning, could we be excused from the morning meeting?"

"I do want to talk you two, but we can get together later, so go."

"Thanks for calling us Detective Romero, we certainly can use all the help we can get."

"To make a long story short," Romero spoke, "a fisherman hooked the body of one Rio Martin out of Lake Cunningham a favorite fishing hole around here, and fortunately, the deceased had his California license on him and we ended up here in this small room in Mrs. Garzas home. What drew my curiosity was the fake gray hair and big horned rim glasses. We found two sets of them. If I remember correctly the person that killed Llamas had worn similar attire. Right?"

"Yes, that's right."

"You wouldn't by any chance have a picture of this man would you?"

"You're right, I wouldn't but I'm sure Mrs. Garza wouldn't object if you took this one," and he walked to the dresser and brought the framed photograph of Rio Martin to Barbara.

"Thank you Detective, this is really important, because we were at dead ends all the way around. But thanks to you and your good memory, we may get somewhere."

"Anytime Grevera, glad to be of service."

Mrs. Garza if someone should come for the photograph, it will be at the Police Station in San Jose."

Barbara and Ed walked to their car.

"What do you think Ed?"

"I wonder if there is a connection between *Rio* Martin and *Leo* Martin?"

"How so?"

They entered the car.

"See what you think about this hypothesis?"

"When Chet and Chip called the number of what we now know was, El Cantina, a tavern, and there's a steady hum emitting from the patrons in the establishment and the bartender answers the phone and someone asks for Rio Martin and because of the chatter, he thinks he hears Leo instead of Rio. He calls

Leo to the phone and Leo hears the directive from the caller. The caller hangs up and Leo sits pondering why someone would call and specifically ask for him. He was sure the call was not for him. Leo probably checked his watch and realized someone would be contacting him at three-thirty. He probably wondered if there was another Leo Martin that came to El Cantina. I'm only guessing but he finally realized he would wait by the phone for the three-thirty call and see if there was *another* Leo Martin that would come to the phone. The phone rings at three-thirty and the bartender yells out for *Rio* Martin. Seconds later, a man comes to the phone and Leo is listening to the minute long call. The man writes something down on a piece of paper and hangs up. Leo probably checks him out and that's about it for my crazy, dubious speculation."

"Wow Ed, that's an amazing summation strictly from such little information."

"I've been told I have a wild imagination, Barbara, so I wouldn't bank on it."

"Let's go see Chet and Chip and see if they recognize Rio Martin?"

"Good idea."

Chip looked at the picture, "I remember the face, but I don't recall if he gave me a name. Do you recall his name Chet?

"I don't remember the face at all Chip."

Chip looked away. "I don't think he ever gave me a name. This Rio character said, 'I'm a friend of Michael Rutledge,' and walked in. That's right, now I remember. He didn't give us a name, because that's the name that was on the package I got on my front porch, and that name was foreign to us. Right Chet?"

Ed nodded.

"Thanks guys," Barbara agreed, "you've helped but I'm not sure exactly how, yet. Let's go see the Chief and see what she thinks, Ed?"

After Barbara finished with a synopsis of the events to this juncture, "so what do you think about our next guest here? And speak of the devil, that's our man coming, Delores."

Leo Martin came walking in, all two and sixty plus pounds and at six foot five…menacing."

"Try not to piss him off, he looks very big and dangerous," Delores said, "and take him to Interview room 2. I'll try and round up a couple of extra cops and observe through the window."

Barbara and Ed approached Leo Martin.

"Thanks for coming Mr. Martin. We'll be interviewing you in Room 2," and Ed took the lead to the room.

Martin followed Ed and Barbara but said nothing.

"Can we stop for a second," he asked.

The two officers stopped, turned and waited.

"I'm not under arrest. Right?"

"That's right, Mr. Martin," Barbara responded.

"I can leave anytime I want. Right."

"Yes," they responded almost in unison.

"Okay," and he proceeded to follow them into Room 2.

They continued into the room that had a table and four chairs and a large one-way mirror. They all sat, the officers on one side of the table and Martin on the other.

"These few words I'll be stating are just police protocol for interviews in California, which are also for your protection, Mr. Martin. My name is Detective Barbara Grevera and this is Detective Edward Talbot. Would you state your name sir?"

"My name is Leo Martin?"

"Thank you Mr. Martin and today is November 4th, 2014 and now we can proceed with our interview."

"Ed would start?"

"Again, thanks for coming in on your own accord Mr. Martin. Do you know a man by the name of Michael Rutledge?"

He shook his head.

"You'll have to put a voice to your answer Mr. Martin."

"No."

"How about any one named Rutledge?"

"No."

"Does the name Carmen Llamas mean anything to you?" Barbara asked.

"No."

"Do you read the Mercury News Paper?"

"Not really."

"Do you patronize the El Cantina tavern on Alum Rock Avenue?"

"You mean, do I stop and have drink there?"

"Yes, that's what I mean."

"Yeah, I do."

"Is it one of your favorite places to get a sandwich and a beer?"

He nodded.

"I need a voice answer?"

"Yeah."

Barbara looked hard at her notebook, "Do you know a man by the name of Rio Martin."

Leo's intimidating eyes peered into Barbara's for a few seconds, but she didn't blink.

"Not really."

"So you've heard the name before."

"Yeah."

"Where?"

He sat up in his chair and his hulking body was daunting and paused, "at El Cantina, but I didn't know him enough to talk to the man."

"You knew him because he had the same last name as yours and you had heard it called out once in while at the El Cantina."

"Yeah, that's right, that's right."

"All right Mr. Martin, that's all I have for you today.

"Do you have anything else Ed?"

"Not at this time."

Leo stood up so quickly his chair fell over backwards.

He muttered, "sorry," almost to himself. "I can go now?"

"Yes sir," Barbara responded, "we might need to talk to you again, but for now, you may go."

"Just a second, Leo we need your friend Dino Tercero's address and phone number," Ed asked.

Leo spit it out quickly and his long strides carried him to the door in only three steps and Leo was gone.

Barbara gathered up her notes.

"He's smarter than I thought, Barbara. I wasn't sure he would admit he knew Rio Martin, but sensed that we knew something and he didn't want to get caught in lie."

"He is really intimidated by the Police Station," Barbara added.

"I sensed the same thing, he was very nervous."

The door opened and Delores came in.

"Why did you stop the interview?" she asked.

"He was on the verge of becoming contentious and I didn't want a confrontation with what I think would be a very formidable adversary."

"I agree with Barbara, he was agitated and could have exploded," Ed added.

"All right, so what did you get from this interview?"

"I don't know what Barbara thought, but I felt like he would deny that he ever heard of Rio Martin. Now I believe he had something to do with Rio swimming with the fishes."

"I definitely believe he killed or knows who did. He's been nervous ever since we showed up at his place of employment. He was uptight the minute he sat down in Room 2."

"Ed, where did I get the name Dino Tercero?"

He leafed through his note pad.

"Rose, Rose Garden, Leo's mother, when we talked to her in her apartment."

"Thank you." *She wondered if she was having some kind lapse from her long standing bout with a bullet to the head."*

"I think we should contact him and bring him in or at least talk to him."

"Delores, we hate to leave you with so many questions but if we can talk to him, I think a lot questions will be answered."

"Go." And she threw her hands up in the air."

"I think she was a little pissed at us Barbara," Ed commented.

"Naw, it's her job. Have you ever wanted to be the chief of some police division?"

"Oh I have thought about it until I see the rough spots they have to walk over. It's a big job with lots of responsibilities and politics get weaved in there. Just being a detective is tough enough. Lot of pressure and I don't think I can handle that kind of stress well."

"Really, you strike me as a solid man. No wife or kids, a job like Delores would fit you well. I bet you don't have bill collectors at your door or live above your means, and I haven't seen you get stressed out so far."

"Thank you for the kind words Barbara, maybe it's the responsibility that gets in the way."

"What was that address again?"

"Let's stop here," Ed recommended, "and walk down to 474 Walker, and I'll take the back door."

Barbara stepped quickly to the front door and knocked. She listened for any sound, and then, knocked again.

The door opened and a rough looking man, growled, "I don't what your sellen, and don't want to know," and he slammed the door shut.

She knocked again.

He opened the door, "I'm gonna call the cops for harassing me, bitch."

"I am the cops Mr. Tercero, may I come in," and she displayed her ID."

"Why didn't you say so," he groused.

Ed followed Tercero to the front room.

"I wasn't going anywhere," Tercero smirked, "I wanted to get some fresh air and I stepped out the back door. That's all."

"Did you want to talk to me or Dino?"

"Your son, Mr. Tercero."

"Good. Can I leave the room?"

Barbara glanced at Ed and he nodded.

"You're not going to leave the house, are you?"

"No."

He left the room.

"How long have you known Leo Martin?"

"Years."

"About how many."

"I don't know, twenty some years, maybe more, he's my best friend."

"Do you know Rio Martin?"

"No. Should I?"

"Do you know why Leo would know the man?"

"I don't think he knows a Rio Martin. Did he say he knew the man?"

"He did."

"So he knew this Rio Martin. So what's the big deal about knowing him?"

"A fisherman recently pulled Rio Martin out of a local lake. And according to our sources he was paid a lot of money to kill someone that we knew."

Dino paused long enough to catch Barbara's attention. Ed was also aware of his hesitation.

"Where were you on October 18 and 19, that would be on a Saturday and Sunday?"

"I don't know. I think I was here." *He'd gone to Salinas with his girlfriend and stayed there Friday, Saturday and Sunday.*

"Rio never had a checking account and probably paid cash for everything and even his land lady said he paid cash for his room. We went completely through his room and never found any monies. Have you noticed if Leo was spending money freely lately?"

"No," he responded quickly. *Thinking he had noticed that Leo paid for his lunch at Chili's with a hundred dollar bill and paid for some drinks at El Cantina with a couple of twenties. The bastard was holding out on him. I need to talk to Leo about the money he's been spending easily, again. He glanced at the clock on the wall.*

"Do you have an appointment Dino?" Barbara asked.

He shook his head, "No."

"Well, we do, so I'd like to thank you for your cooperation and ask you not to leave town. We might want to talk to you again."

"Sure, no problem and I ain't leaving town."

The Detective stood and walked out. They walked to their car up the street and quickly drove away. They reached the corner and Barbara made a 'u' turn and parked.

"Looks like your hunch was right Ed. You think he's going to see Leo?

"Yup."

"Ed, would you mind if we put off going to Leo's house this evening and tackle it tomorrow?"

"Not at all. I don't think we ought to be there tonight anyway. I believe we hit a nerve when we mentioned to Dino if Leo had been spending money lately. I think our behemoth has been doing just that and Dino could hardly wait to go and create a scene."

"So what does your 'wild imagination' grind out now?"

"I'm glad you asked. You see I have a lot more time to try and put this puzzle together. Like you said Barbara. I have no family, no real hobby, but lots of time on my hands. Anyhow, *if* my intuitive power is right," and he winked at Barbara, "and Leo killed Rio Martin, he almost had to have followed Rio in those last few days. Leo didn't hear the conversation but he knew it was important, so he followed Rio out of the tavern to his home. The only problem Leo had was that he didn't know how long he would have to play cop at a stake out. But he was up to the challenge and parked close by. My guess is that Rio had been given orders by an unsub, and I have a vague idea of who it might be, to go to the Stanford Hospital and *off* Carmen Llamas and that in those orders he would be paid *only* if there was proof she was dead. Carmen Llamas was killed late in the evening, if memory serves me, and it was in the Mercury the next day, or the day after. Leo was along through the whole scenario. Somehow our mystery contractor called Rio and informed him where his money would be and he would never hear from him again."

"So how did Leo end up with the money?" Barbara asked.

"Oh yeah, I almost forgot. Well, Leo follows Rio to the workout place on Lawrence and when he comes out of establishment carrying a bulging manila folder stuffed with money, he follows him home, probably ambushes him at his car, puts a bullet in his right temple, according to the crime unit, and dumps him at the local fishing lake and thinks he got away with it."

"Wow Ed, that's incredible. It almost sounds like that could have happened. I'm impressed."

"Thank you, but it's all bull feathers if Leo doesn't have any money or if someone else whacked Llamas."

"I don't think so Ed, you've thought this out pretty well and I for one think you are very close with your conception on what has happened. Now, you said you have a vague idea of who the mystery caller might be."

"Well, originally I thought it was Mr. Milton Taylor, who I believe initiated the contract on Llamas, after the Michael Rutledge demise, and she was killed on a Friday. Mr. Milton Taylor died on a Wednesday. So that meant that someone else was the *caller* and I could only think of one person—"

"Ari Maggio," Barbara articulated without thinking.

Ed nodded, "So you were thinking the same thing?"

"Well, your synopsis gave it direction to the only person it could be, Ari Maggio, the person we initially thought was a straight shooter. He really was quite convincing. Don't you think?"

Ed nodded.

"Let's go see what the Chief thinks about your short story plot? You might consider becoming a raconteur Mr. Talbot."

"Could that be a dirty word wrapped in silk?"

"Ed, when was the last time you heard me use profanity?"

"I never have."

She paused thoughtfully, "Well I have," she intimated, "I guess I've wanted to forget that I have. It was on two different occasions and they are indelible scriptures in my pea-brain. One day I'll be able to tell you, but not now?"

CHAPTER 40

"Well, now what?" The Chief asked.

"I was wondering if you would like to come along, or send a couple of extras with us, just in case Mr. Martin doesn't want to come peacefully," Ed asked reluctantly.

"Hey Ed, she can kick ass with the best of them, I kid you not?"

Barbara looked away with those words from the Chief.

"Well if you think we can do it, then I'll go along with that." Ed responded.

"Are you thinking about going over to his pad tonight?"

"Not tonight Delores. We think Martin is going to have company this evening, and we don't think it's going to be a cordial rendezvous."

"Why?"

"There is no honor among thieves and murderers."

"And Martin was holding out on one of his friends?"

"We think so, right Ed? Thirty K for killing Llamas was a pretty good payoff and we think Tercero believes Martin ended up with that money," Ed responding nodding.

"So you think those two could end up killing each other?" Delores asked.

"They'll put some hurt in that little bungalow that Martin lives in with his girlfriend, *if* they have any conflict about the money. And yes, someone could end up dead, according to one of our informants. We thought about going over there in the morning instead of 'O Dark Thirty,' tonight."

"What about this Maggio person?"
"That would be our next stop."

Barbara and Ed arrived at the Martin home and noticed the car that Dino Tercero had driven the night before, parked in the driveway.
"What do you think Ed?"
"We're here, let's do it?"
Cautiously the Detectives approached the front door, listening for and anticipating any sound of trouble.
Standing at the entrance quietly, "it's pretty quiet in there," she whispered.
He nodded.
She raised her hand to knock and at that very moment there was a loud crashing sound next door and both reached for their weapons.
"You'd think we were nervous," Ed whispered.
They smiled. Barbara knocked on the door and it opened just slightly.
"We're police officers. Is anybody home?" Barbara spoke loudly.
Ed knocked on the door with a little more force and it opened enough to peer inside the front room.

Barbara stuck her head inside. "I think I see a body in the front room."

"That will give us cause to go inside."

Leading with his .38 he walked slowly to the kitchen where Dino Tercero was seated in a chair with his head tilted forward and blood that had oozed down side of his neck and had already clotted.
Barbara had gone to the bedroom and shouted, "clear." There was a small porch that led to the back door. There sat Leo Martin also with a bullet to the back of the head.

"We better call the Chief," she said.

"Looks like a professional did this,"

"The body in the front room must be Leo's girlfriend, and she's got a bullet in the back of her head too, but she isn't tied up. Why do you think she isn't tied up?"

They walked to the front room and Ed kneeled down, scrutinized the body closely and looked ahead as if searching for something in the room. He stood and walked to the end table and picked up a landline telephone.

"She's wearing a light evening sweater, so I believe she arrived late, when our intruder or intruders were busy with one of the vics in the other rooms. She might have called out for Leo, was heard by one of them and when he appeared in the front room, she hurried to that phone and tripped. The killer stood over her as she lay, face down by the love seat and put a bullet in the back of her head. The murderers could have been wearing masks or something that hid their faces. She never put up any resistance."

Barbara nodded her approval and called the Chief.

"Crime Scene is on their way and the Chief will also be here soon."

They both checked the tiny bedroom that had been thoroughly trashed.

"Do you think that whoever did this was looking for the money that Leo stole from Rio Martin?"

"That would be my guess."

There was a knock on the door and both Detectives hurried to the entrance.

"Hi, are you two police officers?"

" Yes. Who are you?"

"Maria Mendez, I live next door. Last night I walked to the store for bread and milk and on the way back I saw a white van stop in front of Sylvia's house here and two men wearing grey masks went to the back of the house. I thought it was strange to see that. I told my husband and he said to leave it alone. I thought about calling the police, but he didn't want trouble from Sylvia's boyfriend. He's a very big man and a mean man."

Barbara wrote all this down. "What time did you see the men go to the back of the house?"

"Maybe twelve midnight or a few minutes after."

"Did you hear any noise coming from this house?"

"No."

"All right Mrs. Mendez, thank you. You said you lived next door. Right?"

"Yes. Is Leticia Morales all right?"

"Is that the woman that lives here?"

"Yes."

"I'm sorry that I can't give you any information on her at this time Mrs. Mendez, and it is in your best interest that you don't discuss what you've told us today with anyone. Do you understand?"

"I think so."

"Everyone should have a good neighbor like you Mrs. Mendez, and again thank you for your input."

"Well, it definitely was an execution type slaying," the Chief expounded, "and I agree with you two, this person or persons knew what they were doing. I did some researching on our man Maggio and guess what? He had some connection with a known Mafia family in New York. I think you should bring him in for a conference."

They displayed their badges to the Doorman.

"I remember you two officers. You were here to see Mr. Maggio. Right?

Barbara paused and wondered about his question.

"Is that going to be a problem?" She queried.

"Not at all, I was thinking of all the anti-police rhetoric and police bashing that New York is experiencing and wondered why police put up with it. The job is hard enough that most people wouldn't do it no matter how much pay they received, and then to have people in power leaning on you too. It's just wrong. The average citizen knows what your position entails- - protecting the public. Anyhow, I would like to shake your hands and say I really appreciate what you do despite all the negative reactions from those who think differently. It's just crazy."

The Detectives shook his hand.

"Thanks for your support, sir," Barbara responded.

"Thanks." Ed nodded.

"I saw him leave with two of his colleagues earlier this morning, but his maid would probably be able to direct you."

"Thank you." Ed acknowledged.

"I'm haven't been a policewoman long enough to see if that problem looms here. Does it, Ed?"

"As you know, I grew up here and I don't think we have that kind of problem, maybe similar minute episodes, but not the big hundreds and thousands of demonstrators that New York draws, however if the people in power push it, that could cause some problems here too."

Barbara rapped on the door, and after a few seconds it opened and Holly the maid stood there, looking a little confused.

"Mr. Maggio isn't here. Did you call him before you came?"

"No we didn't. We just had some questions that we wanted to ask him. Do you know where he went?"

"He didn't say, but sometimes he spends some time at a warehouse that he rents on Java Avenue in Sunnyvale."

"Warehouse?" Barbara probed.

"Yes, he makes things for computers and stores them in the warehouse. Come in and I'll get you the address."

Barbara studied the business card Holly had brought.

"Would you like me to call him to see if he's there?"

"No, it will be alright, Holly…and thank you for the address. It's not that important, and we'll call the next time before coming here."

The elevator door closed behind them.

"Do you think she'll call him?" Ed asked.

Barbara pursed her lips and thought for couple of seconds, "Yes, I think she will. What do you think?"

"Maggio is a very smart man and I think that he might have figured that we might be on to him by now and the doorman said he left with two colleagues. The Chief said he'd been associated with a mob in New York. I think we should go to the station house, discuss a strategy with the Chief, and get some backups to the warehouse."

"I think we're on the same wave length Detective Talbot, although we still don't know if Maggio is even in the storage facility."

"Even more reason to put more heads together and find a viable solution."

After explaining all that Grevera and Talbot presented to the Chief, Rudolph thought they should surround the storehouse and bring him in -- dead or alive.

The Chief went directly to the phone, was able to obtain the help of the SWAT team and the contractor that built the warehouse on Java Avenue.

"What if he's not there? Barbara asked.

"A real situation that is presented and no one gets arrested, wounded or killed is still a very valuable training mission.

An hour and twenty-three minutes later they all converged on Java Avenue and fierce gun battle ensued.

"It could have been worse, Ed. Grevera's in the hospital and two of the swat team were also wounded and all the perps are dead except one, and he got away."

"None of the dead unsubs was Ari Maggio, so he must have been the one that got away," Ed said regretfully.

"That's true, but we did good, Ed, and we know where Ari Maggio might be going. So…this is not the end of this story, not by a long shot."

Also by Joseph Montoya via Amazon.com:

    Ava's Legacy
    The Shade
    Where is Brian Douglas
    The Innocent
    Mysterious Ways
    The Endowment

Made in the USA
San Bernardino, CA
14 April 2015